"Why'd you ki...

The simple questio... ...is life, he didn't think a woman had ever asked him that question.

He had to think. He knew he could give her the glib answer, say something like, *Because I wanted to.* Which he had. But he figured he owed it to Ellie to give her the truth.

"When I saw him knock you to the ground, my heart stopped," he answered quietly. "I jumped him. If not for my damn injuries, I would have had him. You would have been safe, and that piece of trash wouldn't have bothered you ever again. My blood was pumping, but he got away, and I let you down. When I saw you watching me, you looked scared and disappointed and..."

He dragged his hand through his too-short hair. "I wish I was better with words. I'm not saying it right."

* * *

The Coltons: Return to Wyoming—One family's scandalous homecoming

Dear Reader,

I love the Coltons. Yes, I admit it. The Colton family is my guilty pleasure! I wrote *Colton's Christmas Baby* in 2010 and ever since then, I've been hoping I could visit the family again. This time, instead of Montana, we're in Wyoming. And yes, the story does have another baby. And more. In fact, there is so much going on in the little town of Dead River, Wyoming, that writing it was like watching a television drama. Something new lurks around every corner. Fascinating and fun.

I hope you enjoy reading this story—and Theo Colton's journey toward happiness and love—as much as I enjoyed writing it.

Thanks!

Karen Whiddon

A SECRET COLTON BABY

Karen Whiddon

HARLEQUIN® ROMANTIC SUSPENSE

Special thanks and acknowledgment are given to Karen Whiddon for her contribution to The Coltons: Return to Wyoming miniseries.

Recycling programs
for this product may
not exist in your area.

ISBN-13: 978-0-373-27890-9

A SECRET COLTON BABY

Printed in U.S.A.

www.Harlequin.com

As always, to my supportive husband.
He reads every book once it comes out and has
been wonderful about letting me live my dream of
being a full-time writer.

Books by Karen Whiddon

Harlequin Romantic Suspense

The CEO's Secret Baby #1662
The Cop's Missing Child #1719
The Millionaire Cowboy's Secret #1752
Texas Secrets, Lovers' Lies #1773
A Secret Colton Baby #1820

Silhouette Romantic Suspense

One Eye Open #1301
One Eye Closed #1365
Secrets of the Wolf #1397
The Princess's Secret Scandal #1416
Bulletproof Marriage #1484
**Black Sheep P.I.* #1513
**The Perfect Soldier* #1557
**Profile for Seduction* #1629
Colton's Christmas Baby #1636

Harlequin Nocturne

Wolf Whisperer #128
The Wolf Princess #146
The Wolf Prince #157
Lone Wolf #103
The Lost Wolf's Destiny #167
The Wolf Siren #181

Silhouette Nocturne

Cry of the Wolf #7
Touch of the Wolf #12
Dance of the Wolf #45
Wild Wolf #67

*The Pack
**The Cordasic Legacy

Other titles by this author
available in ebook format.

KAREN WHIDDON

started weaving fanciful tales for her younger brothers at the
age of eleven. Amid the Catskill Mountains of New York, then
the Rocky Mountains of Colorado, she fueled her imagination
with the natural beauty that surrounded her. Karen now lives in
north Texas, where she shares her life with her very own hero
of a husband and three doting dogs. Also an entrepreneur, she
divides her time between the business she started and writing.
You can email Karen at KWhiddon1@aol.com or write to her at
P.O. Box 820807, Fort Worth, TX 76182. Fans of her writing can
also check out her website, www.karenwhiddon.com.

Chapter 1

A whisper of sound, so fragile it might have been only a fragment left over from a dream. Another woman might have burrowed back under the blankets, refusing to open her eyes as she willed herself back to sleep. Not Ellie Parker. Not only had the infant recently entrusted to her care awakened every protective instinct she possessed, but her past had made her overly wary.

The noise came again, an echo of a ghost. Heart pounding, she held herself utterly still while waiting for her eyes to adjust to the darkness. Luckily, the full moon brought traces of silver to light the room.

There. Near Amelia's antique crib that had been hastily brought down from the attic. A figure in black, wearing a hoody and a ski mask, reaching for the baby.

Leaping to her feet, Ellie screamed. Loud and shrill. The intruder froze, then ran for the window, yanking it open and racing away.

Baby Amelia began to wail, and Ellie rushed to her on shaky legs, trying to catch her breath.

"What is it? What's going on?" Theo Colton's deep voice, throaty from sleep and full of concern. He flicked on the light switch.

"A man," Ellie gasped, pointing past where he stood,

his broad-shouldered body filling the doorway. "Dressed in black, wearing a ski mask. He was trying to take Amelia."

And then the trembling started. She couldn't help it, despite the tiny infant she clutched close to her chest. Somehow Theo seemed to sense this, as he gently took her arm and steered her toward her bed.

"Sit," he ordered, taking the baby from her.

Reluctantly releasing Amelia, Ellie covered her face with her hands. It had been a strange day, ever since the baby's mother—a beautiful, elegant woman named Mimi Rand—had shown up that morning insisting Theo was the father and then collapsing. Mimi had been taken to the Dead River Clinic with a high fever and flu-like symptoms. Theo had Ellie looking after Amelia until everything could be sorted out.

But Theo had no way of knowing about Ellie's past, or the danger that seemed to follow her like a malicious shadow. "I need to leave," she said to him. "Right now, for Amelia's sake."

Theo stared at her, holding Amelia to his shoulder and bouncing her gently, so that her sobs died away to whimpers and then silence. The sight of the big cowboy and the tiny baby struck a kernel of warmth in Ellie's frozen heart.

"Leave?" Theo asked. "You just started work here a week ago. If it's because I asked you to take care of this baby until her mama recovers, I'll double your pay."

"It's not about the money." Though she could certainly use every penny she could earn. "I…I thought I was safe here. Clearly, that's not the case."

He frowned. "I can assure you…" Stopping, he handed her back the baby, holding her as gingerly as fragile china. Once Ellie had the now-sleeping Amelia, Theo began walking around her room. "How about I check everything out? Is anything missing?"

Helpless to answer, since he obviously didn't understand, she managed a shaky shrug, gently patting Amelia's back. "I don't think he was here for possessions, which I have very few of anyway. He was definitely after Amelia."

"He?" Theo swung around to face her, his stance emphasizing the force of his muscular body. "Are you sure the intruder was a man?"

"Yes." Despite the baby's heat, she couldn't seem to get warm. "Who would try to kidnap a baby, especially with her mother gravely ill?"

"Maybe it just looked that way." He continued checking the room. "Nothing appears disturbed. Any idea how he got in?"

"No. He ran out the doorway into the hall when I screamed." For the first time she realized Theo was nearly naked, wearing only some sort of pajama bottoms low on his narrow hips. His bare chest gleamed. Trying not to stare and failing miserably, she felt her mouth going dry. For one brief second, she allowed the sight of him—so big, so masculine—to make her feel safe.

And then Theo went into her bathroom. He cursed, and she knew. Her stalker had somehow found her.

Pushing to her feet, she placed the sleeping baby carefully back in her crib and hurried over. Theo appeared tense, a muscle working in his jaw. "This seems to be directed to you," he said, pointing. *The only baby you'll be taking care of is OURS* had been written on the mirror with black marker.

Her knees again nearly gave out. She felt as if she'd

been punched in the stomach. "That settles it. I have to go."

"No." He reached out and steadied her. "No, you don't. You're safe here, Ellie. I can help you, protect you. But you need to tell me what's going on."

Despite the fact that she knew sexy Theo Colton couldn't be her knight in shining armor, she took a deep breath. "A couple of weeks ago, I left my home in Boulder, Colorado, because I had a stalker. He seemed to find me everywhere I went, leaving me black roses."

"*Black* roses?"

She nodded. "I don't know why. He also left notes that said things like *No one will ever love you like I do* and *One day you'll be mine forever.*"

"Did you go to the police?"

"Yes, but they said they couldn't do anything unless he threatened me. None of the notes said anything about him wanting to harm me. I couldn't get a restraining order or anything."

He gave her a long look, his green eyes unfathomable. "Yet you felt threatened."

"Yes. Wouldn't you?"

"Do you have any idea who he is?"

"No." She blinked. "And believe me, I tried to find out. I had friends hide and watch me to see if I was followed. No one ever saw him. The note and the roses would appear. So finally I couldn't take it anymore. I left everything in my apartment, packed a small bag and took off. I didn't tell anyone anything, just got in my car and drove."

"You must have been followed."

"I don't know how," she cried. "Honestly, I was very, very careful. When I left Boulder, I drove to Fort Collins, then Laramie, before I headed to Cheyenne. I stayed in Cheyenne for a couple of days before I saw your ad for a live-in cook. My car barely made it here before it died." And as soon as she had the money, she planned to get it fixed.

He nodded. "Don't worry. I'll take care of this." Picking up the phone on her nightstand, he punched in some numbers. "Hey, Flint," he drawled. "Sorry to wake you so early on a Sunday morning, but I need you to come over." Briefly he relayed what had happened before replacing the phone in its cradle.

"You've probably heard that my brother is the police chief in Dead River. He's on his way."

Heart in her throat, she nodded. Despite the fact that police apparently didn't take this kind of thing seriously, maybe the fact that the police chief was a relative of Theo's would help.

If he couldn't, then she was out of here come sunrise, even if she had to take a bus. No way did she want to bring her personal dark cloud down on this family, who'd taken a chance on an out-of-towner with few references. Though Theo hadn't known it, giving Ellie this job had likely saved her life. No way did she want any of them hurt because of her, especially not such a sweet and innocent baby.

Theo stayed with her while they waited for his brother to arrive, leaving her only long enough to go put on a shirt.

Flint arrived a few minutes later. Like Theo, he was tall and muscular, with the same dark hair and striking green eyes. He appeared drained, but that might only have been due to Theo's call waking him in the middle of the night.

"I was on my way over here anyway," he said, a

shadow crossing his face. "I just got word from Gemma at the clinic. Mimi Rand passed away a little while ago."

Both Theo and Ellie gaped at him. Theo was the first to speak. "What was wrong with her?"

"Cause of death hasn't been determined yet." Flint shrugged, his expression weary. "She had a high fever and flu-like symptoms. That's all I know."

Ellie glanced at Theo, watching for signs of grief. After all, if the ranch gossip was to be believed and Amelia was his daughter, then that meant the mother of his child had just died.

While he appeared a bit disconcerted, nothing more, she realized that might be because he wasn't the type of man to show his emotions on his sleeve. She then looked at Amelia, still sleeping soundly, her heart squeezing in her chest. "That poor motherless baby. What's going to become of her now?"

For the first time, Theo seemed uncomfortable. He shifted his weight and tugged at the collar of his shirt, before clearing his throat. "We need to get her checked out to make sure she's not sick like her mother. Mimi's ex-husband is a doctor at the clinic. Our sister, Gemma, works with him. I need to talk to him about all this. We'll work something out."

"Yes," Flint said grimly. "We certainly will."

Ellie got the distinct impression from the way the two brothers exchanged glances that they were saying without words that family stuck together, no matter what. A sharp pang of longing ripped through her, which she quickly pushed away. She'd realized years ago what her parents were and weren't capable of, and being a family wasn't one of those things.

"Now, what occurred here?" Flint asked. "Theo says you had some kind of break-in?"

She nodded. "Yes. I'm pretty sure the intruder was here because of me. For some reason, he wanted to take or hurt the baby to get at me."

Cocking his head, Flint frowned. "Why would you think that?"

Pointing with a shaky finger toward the bathroom, she swallowed hard. "Because he left me a message."

Flint hurried off to check it out. She and Theo waited. A second later, she heard the click and whirr of a camera. When he returned, his expression had gone grim. "What exactly is going on?"

Theo filled him in on Ellie's past, as well as details about what had just happened. Ellie tried like heck not to squirm as both men studied her with identical sharp gazes.

"Tell me exactly what you saw," Flint told her, his serious voice stern but compassionate.

"I'm afraid I can't help much." She wished she could stop shaking or at least get warm. The chill seemed to have snaked into the marrow of her bones. "Even back in Colorado, I've never known my stalker's identity. I've never even seen him."

"You did tonight," Theo reminded her, his gruff voice gentle.

"Not really. It was dark and I couldn't get a good look at his face. Even if I'd managed to turn on a light before he fled, I'm pretty sure he wore a ski mask."

Flint nodded. "Anything else you can tell me about him?"

She thought for a moment. "He was tall and lanky,

but I can't tell you much more than that. It all happened so fast."

Her words came out sounding a little more forlorn than she'd intended. To her surprise, Theo put his big hand on her shoulder and squeezed, offering reassurance. She instinctively leaned into his touch, and when she realized what she'd done, she stiffened and moved away.

Meanwhile, baby Amelia slept on, undisturbed.

"We'll try to find him," Flint said. "Theo, you might look into investing in some sort of home alarm."

"I will," Theo promised.

"Good." Glancing at his watch, Flint put his notepad and pen back in his pocket. "Now I suggest you both get some sleep. We'll talk again after the sun comes up and we're all more rested."

After escorting his brother to the door, Theo returned to Ellie's room to check on her and the baby. Seeing Ellie so terrified and defenseless had awakened every protective instinct he possessed. He'd be lying to himself if he claimed he hadn't noticed how lovely she was, especially since he'd hired her personally. He enjoyed women, especially beautiful ones, and just because that damn rodeo accident had sidelined him didn't mean he had to give up that.

He'd actually figured she'd be a nice diversion while he was stuck here at the ranch. But Ellie Parker surprised him. She'd only been here one week, but when she wasn't working in the kitchen, she might as well be a ghost. Her willowy, athletic good looks had attracted the attention of several of the ranch hands, and Theo had listened to them complain about how she kept to herself. As if she wanted to be invisible.

Which was oddly ironic, because Theo was used to living life in the spotlight, all the attention on him. One damn crazy-ass bronc and he was off the circuit, his season over for the first time since he'd made it into the Professional Rodeo Cowboy Association and started competing with the big boys. He'd loved the rough competition, the mean, hard-bucking broncs and the hefty payout. For the past three years, he'd ranked in the top twenty of the bareback bronc riders and been steadily climbing. This past year had been his best. This year, the PRCA Bareback Riding World Championship had been within reach.

He wanted that title so bad he could taste it. The pinnacle of his career, the real moneymaker. He'd lusted after that ever since he climbed on his first bronc. And he was damn good at it. He had a knack for knowing beforehand which way the animal was going to buck and spin. He'd figured out how to make his eight seconds count.

The money had been flowing in. After all, it was July, with rodeos with such huge payouts they called it the Cowboy's Christmas. There were plenty to choose from. With an eye on the World, he'd chosen to compete in the ones with the biggest payouts since his placement in the standings depended entirely on total money won.

And he couldn't seem to stop winning. Every day, he called PROCOM, the PRCA's computerized system, and got his numbers. As his standings continued to improve, he supposed in retrospect, he'd gotten cocky. So when he'd drawn the one horse no one had ever been able to beat, a beast known by the cowboys as one of the toughest broncs around, a National Finals horse, it had never occurred to him not to try. After all, he was unstoppable.

The instant they'd exploded from the chute, he realized this bronc wasn't like the others. Something was scrambled in his equine brain. After the first crazy sideways leap, Theo remembered nothing until he'd woken up in a hospital bed.

Even in an occupation where injuries are common, everyone had been concerned. They'd told him he was lucky he wasn't dead. At his lowest moments, he wasn't too sure about that. He'd lived for the circuit, spent his time traveling from region to region, pulling his camper behind his pickup. Now he had nothing to live for, not really. Injured, he couldn't ride, and if he couldn't ride, he couldn't win. Injured, he was nothing, his standings slipping with every rodeo he missed.

He'd retreated to his family's ranch to recuperate and lick his wounds. Luckily, due to Slim George, the ranch foreman who'd been in charge since Theo'd been a small boy, the place ran smoothly.

Which was great, since Theo wouldn't have been much help. After his head injury had left him unconscious—they'd used the word *coma*—for weeks, he'd had a long, slow recuperation. Not just his head, but he'd come within a hair of being paralyzed and the discs in his back were fragile enough that he'd have to be careful the rest of his life.

The doctors had said he'd never ride again, never mind compete. He'd told them all to go to hell and checked himself out of the hospital in Cheyenne as soon as he could, despite his broken ribs and bum knee. Flint had picked him up, sharing some grim news. One of Theo's competitors, a cowboy named Hal Diggins who'd had a cold streak for several months, had injected the bronc with some kind of amphetamine to make it go crazy. Hal had been arrested, and, despite Theo's protests, Flint had moved back to Dead River to help take care of Theo while he recuperated. Later, Theo had learned Flint had wanted to get out of Cheyenne and heal his own wounds. Despite Theo asking, Flint refused to elaborate on what they might be.

A good and honest cop, Flint had quickly risen through the ranks in the small Dead River Police Department, becoming chief of police and replacing Harry Peters, who'd left to take care of his terminally ill mother in Denver.

It also helped that their sister, Gemma, was a nurse at the clinic. She'd kept Theo on the straight and narrow, made sure he did his physical therapy exercises and took his supplements.

To all outward appearances, Theo had made a full recovery. He could walk and talk, but not ride. No one knew that a huge chunk of him had gone missing, stomped in the sawdust under that last bronc's hooves. His ribs and knee had healed, as had his concussion. But his back would forever be damaged, and he couldn't take a chance hurting it.

Since he had no choice but to try to make the best of it, he threw himself into helping out around the ranch. Only to learn that he sure as hell wasn't needed around here. The place ran like clockwork without him. Any time he tried to get involved in one of the operations, he pretty much just got in the way. Slim George had taken pity on Theo and asked him to take over the hiring, especially since the ranch cook had quit and they needed to find a new one as soon as possible.

Theo had done so gladly, setting up multiple interviews and planning to find a new cook within days. The instant he saw Ellie, with her innocent eyes and her sensual mouth, he'd known he'd like having her around. Hell, maybe in more ways than one.

As long as she understood he couldn't be serious. He enjoyed women's bodies, and dedicated himself to pleasuring them with as much zeal as he applied to the rodeo.

Women he spent time with knew up front what they were getting. A few laughs and a damn good time. They always left satisfied. No one ever got hurt, at least as far as he knew.

The situation with Mimi Rand had come as a complete shock. Theo had known she still shared intimacy with her ex-husband, Dr. Rand. She'd sought Theo out after a particularly spectacular win in Cheyenne. They'd had a couple of drinks and a night of fun.

In the morning when he'd woken, she was already gone.

He had to confess he hadn't paid much attention to what she did after that. Instead he'd done what he always did, focus on the rodeo.

And then he'd been hurt, come home to recuperate, and bam—Mimi showed up at his door with an infant, claiming he was the father. He'd been flabbergasted, asked her point-blank how she knew and instead of answering, she'd gotten a funny look on her face and collapsed.

Leaving him with a newborn and no idea what to do.

Now she was dead. And he figured since her ex had an equal chance of being the baby's father, Dr. Lucas Rand needed an equal opportunity to care for Amelia.

Back in his own room, Theo clicked off the light and tried to sleep. But, just as it once had the night before a big rodeo, his mind kept whirring.

Somehow he must have fallen asleep. He woke to the

ringing of his phone. Judging from the wealth of sunlight streaming in from behind his window blinds, it was probably mid to late morning. He squinted, trying to read the caller ID, then gave up and answered.

"Hello," he rasped.

"Theo, you need to call Gemma. She's at work at the clinic. She's been there all night, ever since Mimi Rand died." The urgency in Flint's low voice had Theo sitting up straight. His brother was normally the most nondramatic person he knew.

"Why? What's going on? Is she all right?"

"Yes." Flint exhaled. "But more people are ill. And it's not the flu. The CDC is involved. It's some kind of virus, a strain no one recognizes." He started to say something more, but someone else spoke to Flint, interrupting him. "I've got to go," he said to Theo. "Call Gemma. She can fill you in."

Immediately after hanging up, Theo dialed his sister's cell. Sounding harried and stressed, she answered, clearly keeping her voice pitched low and speaking quietly so no one else could hear.

"Is this a bad time?" he asked.

"Right now any time is a bad time. We've got old Mr. Thomas here, sick with the same type of thing that Mimi Rand had. His family is freaking out, worried he's going to die. And two children just came in." She took a deep breath. "The waiting room is packed and the phones have been ringing off the hook. People are getting paranoid. It's bad, Theo. Really bad."

"Flint said something about the CDC."

"Yes. Dr. Rand is working with them right now, despite being pretty broken up about losing his ex-wife. I think he still cared for her."

"Yeah." Theo scratched his chin. "I need to talk to him about that. You know she claims this baby is mine."

"So I've heard. Theo, everyone in town was talking about that before people started getting sick. Apparently she told more than one person."

"I barely knew her," he began.

Gemma cut him off. "I don't have time right now," she said. "You and anyone who came in contact with Mimi Rand need to get checked out. And you especially need to get that baby examined. Something like this would be deadly to an infant."

"I will," he said, but she'd already ended the call.

Pushing himself up out of bed, he felt a flutter of worry in his chest. But he'd never been one to look for problems before they arose. Damned if he'd start now.

Twenty minutes later, having showered and dressed, he made his way down the hall toward Ellie's room. Halfway there, he heard the sound of the baby—Amelia, he reminded himself—wailing.

He increased his speed. Two steps in and the sound stopped. Did babies do that? Frowning, he pushed the bedroom door open, only to see Ellie gently rocking Amelia back and forth.

"Morning." She flashed a tired smile. "She's been kind of restless. She had a bottle an hour ago, but I've used the last can of formula that her mother had in the diaper bag she left, and we're almost out of diapers."

"I'll drive to the store," he promised. With a nod, she turned her attention back to the baby. Even with dark circles under her eyes and her hair a mess, she managed to still look beautiful.

"Have you had breakfast?"

She bit her lip. "No. Neither has anyone else. I overslept and I haven't had time to make it into the kitchen and cook anything, so you probably have a bunch of hungry ranch hands."

He realized he'd need to find either a new cook or a nanny, at least until this thing was resolved. "I'm sure they understand," he lied. "I'll get in there and take care of their morning meal. Heck, I'll tell them it's brunch, since it's nearly lunchtime. They'll survive. And I want you to make sure to get yourself a plate."

A shadow crossed her blue eyes. "I'm sorry. It's just with everything that happened and taking care of the baby—"

"No need to apologize. After I fix breakfast, I'm going into town to talk to Mimi's ex-husband, Dr. Rand. If you'll write down for me what kind I need, I'll be sure to pick up formula and diapers while I'm there."

She nodded, gazing at the tiny infant in her arms. "What do you think is going to happen to her?"

At her question, he dragged his hand across his mouth. "That's what I want to talk to Lucas Rand about."

The rest of the morning flew by swiftly. Still carrying Amelia, Ellie followed him down to the kitchen and directed him in the nuances of preparing the morning meal for six hungry cowboys. She couldn't help but wonder how he managed to look rugged and sexy, even in this setting.

He used two dozen eggs, an entire loaf of bread and two huge slabs of thick-cut bacon. A jug of milk, a huge carafe of fresh, hot coffee and another jug of orange juice completed the setup.

"I usually make them biscuits and gravy too." She sounded apologetic again.

"They'll just have to make do," he said, shaking his head. "Extraordinary circumstances."

Nodding, she crossed to the exterior door and pulled the bell cord, sending the brass bell that hung outside chiming.

Almost immediately after, Theo's hands began filing into the kitchen. A few of them appeared surprised to see their boss there, but once they spotted the food set out on the long wooden table in the adjoining room, they shrugged, grabbed a plate and dug in. If they wondered why the food was so late in coming, no one said anything.

Theo had saved back some of the eggs, bacon and bread and made Ellie and himself a plate. He indicated one of the chairs at the smaller kitchen table and slid her breakfast over to her.

She climbed up, carefully holding Amelia, and once settled, eyed the plate, making no move to pick up a fork.

With a flush of embarrassment, he realized she didn't know how to eat while holding the baby.

"Here. Put her in the bassinette while you eat."

"No." She angled the baby away from him, her chin up, her blue eyes flashing. "You eat first, and when you're finished, you can hold her and I'll have my turn."

For a second, he froze, dumbfounded at the idea of holding such a miniscule little girl in front of everyone. He could do this, he told himself. Surely a man unafraid to climb on the backs of wildest horses wouldn't be undone by an infant. Plus, he'd already held her the night before, though he'd acted solely on instinct.

"Sure," he said, trying for easily.

Ellie rewarded him with a smile that sent his pulse racing. Stunned, he wondered if she knew how adorable she looked. Since she seemed determined, he didn't argue, even though he still felt seriously uncomfortable hold-ing an infant. Instead he started shoveling the food into his mouth, barely pausing for air.

Once he'd cleared his plate, he drained his glass of juice, took a quick gulp of coffee and then held out his arms for the baby, hoping he appeared nonchalant. "Your turn."

One corner of her mouth quirked as she stared at him. "Even they—" indicating the men at the table behind them, who were all intently chowing down "—don't eat that fast."

"I was hungry," he replied, grinning. "Now hand me that baby and eat your food before it gets cold."

Shaking her head, she handed Amelia over, transfer-ring her gently. "Make sure you support her head."

"Yes, ma'am." Once he had her, he gazed down into her tiny sleeping face. She smelled good, like baby powder and milk, and appeared healthy, at least to him. Though fragile. Which made him sort of afraid to move.

"That reminds me," he told Ellie. "There are more people sick with whatever Mimi had. We need to get Amelia checked out."

Fork in midair, Ellie froze. "I didn't think of that." Expression dismayed, she put down her fork. "I don't want her going to the clinic if there are other sick people there. You said Mimi's ex is a doctor. Do you think he'd be willing to check her out here?"

Pleased her concern was for the baby rather than her-self, he nodded. "I'll bring that up when I talk to him today. If not, my sister is a nurse and can do it."

He took a deep breath, hating what he had to say next, but knowing it was necessary. "Listen, Ellie, don't go getting too attached. There's a possibility Amelia might not be here too long."

Her eyes widened. Her voice rose. "What do you mean? You can't be considering giving up your own flesh and blood."

The men at the other table stopped talking and turned to stare at them from the other room. Theo grimaced. "There's a very real possibility she's not mine," he said gently. "Mimi was… Well, let's say she wasn't exclusive."

Her downcast look told him she didn't like what she was hearing. "She has your eyes," she said.

"Yes, but green eyes aren't proof of anything."

"I understand," she replied, clearly lying. "Let me have Amelia back, please."

"You haven't eaten yet."

Taking the baby from him, she nodded. "I've lost my appetite."

No one spoke as she marched out of the room.

Once she was gone, Theo's hands all looked at him. Even from the other room, he could feel their disapproval.

He shrugged. "Come on, guys." Giving their empty plates a look, he pointed toward the door. "Time to get back to work."

Though not a single man argued with him, he could tell from a few of their expressions—belligerent, questioning and yes, disappointed—that they wanted to. He hated that they thought he was acting like a jerk—honestly, he wasn't. But this was his life, and it wasn't up for debate.

If baby Amelia belonged to him, Theo would move heaven and earth to ensure that she wanted for nothing.

However, if Lucas Rand was actually her father, then Amelia needed to be with her daddy. He didn't need to explain that to anyone.

Chapter 2

The drive into town felt as if it took longer than usual. He figured he'd pick up the diapers and formula after he had a word with Dr. Rand.

Dead River looked like a ghost town. Probably because it was Sunday, and most folks were either at church or home with their families. Main Street, usually pretty busy about this time of day while the stores were open, had tons of empty parking spots and only a few people on the sidewalks. But when he turned the corner onto Third and spotted the clinic's overflowing parking lot, he couldn't believe it. Usually, the clinic was closed on Sundays, except for emergencies.

Gemma hadn't been exaggerating. He ended up parking in the street.

As he approached the glass front door of the one-story, white cinder block building, he nearly stopped short as he saw the mass of people milling around in the waiting area. Surely not all of these people had come down with the virus.

Pushing inside, he stopped, checking everything out. No one looked feverish, or was coughing, sneezing or exhibiting any other flu-like symptoms. As far as he could tell, none of these people actually appeared sick.

His suspicion was confirmed when Cathleen Walker, who worked the intake desk, grabbed his arm. As usual, her clothes looked a bit rumpled, as though she hadn't had time to press them. "Theo, are you okay?"

He nodded. "What's up with them?"

"They want a shot." She grimaced, slipping one foot out of the high heels she continually wore to work and stretching it, before sliding it back into her shoe. "Not a flu shot either—most everybody has already had that. I don't know why, but someone heard we had received an inoculation against whatever killed Mimi Rand and got the others sick."

"And you don't even know what it was, do you?"

"No. But none of these people will leave." She heaved a frustrated sigh. "More and more keep showing up. I've told them, Dr. Moore has told them and even Dr. Granger."

"What about Dr. Rand?"

Her expression changed, softening. "He's in the back, writing up a report on the latest people to fall ill. The poor man is grief-stricken over losing Mimi. He acts like it's his fault he couldn't save her."

"I need to talk to him." Again he glanced at the packed waiting room. "People," he said, raising his voice. "If you're sick, please raise your hand."

Not one hand went up. Exactly as he'd suspected. "Everyone else, go on home. You don't want to risk being exposed to whatever this virus is." He glanced around, picking out individuals among the crowd and meeting their eyes. "Do you understand what I'm saying? If you're healthy, not only are you using resources that could better be directed toward helping those that are sick, but just being here puts you in very serious danger of becoming infected."

At his words people began exchanging glances, some chastised, others suspicious, a few even hostile. One or two hurried toward the door, and then a couple more followed. Pretty soon, it became apparent the place was going to rapidly empty out.

"Oh, thank you." Cathleen sagged against her desk, clearly relieved. "Dr. Granger has been saying if too many more get sick, we're going to have to set up an isolation area and keep the virus victims separated from everyone else."

Which made sense, since the clinic was the main place for medical care in Dead River.

"Come on," Cathleen said, giving him a tired smile and finger-combing her slightly mussed blond hair. "I'll take you back to see Dr. Rand."

He followed behind, her high heels clicking on the linoleum. They went past the reception area to where the older patient-records were stored in manila folders. For years, Gemma had claimed Dead River Clinic wanted to go entirely electronic. Apparently they had not yet completed the task of doing so.

"Here we are." Once again all professional, Cathleen stopped and pointed toward one of the offices. A brown and gold nameplate on the door stated it belonged to Dr. Lucas Rand.

"Thanks." He lightly squeezed her shoulder, making her blush, which sort of surprised him since they'd known each other from the fifth grade.

Moving forward, he peered into the small office. Dr. Rand spoke into a handheld dictation device. His usually perfect dark hair looked as if he'd been dragging his fingers repeatedly through it.

Theo knocked lightly on the door.

The doctor looked up, his dark eyes full of pain. He clicked off his machine and stood, holding out his hand. "Theo."

Theo shook his hand, trying to figure out the best way to word what he had to say. Finally, he decided the hell with it. He'd talk to Dr. Rand man-to-man.

"About Mimi," he began.

"I can't believe she's dead."

"Me, either." Theo dug his hands down into his pockets and resisted the urge to shift from foot to foot. "I'm guessing you know she had a baby?"

The other man nodded. "Of course. When she first got pregnant, I wrote her script for prenatal vitamins." He choked up, averting his face and swallowing hard as he tried to get himself under control. "I can't believe she's gone."

"I'm sorry."

Dr. Rand sighed. "I tried my best to save her. I couldn't. I let her down. And now her newborn child is motherless."

"About that." Theo tried to figure out the best way to say it, and then decided to just blurt it out. "Is the baby— Amelia—yours?"

Dr. Rand stared at him, his expression a mix of surprise and horror. "Good Lord, no. Mimi and I haven't been together like that in at least a year." He blinked and peered at Theo the same way a scientist might inspect a particularly interesting petri dish full of bacteria. "Um, Theo? I don't know what you're getting at, but it's my understanding that Amelia is your daughter." He flushed and looked away. "At least that's what Mimi told me. And she had no reason to lie."

Mine. For a split second, it seemed to Theo everything tilted sideways. The room suddenly felt too warm. Treading carefully, as it was common knowledge that Dr. Rand had still cared for his ex-wife, Theo cleared his throat.

"Look, Dr. Rand—"

"Call me Lucas."

Theo nodded. "Okay. Lucas. This is awkward, but Mimi never contacted me about being pregnant. I would have helped her."

"I took care of that. I've been paying spousal support anyway, so I just added to it. I don't think she ever intended you to find out, at first. Clearly, she changed her mind."

"That doesn't make sense." Frowning, Theo couldn't make sense of any of this. "Besides, she and I were only together a couple of times. I sincerely doubt that I could be Amelia's father."

Some dark emotion flashed across Lucas's face, before he looked down. When he raised his head to meet Theo's gaze, he expression was calm. "One time is all it takes. You know that."

Theo found himself at a loss for words.

"Look, Theo." Lucas gripped his shoulder. "I've always thought you were a good guy. And little Amelia is a Colton. You should be raising her. Obviously, since Mimi came to you when she realized she was ill, that was her last wish for her baby girl. Amelia needs to be with her family. I work all the time, here at the clinic. I have nothing to offer her, while you…you have a rich heritage, a large family and plenty of support."

Put that way, Theo knew Lucas was right. But how

could Theo be a father? He had no idea how. His own father had been an abusive drunk, who'd only shown up when he needed something and stayed just long enough to break his young children's hearts.

His father's mother—Grandma Dottie—had raised all three of them, and Flint, Theo and Gemma worshipped the ground she walked on. Maybe she could help, Theo thought. Or at the very least, explain to him how a good father should act.

Still rattled, he nodded and turned to go. Lucas tightened his grip on Theo's shoulder, stopping him.

"Theo, I swear I will find the medicine to treat this thing," Lucas vowed. "Or a cure, if it comes to that. In the meantime, have Gemma check you out. I want you to bring Amelia by immediately if she starts showing any flu-like symptoms. Same with you or anyone in your house. We need to treat early, before symptoms become life-threatening."

The other man's choice of words worried Theo. "You talk like this is some new kind of disease."

"It might be." Lucas appeared to be choosing what he said carefully. "I'm doing everything I can to figure it out."

"You're a good man, Dr. Lucas Rand." Theo moved away. "I'll go have a word with Gemma now."

"She's in the back with the sick children." Lucas frowned. "I don't want you going back there. It's not safe."

"Then why is my sister there?" Theo asked sharply.

"She's taking the proper precautions—she has on a mask and gloves. Let me page her and see if she has time to come out."

Theo waited while Lucas did that. After a moment,

Lucas's cell phone rang. He answered, spoke a few words and hung up.

"She said she'll call you later, once her shift is over." A sudden weariness appeared to settle over the doctor. "Thanks for stopping by, Theo. You know the way out, right? I need to get back to work."

Summarily dismissed, Theo took his leave. When he reached the front desk, he saw the waiting room had once again begun to fill up.

This time, he simply made his way to the door. He had a lot to think about, but most important, he needed to pick up formula and diapers.

Once that was done, he headed home.

On the drive there, he called his grandmother Dottie. If he remembered her schedule right, she should be home from church by now. Though she was seventy-five years old, she played canasta with several other widowed women once a week. She'd never remarried, but she kept busy. She ate lunch out with her church friends on Wednesday, and then went to Bible study that night. Church on Sunday, a reading group on another day—he couldn't keep up with her schedule.

The phone rang six times before she picked up. "You're there," he said, relieved. "I thought I missed you and was about to disconnect the call. How are you, Gram?"

"Not too good," she answered, surprising him. "I think I might be coming down with something."

He felt a flash of alarm. "Promise me you'll go to the clinic and get it checked out."

"It'll probably pass." She didn't sound too worried. "If not, I'll have Gemma check me out. If she thinks I need to see a doctor, I will."

Relieved, he asked her if she was sitting down.

She laughed, or attempted to. Instead she made a sound that turned into a hacking cough.

Instantly alarmed, Theo felt his stomach twist as he remembered what Gemma had told him earlier. He told Gram she needed to go to the clinic immediately and get checked out.

"Don't be silly," she replied, after she regained her voice. Even over the phone, Theo could tell she wasn't well. "It's just a cold," she continued. "Nothing to stress about."

"Gram, please. I've got enough on my plate. Don't add having to worry about you to my list." He knew making it be about him was the only way she'd consider doing something for herself. That was his gram Dottie. Always doing for others.

"What do you have on your plate?" she asked, instantly concerned. Of course. He chastised himself. She'd immediately pick up on that.

"A woman named Mimi Rand showed up on my doorstep yesterday morning with an infant. She claimed the baby girl is mine. And then she collapsed." He swallowed hard, almost afraid to tell her the rest. "She was rushed to Dead River Clinic, but she passed away last night. She had a virus. That's why I'm so worried about you. It starts out a lot like the flu. Fever, chills, body aches. A cough, sore throat, maybe even vomiting or diarrhea. Do you have any of those?"

"No."

"I still want you to get checked out. I love you too much to lose you."

"Fine." She sounded grumpy, though touched too. She knew Theo as well as he knew her. "I'll try to go tomorrow. If I start feeling worse, I'll call Gemma and ask her to stop by and check on me."

"Perfect."

"Now, Theo, tell me the truth. I know—knew—Mimi Rand. She was well dressed and well mannered and acted as if she was used to the finer things in life. Probably because she was Dr. Rand's ex-wife. I can't imagine..." She took a deep breath. "Dead?"

"Yes. And Gemma says no one knows what it is exactly that killed her."

Silence while she digested this. Then she cleared her throat and spoke. "Theo, tell me the truth. Is this baby really yours?" She sounded deeply disappointed, which still had the power to crush him.

"I don't know." He told her the truth. "But after talking to Dr. Rand today, it's appearing likely."

"Well, then." Disappointment gave way to her normal, brisk, take-charge attitude. "I'll do whatever I can to help. I wouldn't mind having a young'un to cuddle again. Once I get over this cold, I'll come by and meet... what is her name?"

"Amelia. She's really tiny."

"Amelia. I like it." She coughed again. "I can't wait to meet her."

He hung up, smiling although her cough still worried him. But she was a tough old lady and he figured she knew if she was seriously sick or not.

Ellie had always avoided cocky men who were full of themselves. A lot of cowboys were like that. But from what she'd seen of Theo Colton in the short time she'd been here at the ranch, while he had swagger, and the same rough-and-tumble sex appeal, he wasn't conceited or arrogant. There was a fine line between self-assurance and smug self-importance, and she thought Theo was merely confident and comfortable in his own body. She believed this despite the stories she'd heard the one night she ventured into town to have a drink at the Dead River Bar.

But this morning, hearing how he'd spoken of this precious little innocent baby—*his* baby—at that moment, she'd wondered if she'd been wrong about him after all.

Once he'd left to go to town, she realized he must be terrified. He'd been a big-time rodeo cowboy, a bareback bronc riding champion. She'd spent enough time around horses in her hometown of Boulder to know rodeo cowboys were footloose and fancy-free. They had to be, since they made their living driving from town to town, rodeo to rodeo.

She also knew women of all kinds flocked to them, the way groupies hung on to musicians. All kinds of women. Mimi Rand was proof of that, may she rest in peace.

Now Theo was dealing with the fallout. For him, just knowing that his injuries had cost him all that, everything he'd ever known, must have been bad enough. Now this—finding out he was a father. By a woman who, from what he'd said, he'd barely known.

Gazing at Amelia while she slept in the car seat she'd been brought here in that converted to a portable bassinette, Ellie thought she'd never seen a more darling baby. Wisps of curly dark hair framed her chubby-cheeked face. As she'd done several times over the past hour, Ellie lightly touched the infant's forehead, checking to make sure there were no signs of fever.

So far, so good. No sign of whatever mysterious illness had plagued her mother.

For some reason Ellie thought of her parents. She knew what they'd do in this situation. As lifelong evangelistic missionaries on the African continent, they'd elevated the act of prayer to a fine art. She only wished they'd devoted as much effort to being parents and making them all a family. She hadn't seen them in years, and even in her younger days, she'd stayed with a neighbor while they were off saving the world. They were too busy, too full of what they considered their life's work, to spend time raising a daughter.

Ellie had often wondered why they'd even had her. Most likely, she'd been an accident. Ah well, dwelling on the past never changed anything. And she no longer prayed, because she'd spent her entire childhood praying her parents would want her. When her prayers had gone unanswered through the years, she'd sworn never to pray again.

Even though they'd had a late breakfast, soon it would be lunchtime on the ranch. As the only cook, Ellie knew she had to come up with something to feed the hardworking, hungry ranch hands. Luckily, she'd started on a big pot of chili the day before, and all she had to do was place the large cooking pot on the stove and break out a couple of bags of Fritos and shredded cheddar cheese.

Relieved that she could do this and still take care of Amelia, she knew the evening meal might be more of a challenge. She needed to do prep work now. A couple of days ago, she'd moved four whole chickens to the fridge from the freezer. She could roast those and make a pot of pinto beans and a huge bowl of rice. Simple but efficient.

She gave the chili another stir with the wooden spoon and returned to gaze at the sleeping baby. Footsteps in the hallway made her turn, wondering if the crew had broken for lunch early.

Not the ranch hands. Instead Theo, gazing first at her and then the baby. Ellie's heart did a little stuttering dance as she stared at him. Broad shoulders, narrow waist, muscular arms. And that face, craggy and masculine, with that cute little bump on his nose where it had been broken. He was handsome and sexy, and so far out of her league it wasn't funny. Even knowing this, she couldn't keep from drinking him in with her eyes, even as she tried—and pretty much failed—to appear nonchalant.

"How's she doing?" he asked, his gaze on Amelia.

"Fine." She found a sudden need to turn away and stir the chili. "I've been watching her and there's no sign of a fever. I'm guessing she's not hungry yet since she's been asleep since you left. Did you bring the formula and diapers?"

"I did. They're on the counter." The edge of huskiness in his voice made her look at him. He was still staring at the baby, something very much like tenderness flashing in his amazing green eyes.

Chest tight, she turned back to the simmering pot. "Lunch is almost ready. The ranch hands should be here any moment."

"I told you that you didn't have to cook since you're taking care of the baby."

"Then who would?" Her tone came out sharper than she'd intended. "If I don't, the hands won't have anything to eat."

"Thank you." He came to stand next to her, making every nerve in her body quiver. "I'm sorry. I thought I'd made it back in time to get the noon meal ready."

She didn't comment. It was eleven-thirty and the men ate at straight-up twelve.

When he touched her arm, she gave a little jump. Inhaling sharply, she took a step back from him, hoping if she put a little distance between them, she could regain her equilibrium. When she'd first applied for the job, she was so desperate for work, she'd barely noticed his rugged good looks. After all, she'd been nearly broke with nowhere to live but her car.

Now, almost a full week later, every time Theo came anywhere near her, she went weak in the knees and her entire body tingled.

Cleary, she needed to get over this.

"I've talked to my grandmother." He frowned. "I wanted to ask her to help with the baby, but she sounds like she's coming down with a cold."

"That's not good." Ellie kept her voice steady, a bit startled at the odd rush of possessiveness she felt at the thought of someone else taking care of Amelia. "Maybe it would be better to see if you can find someone else to cook, at least until your grandmother gets better. I don't mind."

He gave her a long look, his green eyes keenly observant. "We'll see. In the meantime, I'll help you with dinner," he said. "How about that?"

"Let's get through lunch first," she said. "If you don't mind, I'll get Amelia changed and fed. There are corn chips on the table, shredded cheese in the fridge and all they need to do is ladle the chili into their bowls."

He nodded. "I can handle that."

"Thank you." Moving briskly, she washed her hands and then grabbed one of the cans of formula and read the instructions, just to make sure.

Once everything was mixed up in one of the bottles, she warmed it slightly in the microwave and shook it to make sure the heat distributed evenly. She squeezed a drop on her wrist, something she thought she'd seen on TV. "Perfect."

More relieved than she'd care to admit, even to herself, she crossed over to where Amelia still slept. One quick glance at Theo, and the knot was back in the pit of her stomach. "I'll just take her upstairs and feed and change her."

"Sounds good." Theo glanced at the clock. "The less exposure she has to others, the better, at least until we get her checked out. I'm going to see if Gemma can come by tonight after work, though I might have her stop by Gram Dottie's first."

The worry and affection in his voice when he spoke of his grandmother warmed her. "Just let me know," she said. "I think I hear the guys."

He gave her a panicked look, nearly making her laugh. Instead she picked up Amelia's carrier, tucking the warm baby bottle on one side. She looped the bag with the diapers over her arm and hurried upstairs just as the back door opened and the hungry ranch hands began filing in.

Amelia woke with a startled little sound when they were halfway up the stairs. After one quick gasp, she scrunched up her little face and let out an ear-piercing wail. By the time Ellie had reached the landing, Amelia had begun to cry in earnest.

Making soothing sounds, Ellie hurried to her room. Once there, she dropped the diapers on the bed and hurried to get Amelia out of the carrier. No amount of rocking or murmuring endearments would soothe her. But the instant Ellie pressed the baby bottle against her lips, Amelia latched on, drinking so fast she hiccupped.

"What a beautiful baby you are," Ellie murmured, her heart full. "I'm so sorry your mama won't get to see you grow up."

Cradling Amelia while she finished her bottle, Ellie wondered at this newfound surge of maternal emotion. She hadn't spent a lot of time around babies, and it amazed her how tiny this one seemed.

Once Amelia finished her bottle, Ellie burped her, again copying something she'd seen on television. Amelia let out a satisfied belch.

Ellie kicked off her shoes and climbed onto her bed, holding Amelia close. She propped up a pillow and leaned back, resting while she gently rocked her charge.

A few seconds later, Amelia had gone back to sleep. Smiling, Ellie watched her. Once, before her stalker, she'd settled into a sort of Bohemian existence working at a bookstore in Boulder. She'd had friends, she'd been happy, though she'd often felt like she was floating along through life. Her stalker had changed that, and the constant panic had forced her to go on the run. Now she'd landed here. She wasn't sure why, especially since she'd always wanted to travel, but she hadn't felt this content in a long time.

By the time the lunch hour was over, Theo had a newfound respect for the job of ranch cook. Since coming back home, he hadn't had to do much, Mrs. Saul had worked in the kitchen for over twenty years. When the plump white-haired lady had come to him and announced she wanted to retire, the entire ranch was caught off guard. She'd promised to stay until he'd found someone to replace her, and so she had. The transition from Mrs. Saul to Ellie Parker had gone seamlessly.

One tiny baby and everything had been thrown off balance. That was okay, he told himself. Once Gram Dottie took over nanny duty, everything here would be right back on track. He'd just have to pitch in until then. At least he had plans. Big ones, actually. He just had to find the right stock to get his breeding program underway.

Most people didn't realize that the majority of broncos in the rodeos were bred specifically for that role. The best buckers had good confirmation and breeding. Theo figured if he couldn't ride 'em, he'd breed 'em.

Until then, he'd help out in whatever way he could, including cooking. The men had been surprised to see him in the kitchen, but they'd been hungry and dug into the chili. Theo had fixed himself a bowl too, and taken a seat at the table in the other room to eat with them. All the talk was on the upcoming Tulsa State Fair and Rodeo in Oklahoma.

Pretending it didn't bother him talking about something that had been his favorite activity in the world was something he had gotten better at. Theo laughed and joked, argued about who he thought was the best bull rider, hoping and praying they didn't ask him about the bronc riders, whether saddle bronc or bareback. Bareback had been his sport, and even thinking about what he would be missing usually filled him with a brooding kind of anger.

Maybe they had heard this, or perhaps his hired cowboys had a lot of common sense, because bronc riding never came up.

Most of them had seconds, complimenting Theo on the chili. He smiled and told them to thank Ellie. No one asked about the baby, no doubt remembering the way the conversation had gone that morning.

Finally, one by one, they pushed back their chairs and headed out to get back to work. Relieved, Theo gathered up the dirty dishes, rinsed them off and put them in the dishwasher. He made sure the burner was off and left the pot on the stove to cool.

He made a quick call to a local alarm monitoring service and left a message on their answering machine asking for an appointment the next day to have motion detectors and whatever else came with a home alarm installed.

Someone called him back in two minutes, confirming the appointment for Monday afternoon. He imagined they didn't get much business. Here in Dead River, the country folks rarely even bothered to lock their doors.

Theo had been the same. In the past. No longer. He planned to make sure the house was locked up tight each night before he went to bed. An alarm would be additional insurance. Whoever had broken in, whether he'd been after the baby or Ellie, wouldn't be able to get in so easily next time.

As he tried to decide whether or not to take Ellie her lunch upstairs, his cell phone rang. The caller ID showed Gemma.

"Hey," he answered. "I thought you weren't going to call until after you got off work."

"I wasn't," Gemma answered, sounding stressed and more upset than he'd ever heard her. "But Gram Dottie just came in."

"Good. I told her to get her tail in there if she didn't start feeling better."

"Oh, Theo." To his shock, he could tell his sister was

on the verge of tears. "She walked in the front door, and then she collapsed. We've moved her back to the isolation area. The doctors think Gram Dottie has the same thing Mimi Rand had."

Chapter 3

Stunned, Theo wasn't sure he'd heard correctly. "What? I just talked to her and she didn't sound that sick. Now you're telling me… How is that even possible?"

"I don't know. No one even knows what this disease is, never mind how it's transmitted. Dr. Rand thinks it's a virus. Either way, it's not good. She's in really bad shape, Theo."

"I'm on my way down there," he said, pacing the length of the kitchen. The rich smell of the chili now made him feel queasy.

"No. You can't. There's a reason we have the victims isolated. You can't risk exposing yourself."

"I don't care about myself." He swore. "You know how much Gram means to me."

"We all feel that way," Gemma said. "And you may not care about yourself, but you have to think of the baby. You can't risk her." She took a deep breath. "Right now you'd be denied entrance anyway. Only essential medical personnel are allowed in, and we have to put on protective-wear as a precaution."

Theo cursed again. "How bad off is Gram?"

"Right now she's stable." Another shaky breath, the sound coming through as more of a warning than any words could be. "The CDC is sending a team. Flint knows this already, but they're talking about a quarantine."

Theo stopped pacing, trying to understand. "A quarantine? Of what, the clinic?"

"No. Dead River. The entire town." And then Gemma, his normally unflappable sister, began to cry.

Theo did his best to console her, well aware she most likely hadn't shared every detail with him. "What about the baby?" he asked, taking a deep breath. "She was with Mimi right before she died. We need to get her checked out."

"You're right," Gemma said. "And you and anyone else who might have come into contact with her. I can't come by tonight, but I work the afternoon shift tomorrow, so I'm off in the morning. How about I swing by the ranch and check her out then?"

"That'd be perfect."

"Then that's what I'll do." With that, Gemma told him she had to go back to work and ended the call.

Stunned, Theo could only stare at his phone. He felt he needed to do something, anything, but he didn't know what. If this virus had been a bronc, he would have climbed on and ridden it into submission. But it wasn't, and in reality, there was nothing he could do but stand by helplessly and watch.

And that summed it up. He was a rodeo cowboy, a bareback bronc riding champion, and not much else. He couldn't even help his own grandmother—the woman who'd raised him—when she needed assistance.

But he could—and would—protect Amelia. His tiny daughter had no one else. He'd somehow figure out a way to be a good father, even though he had no idea how. Again the spicy scent of chili filled his nostrils.

This time, the smell filled him with purpose. Ellie had done nothing but work all day. She had to be starving.

He found a cookie sheet that would work as a tray and filled a bowl with corn chips before ladling the chili over that. Topping if off with a generous amount of shredded cheddar cheese, he folded a paper towel to act as a napkin, grabbed a spoon and a can of cola and carried the tray up to Ellie's room.

It was impossible to knock with his hands full, so he didn't bother. The door was cracked. He used his elbow to nudge it the rest of the way open.

Carrying the tray, he paused just inside the room. Both Ellie and the baby were asleep on the bed—Ellie sitting up, her back supported by both pillows, still cradling the infant securely in her arms.

Carefully and quietly, he placed the tray on the dresser and stared at the pair. Bathed in the soft light from the window, Ellie looked almost angelic. Looking at her and the sleeping baby made the back of his throat ache.

Shaking his head, he scoffed at himself. Still, there was a particular glow about her. Maybe it was one of those things females got when they were around babies. Who knew?

He took the opportunity to study her—and his child too. Something about the scene calmed him, the way beauty always did. Ellie's exotic, high cheekbones caught the light, bringing a soft flush to her creamy skin. The delicacy of her face seemed almost at odds with her lean, athletic body. She'd pulled her hair, a soft brown color, back into a ponytail. The soft strands that had escaped framed and highlighted her face.

And the baby… Chest tight, he moved closer to examine her. Perfect little rosebud of a mouth, dusky skin like her mother's. Innocent and perfect, too much so for the likes of someone like him. What did he know about being a father? His dad had become a drunk after their mother was killed in a car accident. His father had been in and out of their lives, showing up just often enough to humiliate his sons. He'd finally abandoned their family, much to everyone's unspoken relief. Gram had taken over, filling the void as best she could. She'd been both mother and father, grandmother and teacher to Flint, Theo and Gemma.

Standing there in the quiet room, midday sunlight warm on his arm, Theo faced the fact that the world he'd taken for granted continued to crumble down around him. Losing the ability to rodeo had seemed like the worst thing that could ever happen, even though everyone had kept telling him he should consider himself lucky that he'd survived.

But now his beloved Gram was seriously ill, and this tiny, helpless human had been entrusted to his care. Him, of all people, who had always taken a certain sort of pride in being the least settled person he knew. Despite his satisfaction with the life he'd chosen, he'd never wanted to fail his grandmother, though deep down inside, he knew he had. Gram had loved him anyway. Now, no matter what, he knew he couldn't let his daughter down.

"Theo? Are you all right?" Ellie's voice, husky with sleep, startled him. Her bright blue eyes were fixed on him, though still groggy with sleep.

"I hope I didn't wake you," he said, feeling surprisingly awkward. "I brought you lunch."

She shifted, sliding back to sit up, careful not to disturb the baby. "Are the hands all fed?"

"Yep. And I cleaned everything up. Later, I'll need

you to tell me what I need to do to prepare for the evening meal."

"I will." Her heavy-lidded gaze slid past him to the tray. "But right now I'm famished. Would you mind taking Amelia so I can eat?"

"Sure." This time he didn't hesitate. He figured if he did this often enough, soon he'd be completely comfortable with holding the baby.

The transfer could have been awkward, but Theo just held out his arms and let Ellie take care of it.

"I've got her," he said, half smiling, barely noticing as Ellie moved to take the bowl of chili from the tray and begin eating with a quiet and intent efficiency.

The rumble of his voice caused Amelia's eyes to open. Colton green. Of course. He'd read somewhere that less than five percent of the world's population had green eyes.

"Hi there, little baby," he crooned, trying not to feel foolish.

Looking up from her meal, Ellie made a sound.

"What?" he asked, reluctantly dragging his gaze from the baby.

"She has a name." Ellie's soft voice carried a bit of steel. "Amelia. You don't have to always call her baby or the infant."

"I wasn't aware I did." He shrugged, refusing to let a small detail like that bother him, despite what Ellie thought it revealed. "Sorry."

Too busy finishing her lunch, Ellie didn't respond, though he could feel her gaze on him as he gently rocked the baby. Gram Dottie would love Amelia, he knew. Now she just had to get well so they could meet.

Something of his worry must have shown in his face.

"Are you all right?" Ellie asked again. "You look… Is something wrong?"

"Yes." He took a deep breath, needing to get it off his chest. "My sister called while you were asleep. Gram Dottie collapsed at the clinic." Despite his best intentions, his voice cracked a little. "The doctors think she has the same thing that killed Mimi Rand. They've got her in isolation."

"Oh, Theo." Ellie's eyes widened. "I'm so sorry."

He nodded, working really hard to keep his expression neutral. "Gemma says they think it's some kind of new virus. The CDC is sending a team and they're even talking about quarantining the entire town."

"What?" Ellie hand moved to her throat. "I've never heard of them doing that, except maybe in movies. It must be really bad."

"Don't panic." His words were for both of them. "We've got some really sharp doctors at the clinic, and Dr. Rand vowed to find a cure. He's working around the clock, despite being really broken up by the death of his ex-wife."

Ellie nodded, her blue eyes huge in her suddenly pale face. Her cheeks flushed, she looked away. "You're right. Of course. There's no need to let my imagination get the best of me. I hope your grandmother gets well quickly."

"She will," he said with a confidence he didn't feel. "Anyway, Gemma is going to come by tomorrow and check us all out. I can't risk the baby's—Amelia's— health by taking her down to the clinic."

"I agree." Her brow creased in a dainty frown. "But it's still safe to go into town, isn't it?"

"Of course."

"Good. I need to pick up a few things." She hesitated,

and then continued, sounding a bit sheepish. "Though now that my stalker might have found me, I'm a little bit scared to go."

"Don't be." Here Theo could speak with confidence. "I've called a company to come out and install an alarm. They'll be here tomorrow. And as far as going into town is concerned, I'll go with you, like a sort of bodyguard."

He could tell his words pleased her from the dusky rose that suffused her face. "Thank you," she said. "If you don't mind, I need to make a trip in the morning, as long as it won't interfere with the alarm installation."

"They're supposed to come around two, so if we go early, we should be fine. I'll need to find out what time my sister plans to stop by, but we can work around that. I want to make sure none of us is sick before we leave the ranch and risk infecting others."

She nodded. "Good point. Do you have any idea what the early symptoms are?"

"It's flu-like. From what I remember Gemma telling me, it'd probably be fever and nausea, weakness or tiredness, cough, sore throat, runny or stuffy nose and maybe body aches."

She nodded. "That's kind of what I thought. So far, Amelia hasn't exhibited any of those."

"What about you?"

"Nothing." Tilting her head, she studied him. "And you? Have you been feeling all right?"

He started to answer, then checked himself. "I'm still dealing with fallout from my rodeo accident, but no flu-like symptoms yet."

"I'm sorry." Her soft voice matched the softening in her blue eyes. "What exactly happened to you?" She blushed, then shook her head. "I'm sorry. I don't mean to pry."

Even now, six months later, he could still barely talk about it. To anyone else. But for some reason, he wanted to tell her. "I got thrown by a horse. A crazy, completely out of control bronc. My skull was broken, I had a right clavicle fracture, messed up my hip and my ankle was shattered."

He took a deep breath, forcing himself to continue. "But the worst thing was that my spine got messed up. All the other injuries were fixable. Meaning, I could heal and go back to competing. But that damn spinal cord injury nearly paralyzed me. They told me I can never ride again. I'm lucky I'm even able to walk."

"You don't sound as if you think you're lucky," she commented.

Which meant he hadn't successfully hidden the bitterness. How could he, when it rode so close to the surface?

"Rodeo was my life," he said quietly. "With that gone…"

Her chin came up. He was starting to recognize that habit of hers. Gesturing at Amelia, still cocooned in his arms, she gave him a look that reminded him of Gram Dottie when she was about to make a point.

"With that gone," Ellie threw his words back at him. "You now have time to focus on something else. *Someone* else. Amelia. Your daughter."

Ellie hadn't meant to be so bold. Judging from the total shutdown on Theo's rugged face, she'd gone entirely too far. Still, she didn't regret her words, nor would she call them back.

Amelia had just lost her mother. She deserved a father who'd give her 100 percent.

Theo had given Ellie a hard stare and then turned without a word, placed Amelia in her bassinette and walked away.

Apparently she'd touched a nerve. Well, baby Amelia's situation touched Ellie. She knew better than most how it felt to have parents who treated you as an afterthought. She'd do everything she could to make sure Amelia didn't suffer the same fate.

The rest of the day passed quickly. She bathed and changed Amelia, before taking her down to the kitchen so Ellie could resume the rest of her duties. Despite his offer to help, Theo didn't put in an appearance. Ellie wasn't really surprised, though she was disappointed.

Since Amelia had gone right to sleep, Ellie was able to work unencumbered. Dinner went off without a hitch— she'd placed the chickens in the oven to roast along with some potatoes, carrots and onions, and opened several cans of rolls and baked them just before it was time to eat. For dessert, she'd made a cobbler using baking mix and canned peaches. Not exactly gourmet fare, but it would fill their hungry bellies. She'd fed Amelia while everything cooked.

The meal turned out delicious and the cowboys were loud and appreciative. Theo arrived just after everyone had started to eat. A few of the men paused, but Theo waved them to continue. So they did, still raining compliments down on Ellie.

She smiled, told them thank you, and waved them back toward their meal.

As had been her habit, Ellie stayed slightly apart, near Amelia's portable bassinette. She watched from near the oven, having just made herself a plate and about to sit down at the smaller dinette table. She'd fed and changed Amelia earlier, and despite her earlier nap, exhaustion battled to claim her.

Theo crossed the room to stand near her. Conversation at the long table briefly ceased. But a quick look from Theo and it resumed, though several of them men made no secret of the fact that they were watching.

"I'm sorry," Theo said, pitching his voice low so the others couldn't hear. "I promised to help you with the evening meal and I forgot." He rubbed his leg as he talked to her, making her realize his injuries were no doubt hurting him.

"That's okay." Surprised that he'd even apologized, she slid the plate she'd just filled toward him. "Go ahead and eat. I'll make another plate and join you."

He glanced at Amelia, who, with her tummy full, slept contentedly. "How is she?"

"Still fine." Turning, she busied herself filling a plate with food. Once she was done, she carried it over to the smaller table that sat in the kitchen proper.

After a moment, he followed and took the chair opposite her, his expression shuttered. "I talked to my sister. Gemma's going to be here about eight-thirty tomorrow morning. That'll give her plenty of time to check us all out. The stores in Dead River don't open until ten anyway."

"Sounds great." She glanced at the still-sleeping baby. "What about Amelia? After she's cleared as healthy, can we bring her with us? I can't exactly leave her here alone."

"Of course not. I'll help you with her." Flashing her a preoccupied smile, he dug in. The muscles rippling under his button-down shirt made her mouth go dry. Even here,

Theo radiated masculinity and sex appeal. And tension, though he appeared to relax a little as he began eating. "This is great," he said. "How did you manage to make all this and still look after the baby?"

Secretly pleased, she shrugged. "It's nothing fancy, that's why."

"It's good food. Thank you for managing to act both as cook and nanny. I promise I'll make it up to you as soon as I can."

He sounded earnest and charming, and the sparkle in his emerald eyes was pretty damn close to irresistible. Dangerous thinking, she chided herself. "I may hold you to that," she replied lightly. "Now eat up. There's peach cobbler for dessert."

He made a moan of delight and again she blushed. When she got the warm cobbler out of the oven, the men cheered. She served it herself, wanting to make sure there was enough for everyone.

After the hands had taken themselves off to the bunkhouse, Theo guided her toward the living room couch, handing her the remote before going back to fetch the bassinette, which he placed near Ellie.

"Sit. I'll clean up," he said. "And for breakfast tomorrow morning, Gram Dottie used to make us this baked egg dish that you can refrigerate and just pop in the oven. I helped her once or twice, so I think I remember how to do it."

Surprised and touched, Ellie nodded. "Thank you."

"You're welcome." He flashed a grin so devastating her breath caught in her chest. "Now relax and watch something on TV. I'll join you once I'm finished in the kitchen."

Strange. Too tired to comment, she glanced at Amelia, who still slept. Perfect baby. Leaning back into the overstuffed couch cushions, she pressed the power button on the remote. Since she still didn't know the television channels for this area, she pressed one at random. A legal drama was on, one she thought she might have caught a few episodes of in the past.

The next thing she knew, Theo was shaking her shoulder. "Ellie, wake up. It's late and you need to go on to bed."

Groggy, she blinked up at him, trying to understand. "What...what time is it?"

His lazy smile touched her like a sensual caress. "A little after ten. You fell asleep and looked so peaceful. I didn't want to bother you."

"Amelia." She looked for the baby, not finding her. "Where's Amelia?"

"I carried her upstairs a minute ago. She needed a diaper change and I think I figured out how to do it." He lifted his shoulder in a sheepish shrug. "Though you might want to double-check my handiwork. She's asleep in the crib."

He'd *changed Amelia?* Talk about giant strides, especially from a man who'd barely been able to say his daughter's name. Wisely, she kept her sentiment to herself. She sensed if she made a big deal about it or even commented, Theo would shut down.

"She's going to want her nighttime bottle soon." Pushing herself up off the sofa, she stifled a yawn. "I'll just go ahead and make it, so I'll have it when she wakes."

He eyed her. "How do you know how to do all this, anyway?"

"My parents were very active in the church," she said, shrugging. "When they went off to be missionaries, I stayed with a neighboring family who had triplets. Mrs. Anderson needed all the help she could get. I learned not only how to take care of babies, but I also learned how to cook."

And Ellie had felt glad to be needed. Even if later, as she'd grown older, she'd come to understand she was being used as an unpaid nanny and cook. She hadn't truly minded, as she'd come to love the triplets, but when she'd needed to get a job to earn her own money, she'd asked to be paid. Instead, she'd found herself out on the street. Luckily, one of her high school friends had taken her in until she could find a job and save for a place of her own.

Taking her arm, he guided her into the kitchen and over to a chair. His slow smile made her mouth go dry. "Sit. Tell me what to do and I'll make the bottle."

Wondering if she was still asleep and dreaming, she gave him instructions, unable to resist the tiniest bit of flirting. "It would seem you have a natural talent," she told him, smiling shyly. His answering grin made her feel warm all over.

When the bottle was ready and he'd tested the temperature with a drop on his wrist, the way she'd told him, he handed it over, his fingers brushing against hers and lingering a second too long.

Telling herself it was in her imagination, she took it and pushed to her feet, again swaying slightly. He reached out to steady her, and somehow she ended up pressed against the muscular length of him.

Instantly, her senses leaped to life as she came deliciously awake. Breasts tingling against his rock-hard chest, her entire lower body began to melt as she stared up at him.

Green gaze dark, he lowered his face as if about to

kiss her. She caught her breath, her heart lurching crazily, her mouth already throbbing. She wanted him so badly in that moment she shivered, dizzy with longing.

And then he released her, shaking his head, one corner of his sensual mouth curving. "Sorry. Old habits."

Somehow she managed to make it out of that room and into hers without collapsing. Only when she'd closed the door and dropped down onto her bed and covered her face with her hands did she let herself think about what had just almost happened.

The only reason it hadn't was that Theo had enough sense to back away.

Though she had to admit, the casual *old habits* had stung. But then, she chastised herself, what the hell had she expected? Theo Colton wasn't for her. She needed her job and the protection Theo had promised from her crazy stalker. Which meant she needed to get herself under control and forget even thinking about being attracted to him.

Amelia began making snuffling sounds, which meant she was about to cry. Ellie scooped her up, gently pressing the bottle's nipple against her perfect, bow-shaped lips. The baby latched on, suckling like a champion, which made Ellie smile.

Once Amelia had finished, Ellie burped her. One final check of her diaper, which had been put on perfectly, and she put the baby back in her crib, amazed at how quickly Amelia dropped into sleep.

Attending to her evening preparations as quickly as she could, Ellie brushed her teeth, washed up and changed into her pajamas.

She climbed into bed, ready to fall asleep, even though

she knew she'd probably dream of Theo. She resolved, if she did, to promptly forget all about them in the morning.

That night and the next morning, Theo refused to even think about what foolish urge had made him almost kiss Ellie Parker. He'd been without a woman too long; that had to be it. After all, Ellie wasn't even his usual type. He preferred his women curvy and flirty and casual. With her willowy, athletic figure, Ellie not only wasn't his type, but was too serious by far.

And too sweet, he thought. The kind of woman who needed a white picket fence and a husband who was content to work a nine-to-five and come home to her each night.

In other words, everything Theo was not. Little Miss Serious would want it all, including love. He wasn't in the habit of intentionally breaking hearts, and he didn't intend to start now.

Rushing through his shower, he hurried downstairs to get the egg casserole baking in the oven. He also made a pot of coffee, waiting impatiently for it to finish brewing. Outside, the sun hadn't yet risen, and he could tell the outside air would be crisp. His favorite kind of morning, back when he'd wake up and drive out to the rodeo grounds to check out the lay of the land. He'd walk the grounds, a cup of java steaming in his hands, looking for the other cowboys who were out there doing the exact same thing.

Shaking his head, he ruthlessly pushed that thought away the same way he'd quashed his surprising desire for Ellie.

Pretty soon the kitchen smelled like eggs and sausage and coffee. The hired hands begin to drift in, one by one, hanging up their jackets and wiping off their work boots on the mat just inside the back door before heading to their table in the adjoining room.

The casserole seemed to be a big hit, judging from the appreciative comments and requests for seconds. He'd already put the second one in and it had finished cooking just as he scooped the last bit out of the first pan.

The hands finished eating, several of them joking and laughing and clapping him on the back, calling him a damn good cook. As they filed out, Theo began to wonder why Ellie hadn't yet put in an appearance.

Surely what had almost happened last night hadn't made her skittish?

Fear stabbed him. What if she was sick? Or Amelia? Gemma wouldn't be here for another hour or so. Trying to contain his rising panic, he rushed to Ellie's room, finding the door closed. Taking a deep breath, he tapped lightly. When he received no answer, he went ahead and opened the door.

Inside, he heard water running and realized she was in the shower. Amelia gurgled, awake in her crib. He went closer and swore she smiled at him, flailing her tiny hands. Glancing toward the open bathroom door, Theo leaned over the crib, reaching for the baby. His hands looked huge even to him as he unbuttoned her Onesie so he could check her diaper. It was dry, which meant Ellie had changed her. He noticed two empty baby bottles on the dresser. One had to be from last night. The other meant Ellie had already been downstairs to make her formula and fed her. He had no idea when, but it had to have been before sunrise.

Amelia cooed, and Theo felt his smile widen. He'd

never been much for babies—hell, what guy was—but this one seemed cuter than most.

"Well, good morning," he said, in what he thought might be a reasonable facsimile of baby talk. "You look mighty pretty this morning."

And then he'd be damned, but Amelia latched her teeny, tiny, wrinkled pink fist on to his finger and held on as if she knew what she was doing.

Throat tight, he stood still and let her.

A moment later the shower cut off. "I'm in here with Amelia," he called out, just in case Ellie planned to walk out here naked or something. For his own protection as well, because baby or no baby, he wasn't sure he'd be able to resist a nude Ellie. In fact, even thinking about it...

He forced his thoughts back to the baby, picking her up and holding her close as if she were also a shield.

"Morning." Ellie wandered into the room, wrapped tightly in a towel, wearing another on her head like a turban. She looked pink and young and absolutely delectable.

Glad he was holding the baby, he managed a friendly smile. "I got worried when you didn't come down for breakfast."

"I'm sorry." She sounded anything but. "I got up early to take care of Amelia and then came back up here and feel asleep. You'd promised to take care of feeding the hands, so I decided not to worry about that."

Her gentle dig made him want to laugh. Instead he nodded. "There's still some egg casserole left if you're hungry."

"I'm starving. I'll come down and warm it up after I finish getting ready. Do you want to take Amelia with you or..."

A not so subtle request for him to go. He almost offered to take the baby with him, but then he realized he wouldn't know what to do if she cried or needed something. No, he'd need a bit more practice and experience before he tried handling her alone.

"I'll just put her back in her crib," he said, pretending not to notice her disappointed expression. "Come on downstairs when you're ready. Gemma will be here in a couple of hours."

"Ninety minutes," she corrected automatically. "You said eight-thirty. It's seven now."

"Right." Once he had gently placed Amelia back, he carefully avoided looking at Ellie or going anywhere close to her. His hands were empty now and already he was itching to fill them.

Giving himself a mental shake, he hurried from her room and back down to the kitchen.

Chapter 4

Only when Theo was gone, closing her door behind him, did Ellie release the breath she hadn't even realized she was holding. She didn't know what it was about the man, but he made her want things she had no business wanting.

She'd never met anyone like him. So confident in his masculinity, with sex appeal practically radiating from his skin. She could well imagine how many women he had begging for his touch. The way Amelia's mother apparently had.

No way did Ellie plan to become one of them.

No way.

She hurried through the rest of her preparations, taking a little extra care with her hair, since she'd be meeting Theo's sister as well as going into town.

When she went downstairs, Amelia in her carrier, the empty kitchen had been cleaned and appeared spotless. A plate sat on the stove, covered by a paper towel. She peeked under and saw it was the egg casserole, which looked fantastic.

A quick zap in the microwave, and she sat down to eat, her stomach rumbling.

Her first mouthful had her rolling her eyes in delight. It was good. More than good. Chewing slowly so she could get every ounce of flavor, she finished off her plate in record time and wished there was more.

"Did you like it?" Theo appeared. "It won't hurt my feelings if you didn't."

She had to smile at that. "I need your recipe," she said, paying him the highest compliment anyone could give a cook. "That was absolutely restaurant quality."

He nodded. "Thank you."

"Where is she?" a feminine voice called from the other room. Ellie straightened, turning toward the doorway. A tiny woman with long blond hair breezed into the room.

"Gemma." Theo smiled. "Ellie, this is my sister, Gemma. Gemma, Ellie. She's been taking care of Amelia."

"Pleased to meet you." Green eyes exactly like Theo's flashed as Gemma smiled at Ellie. Spotting the bassinette, she gasped. "Oh, there she is!"

Gemma rushed over, staring down at Amelia while she slept. When she raised her head to look at Theo, her eyes shone. "She's beautiful. I can see Mimi in her some, but mostly she looks like you."

Theo shrugged. "Maybe," he allowed. Ellie considered that great progress, since just yesterday he'd been talking about a DNA test.

Gemma turned to Ellie. "Tell me about her." Quietly intense, she focused on Ellie. "How's she been acting? Any problems taking her bottle? How's her poop? Is she sleeping okay? Or too much?"

"Whoa, take it easy." Theo held up a hand before Ellie could even begin to formulate a response. "Gemma, Ellie's not used to you like we are. Go easy at first."

"It's okay," Ellie spoke up, amused. "Gemma, Amelia seems fine to me. She sleeps a lot, but she's still a newborn. She's eating fine, her poop looks like baby poop and she hasn't been running a fever."

"Thank you." Expression satisfied, Gemma lifted Amelia in her arms. "Is there someplace I can examine her?"

"Sure." Ellie got up. "We can take her to my room. Her crib is set up there."

Leading the way, when she turned to show Gemma into the room, she realized Theo hadn't followed.

Gemma noticed where Ellie was looking. "Don't worry. I'll check him out after this. He knows I've got to examine you, so I'm sure he wanted to give you some privacy."

Feeling herself flush all over for no good reason, Ellie was glad Gemma had begun to undress Amelia.

"Her skin looks normal," Gemma said. "No rashes." She turned the baby over with practiced ease and reached into her satchel for a thermometer. "Let me check her temp."

Ellie waited while Gemma silently counted. She found herself holding her breath as the other women withdrew the thermometer and checked it.

"Normal," Gemma pronounced. "I'd say she's as healthy as could be."

"That's wonderful." Grabbing a clean diaper, Ellie moved forward, only to have Gemma take it from her and change the baby herself. She even buckled Amelia back into her Onesie, crooning nonsense to her the entire time. Amelia loved it, gurgling and cooing back, all smiles.

"You have a way with babies," Ellie said.

"Thanks." Still focused on her niece, Gemma barely looked up. "How often are you feeding her?"

"Every couple of hours," Ellie responded. "I looked

it up on the internet and saw she's supposed to eat eight to twelve times a day for the first month."

"Is she eating well every time?"

"Yes." Ellie smiled. "She drains the bottle every single time."

"Definitely healthy." Straightening, Gemma fixed Ellie with a practical eye. "Now it's your turn. How are you feeling?"

"Fine. No fever, I'm eating well. No nausea or sweating. Whatever this virus is, I haven't caught it."

"Do you mind if I take your temperature?"

Smiling, Ellie pointed at the other woman's bag. "As long as you don't use the same thermometer you used on Amelia."

Gemma laughed at that. "No worries. Though that one has been sterilized."

A few minutes later, the examination complete, Gemma also pronounced Ellie healthy. She left Ellie and Amelia and went to check out Theo.

Meanwhile, Ellie took Amelia into the kitchen and fed her another bottle. She had just raised her to her shoulder to burp her when Theo and Gemma returned. Next to his petite sister, Theo appeared even larger and more powerful, the essence of masculinity.

"We have the all-clear," Theo announced. "And now we can go into town and pick up supplies."

"Into town?" Looking from one to the other, Gemma frowned, appearing concerned. "I'm not so sure that's a good idea."

"Why not?"

"The virus," Gemma answered simply. "While it hasn't reached epidemic status yet, it shows signs of heading that way. The CDC is concerned and you should be too."

"We have to get supplies," Theo said. "And unless it turns into some sort of plague, we're not going to stay holed up here like a bunch of paranoid doomsday nuts."

He had a point, Ellie thought. But then again, so did Gemma.

"Stock up on your supplies, then," Gemma told them. "And stay away from the general populace as much as you can."

"You're a fine one to talk." Theo ruffled her hair, earning a sharp look of rebuke. "You're working in the clinic, right there in the middle of all the sick people."

"Fine." Throwing up her hands, Gemma gave in. "But at least keep Amelia away. Can you do that?"

Ellie looked from her to Theo and back again. "We don't have anyone else to watch her."

"Gram was going to help out, but she got sick," Theo added.

"Why can't Ellie go to town alone and you watch Amelia?" Gemma asked.

At a loss for words since she didn't want to go into details about her stalker, Ellie looked helplessly at Theo.

"She can't," Theo said. "And that's that. So we have no choice but to take Amelia with us."

"Then I'll keep the baby," Gemma said brightly, her sharp green gaze going from one to the other. "I'd love to spend some time getting to know my niece, and honestly, I'd feel better if she stayed away from town until we get a handle on this virus."

"Are you sure?" Ellie asked, hesitant to shirk her duty. "I really don't mind."

"Amelia can stay here." Theo took Ellie's arm. "Let's

get going so we can get back before Gemma has to go to work."

He hustled her from the room before she could protest. "And make sure you bring your sense of humor."

Dumbfounded, she froze, staring at him. "What do you mean?"

"I know you're worried about the stalker. But for today, I'd like you to try and forget about him. You deserve to have a good time."

"Do I?" She frowned. "If not for me—"

"Shhh." Pressing a finger against her lips, he shook his head. "That's what I'm talking about. I want you to promise."

Staring up at his rugged profile, she felt the weight on her shoulders slide off. "You're right," she said. "At least for today, I'm going to try to enjoy myself."

"Good." The approval in his voice increased her determination to try to pretend her stalker didn't exist. At least for a few hours. She knew she'd have to go back to normal soon enough.

"Do you have everything you need?" he asked.

"Let me grab my jacket." Once she did, she put it on and smiled up at him. "I'm ready."

"Really? What about your purse?"

She shrugged. "I rarely use one. I just stuffed my wallet in my jacket pocket and I'm ready to go."

"What about your lipstick and perfume and all the stuff women always have to carry around with them?"

"I have my ChapStick." She pulled it out to show him. "That's all I need."

The way he looked at her, she wondered if she might have grown two heads.

"Okay," he finally said, grabbing a black cowboy hat from the coatrack and jamming in on his head. "Let's go."

He drove a large black Dually pickup truck, with shiny chrome wheels and an NPRA decal on the back window. When he started it up, the engine rumbled like a hot rod. Inside, there were leather seats, wood-grain trim and every luxury you could get.

She couldn't help laughing.

"What so funny?" he asked, glancing sideways at her.

"I've never seen a vehicle that matched someone's personality as much as yours does."

Putting the shifter in Drive, he shrugged, though he looked pleased. "I spent a lot of time in my truck. I needed to make sure it had everything I liked."

She nodded. "I bet it works great when the snows come."

"It does." He tipped the front of his hat with his index finger. "I know you said you'd just arrived in town when you applied to work at my ranch, but did you get to do any exploring?"

Town. Other people. Maybe even crowds. Just like that, her nervousness slammed back into her, full force. "You know, maybe we should reconsider this."

He glanced at her, and then squeezed her shoulder. "Focus, honey. I asked you if you were able to check out Dead River."

Honey. Even aware the word was a mindless endearment that came naturally to a man like Theo, Ellie felt warm inside.

"Focus," he repeated. "We're talking about town."

After a deep breath, she nodded. "Ok, fine. To answer your question, I was really low on funds. So, no.

But I have to say, from what I did see of it, it looks like a nice place."

At that, he laughed. "Nice, huh? That's what I always thought. One of the reasons I couldn't wait to get out of here."

"Nice doesn't always equal boring," she felt compelled to point out.

"Maybe not, but Dead River is exactly that. Dead. The lights go out and the sidewalks roll up as soon as the sun sets."

Surely, Theo exaggerated. "You're telling me there are no bars?" she asked dryly. "I find that hard to believe."

One corner of his sensual mouth lifted. "You equate bars with fun?"

Shaking her head, she laughed. "Isn't that what you meant?"

Shrugging, he looked sheepish. And adorably sexy too. She'd never really had a thing for men in cowboy hats, but Theo looked amazing in his. Ellie hoped that with time, she'd manage to become immune to his over-the-top charm.

As they rumbled from the dirt road to the blacktop, old-school country music wailing away softly on the radio, she couldn't help marveling at the odd twists and turns her life had taken to get her here.

"I need to ask a favor," Theo said, sounding oddly hesitant, which was unlike him.

"Okay." She twisted in her seat as much as the seat belt would allow, and faced him. "What's up?"

"Would you stay and take care of Amelia on a permanent basis?"

"Permanent?" She swallowed hard, not wanting to tell

him as long as there was a stalker out there, she pretty much lived her life day by day.

"Yes. You're good with her, and Gemma cleared you as healthy. I know I hired you as cook, but I can easily find someone else to fill that position."

"No." Surprising even herself with her vehemence, Ellie shook her head. "I can do both." She took a deep breath, daring herself to go for the gusto. "But I'll need an increased salary."

A dimple flashed in his cheek. "How much of an increase?"

"How much would you be paying someone else to come in and cook?"

He laughed. "Touché. So you want me to double your salary."

Trying not to wince, she nodded. "Yes."

Flashing her an amused look, he drummed his fingers on the steering wheel as he made a right turn. "Are you up to working two full-time jobs? You know that baby is going to be keeping you up some nights. Getting up before sunrise to make sure breakfast is ready might be a bit of a stretch."

"I need the money." Though her parents had drilled into her the importance of living a Spartan existence, ever since she realized someone was stalking her, Ellie had dreamed of making enough money to fly to another country and disappear. Make that another continent. She wanted to start over, as it were. Maybe doing so would be running away, but she didn't care. She was tired of looking over her shoulder.

She didn't even think she'd let her mother and father know where she was. She wasn't even sure they'd care.

"How about this?" Theo said. "I'm willing to give it

a shot, on a trial basis. Provided you promise to tell me if doing two jobs gets to be too much. Taking care of Amelia has to be your number-one priority. Cooking will have to come in second. As long as my hands are fed on time and the food is reasonably tasty, we'll have a deal."

Trying not to be insulted by the reasonably tasty part of his remark, she stuck out her hand. "Deal."

When he slid his big fingers into hers, she felt a jolt. The same kind of shock she'd noticed the few times she brushed up against him, as if his body contained some sort of electromagnetic pull, drawing her to him.

Fanciful and stupid, she chided herself. She needed to focus on reality. This double job, double paycheck would be a good thing. With no living expenses other than clothing and toiletries, making a hefty salary would enable her to sack money away, after she fixed her car. She'd long dreamed of going to Australia. Maybe now she could even start planning.

When they turned the corner onto Main Street, she sat up straighter. Dead River. What a name. Despite that, something about this town called to her, which was the entire reason she'd stopped here in the first place. And then, of course, her car died.

All she'd been thinking of was escaping her life and her stalker, so she'd headed north, planning on traveling through Wyoming on her way to Montana or maybe even Idaho.

But the instant she'd stepped foot in Dead River, she felt as if she was home. Foolish? Maybe. But so far she'd managed to survive by relying on her gut instincts, and they hadn't failed her yet.

She'd seen the help wanted ad clipped on a bulletin board in the coffee shop. She'd called, gotten an interview and here she was. She'd always had an aptitude for cooking. Apparently she also had a knack with babies.

Since she really liked Amelia, and had always loved to cook, it was all good. At least, until her stalker had found her. Now, her very presence here could put them all in danger.

Focus. Theo's admonition had her pushing her worries about what she might have brought to the Coltons' doorstep out of her mind. She'd gotten to go to town with a hunky cowboy. Might as well let herself enjoy it.

Parking in front of a hardware store, Theo grinned at her as he pointed across the street. "See? There's the bar."

Unable to resist the power of that grin, Ellie smiled back as she got out of the truck.

A few people waved at Theo. She noticed most of the men wore either cowboy hats or baseball-type caps. Doug Gasper, one of the guys she'd worked with in the bookstore in Boulder, had called them tractor caps.

She caught a few people eying her with open curiosity, but it felt friendly, in keeping with the overall vibe of the town.

Though the cool air felt crisp, it also felt fresh. She inhaled deeply, a bit of a spring in her step. Pure, like the air near her hometown. But Dead River had a more old-fashioned, close-knit sort of feel.

"I'm going to run in here," Theo said, indicating a barbershop with an old-fashioned barber pole outside the door. "I need to get a trim. You're welcome to come with me, or you can take care of your own shopping. Up to you."

She almost opened her mouth to ask him not to cut his sexy, tousled hair, but she realized she didn't have the right to say she liked his hair the way it was. "I think I'll head over to the drugstore. Meet you back here?"

He grinned. "Either way. If you get done first, that's fine. Otherwise I'll find you up there."

"Sounds good." Before she stepped away, she couldn't resist glancing around. Not that she expected her stalker to show his face in broad daylight, but still. The intruder in her room had made her extremely nervous.

Theo noticed. "Hey, would you rather I go with you? I can always get my hair trimmed another time."

Heaven help her, she actually considered it. But she'd never been timid, and she sure as heck didn't intend to start now. "No," she said, squaring her shoulders. "It's broad daylight. Go ahead and get your haircut. I'll be fine."

A knowing look flashed in his eyes. "Are you sure?"

"Yes." To prove it, she started off in the direction of the Dead River Pharmacy. "See you in a little bit."

Halfway there, she glanced back. Theo still stood outside the barbershop, watching over her like her personal guardian angel.

Inside the drugstore, she turned and looked around. Unlike the huge chains, this small one seemed homey. Clean and well lit, each aisle clearly marked. Relaxing, she grabbed a small basket and headed toward the cosmetics section.

"Can I help you?" An elderly woman in a white coat stepped out from behind the pharmacy counter. "I'm Gloria Hitch."

Ellie shook her hand. "I'm just stocking up. I'm working out at the Colton Ranch."

A smile creased Gloria's lined face. "I thought you were new in town. Welcome to Dead River. Though you picked a mighty bad time to come. I'm sure you've heard about the virus."

"Yes, ma'am." Ellie glanced at a large bottle of Vitamin C tablets. "I'm thinking about taking some preventative measures."

Gloria snorted. "Pills can't help with a virus, honey. Maybe keep a cold away. I'm just hoping one of those doctors at the clinic can figure something out before this thing turns into an epidemic."

The bell over the front door tinkled. Ellie turned, but it wasn't Theo. An older man in a cowboy hat came inside. "Morning, Gloria." He squinted at Ellie. "And who do we have here? Are you one of Brenda Forest's children?"

"She's not," Gloria put in before Ellie could answer. "She working at the Colton Ranch. She hasn't even been in town all that long."

"Where you from, honey?" the old man asked. "My name is Horace, by the way. Horace Gunn."

"I'm Ellie Parker. I'm from Boulder, Colorado," she answered.

"Ellie, you're the second newcomer from that town," he said. "I met a young man at the café yesterday who said he was from there too. Is he here with you?"

A chill snaked down Ellie's spine. "No. Did you happen to catch his name?"

His bushy gray eyebrows drew together in a frown. "I don't think he gave it to me."

Struggling not to show her disappointment, Ellie sighed. "Oh well. I was hoping it was a friend of mine. He was supposed to meet me here," she lied. "But he hasn't made it yet. What did this guy look like?"

"Out of place," Horace answered promptly. "He wasn't a cowboy, that's for sure. Not that everyone around here is, but he looked like one of those dope-smoking, hippy types."

So did half the people in Boulder. "You mean like a college student?"

"Nah, he was older than that." He peered at her, his faded blue eyes sparkling. "Does your friend have long, reggae hair?"

"Reggae hair?" Confused, Ellie tried to understand. "You mean like dreadlocks?"

Horace shrugged. "I guess. I think it was some kind of wig. Is that your friend?"

"No." Ellie tried to sound casual, though she thought she probably failed miserably. "That probably wasn't him."

"Unless he's wearing a disguise," Gloria put in.

"Why would he do that?" Horace's frown deepened.

"So he could surprise her, silly." Gloria turned back toward the pharmacy counter. "Maybe he doesn't want you to know he's in town yet."

Ellie nodded. Gloria was closer to the truth than she realized. Though why anyone would care to wear dreadlocks in a small Wyoming ranching town was beyond her. He'd fit right in if he was in Boulder. Here, he'd stick out like a donkey in a herd of horses.

"Can you describe anything else about him?" she asked, remembering the outline of the intruder who'd been in her room. "Was he tall and lean? Or short and stout?"

"Tall," Horace answered promptly. "And he was a skinny feller. I did notice he had a lot of freckles, if that helps. Does your friend have freckles?'

"No." Pretending disappointment, Ellie shrugged. "That must have been somebody else."

"Horace, your blood pressure pills are ready," Gloria called, winking at Ellie. "Come get them, and let that girl finish her shopping."

Shaking his head, Horace dipped his chin at her and shuffled over to the counter.

Since she had a few more things she needed, Ellie gathered up shampoo and conditioner, a new blow dryer, as hers had given up the ghost right after she'd started working at the ranch and a bottle of generic multivitamins.

She waited behind Horace, who was leaning on the counter telling Gloria all about some dog he'd had back in the 1950s. Clearly having heard this same story numerous times, Gloria rolled her eyes and motioned Ellie up to the register.

Gloria and Horace made a big deal out of Ellie's reusable cloth bag, which Ellie found amusing. In Boulder, people were shocked if you asked for paper or—heaven forbid—plastic.

After she'd paid, she waved goodbye and headed out the door toward the barbershop. On the way there, she stopped to admire the window display in the florist shop. She had just started to turn away when someone came out of nowhere and tackled her, knocking her to the ground.

She hit hard, with a little scream. Panicked, she raised her head, trying to get a good look at her assailant. She saw a black hoody and battered tennis shoes, but since he had the hood up, she couldn't get a good look at his face.

"You belong to me," he snarled, looming over her as if he meant to kick her while she was down. And then, as she opened her mouth to scream for help, someone else came out of nowhere, tackling him.

Theo. He swung at the guy and connected. Wincing

with pain, Theo twisted and tried to grab the other man. Instead, Theo crumpled to the pavement.

Taking advantage of this, her attacker ran off.

Shakily, Ellie got to her feet. Her jeans were ripped at the knees, and one knee was scraped and bloody, as were her palms.

The bag she'd been carrying had remained intact, though some of her purchases had been disgorged. Slowly, methodically, she picked them up, tears pricking at her eyes. Broad daylight was all she could think. Her stalker had attacked her in broad daylight.

A lot slower getting up, Theo stood hunched, clearly making an effort to straighten. "Are you all right?" he asked her, limping over to try to help.

"I should be asking you the same question." The instant she spoke, she regretted it.

Though his expression hardened, he exhaled. "It's my damn back. If not for the rodeo injury, I would have had him."

Oddly enough, she felt the urge to comfort him. "It's okay," she began. "He took us both by surprise. Not your fault. I think—"

Hauling her up against him, he kissed her. Hard and punishing, as though he meant to make them both suffer. Stunned at first, she returned his kiss with a recklessness born of adrenaline. When he broke away, leaving her mouth burning as if on fire, they were both breathing faster.

Knees weak, Ellie leaned against the brick wall, trying to regain her bearings.

"We're going to the police station," Theo said to her, as if he hadn't just completely rocked her world. "Come on." Keeping a firm grip on her arm, he steered her back toward his pickup. "Flint should be on duty now. He definitely needs to know about this."

Despite her protests, he loaded her up in his truck and drove her the few blocks to the police station. The one-story, redbrick building looked professional and Spartan, hedges trimmed nicely and the paved lot clean.

After he parked, Theo rushed over to Ellie's side, opened her door and helped her down as if he thought she'd suddenly gotten fragile.

"I'm not badly injured," she said, amused and appreciative all at once. "I can walk."

"Good to know," he said, yet he didn't let go of her arm.

Once inside the glass doors, Ellie looked around with interest. Standard-issue police station chairs, check. There were only six of the plastic and metal monstrosities, separated by a few cheap end tables.

A Formica counter separated the receptionist from the waiting area. The stout, middle-aged woman stood, shaking her curly black ringlets and grinning at Theo. Her name tag said she was Kendra Walker, Dispatcher.

"Theo Colton." She reached across the counter for a hug. "It's been way too long since we've had the pleasure of your company. What are you doing in town?"

"Unfortunately, today I'm here on business, not pleasure," he said, moving enough so she could get a good look at Ellie.

"Oh my." Her heavily made up eyes widened. "What on earth happened to you, honey?"

"We need to talk to Flint," Theo put in before Ellie could speak. "Is he here?"

"Sure." She buzzed them in. "You know the way to his office."

The back area looked like a stereotypical, small-town police station. The same cheap chairs, a couple of metal desks and a few rooms with doors. Theo led Ellie to one of these. A nameplate on the door proclaimed Flint Colton, Chief of Police.

"Theo!" Flint stood when they entered, his face breaking into a welcoming smile. Then he caught sight of Ellie and frowned. "What happened?"

"Someone jumped her. We think it might have been her stalker." Theo swallowed. "I tried to get him, but with this bum back, he got away after knocking her to the ground."

"Are you all right?" Flint asked Ellie. "Do you need medical attention?"

Theo cursed before she could answer. "I should have gotten her checked out at the clinic before I came here."

"Hello?" Ellie waved her hand in front of Theo. "I'm right here. And I haven't lost the ability to speak. Flint, I'm fine. Just a little shaken up, that's all."

Indicating the two chairs in front of his desk, Flint waited until they were seated before taking his own seat. He grabbed a pad of paper and a pen. "Can you give me a description?"

"Not really. He had on a black hoody, and I couldn't get a good look at his face." She took a deep breath. "He's never attacked me before. He just followed me around and left creepy notes and black roses, stuff like that. Until he showed up in my room here, I've never even caught a glimpse of him. And now this."

"Ellie, we're not even sure it's the same guy," Flint cautioned.

She stared at him in disbelief. "Who else could it be?"

"That's what we're trying to find out." His calm and

measured voice helped her regain her admittedly shaky self-control. "Granted, Dead River doesn't have a lot of crime, but we have some. The guy today might have been a purse snatcher."

"I don't carry a purse." Ellie remembered the old man in the drugstore and snapped her fingers. She relayed what he'd told her about meeting someone from her hometown.

"Horace met him at the café," she finished. "And he had a pretty good description."

"Horace Gunn?" Theo asked. When she answered in the affirmative, he smiled. "Figures. He's a fixture at the pharmacy. He's sweet on Gloria Hitch. She's the pharmacist."

"I met her." Turning back to Flint, she waited until he'd finished writing.

"A white guy with dreadlocks?" Flint shook his head. "Someone like that would stand out like a sore thumb in Dead River. If he's your stalker, he'll be pretty easy to find."

"Not if he wears that hoody," she put in. "Whoever broke into my room at the ranch wore a hoody and a ski mask. Plus, today he said I belong to him. So it's a pretty sure bet it's the same guy."

"All right." Putting down his pen, Flint steepled his fingers on the desk in front of him. "For now, we'll assume this guy is your stalker. The fact that he attacked you is not a good sign. It could mean that he's escalating. If so, you will be in danger until he's apprehended."

Chapter 5

In danger. Theo tensed at the words, the rush of protectiveness he felt surprising him. "I'll protect you," he declared.

Both Flint and Ellie turned to look at him. Ellie with disbelief, Flint with surprise.

Even as he'd said the words, Theo realized he shouldn't have spoken. Because of his back injury, he hadn't done such a good job protecting her at all. This infuriated him. After all, he'd been told he couldn't even ride a horse—not a bronc, but a regular, tame, saddle horse. Why did he think he could protect Ellie? Most likely, he'd fail.

For a guy who'd never backed down from a fight, this news was sobering.

"I need to go," Ellie said. "As in, leave town. I'm sorry, Theo. But I can't risk putting Amelia or anyone else in danger. If you'll just pay me what you owe me, I'll be moving on."

"You quit?" Theo dragged his fingers through his freshly shorn hair. "We just reached a new agreement. You can't quit without giving me some sort of notice."

Ellie bit her lip. "These are extraordinary circumstances," she began.

"For everyone," Theo put in. "I need your help. I don't

have anyone else to take care of Amelia. You can't let her down."

"How can I risk her?" she shot back. "If this guy, whoever he is, is bent on hurting me, he won't let a tiny baby stop him."

"I'm having security installed this afternoon, you know that." Theo heard the edge of desperation in his voice, but it couldn't be helped. With Gram sick, he literally had no one to help him take care of Amelia. He knew absolutely nothing about infants—what little he'd learned had been from watching Ellie. "No one will be able to get into the house undetected."

"That's fine, but what about the rest of the time? I have to come into town occasionally. I can't be a hermit at the ranch."

"When you do, I'll go with you." Theo tried not to let his frustration show. "You'll never be alone. I'll protect you."

Flint cleared his throat, making them both look at him. "Are you two done?"

Looking abashed, Ellie nodded. Crossing his arms, Theo smiled thinly and waited.

"I'll have my men look for either a guy with dreads or a guy in a black hoodie. Meanwhile, why don't you both finish up whatever shopping you have left and head back home? Ellie, are you sure you don't need to go by the clinic and have yourself looked at?"

"I'm sure," she answered. "Just a bunch of scrapes. I can fix them myself at the ranch."

"What about you, Theo? Is your back okay?"

"Fine," Theo growled. "Just fine."

"Okay, then." Flint stood and met Theo's gaze. "I'll call you when I find out anything."

"Sounds good." Again Theo took Ellie's arm. This time, she shrugged him off. He sensed she was furious with him, probably because of the kiss, though it might be because he'd failed her.

He couldn't blame her. He'd not only failed her, but failed himself.

Barely speaking, he drove them to the supermarket and picked up more diapers and another case of formula, just in case. Ellie had wanted to stay in the truck, claiming to be self-conscious about her torn jeans and scrapes. He let her, making sure the doors were locked, glad of the time alone to get his shit back together.

She'd be fine, he told himself, wishing he could believe it. Sunlight, busy parking lot and locked truck would all combine to keep her from harm.

Nevertheless, he rushed through his shopping, and made it back outside in record time. This protective feeling was new and felt…strange. But good. As the older brother, Flint had made sure Gemma and Theo never lacked for anything. Of the three siblings, Flint had been the protector, Gemma the nurturer, and Theo'd been the cool, fun one. He'd never had anyone to look after other than himself. Now he had two people. Amelia and Ellie.

And he'd make damn sure to keep them safe. Back or no back. No matter what it took.

"We need to talk," he said, once they were on the main road heading back to the ranch. "I don't want you to leave. Baby Amelia needs you." Swallowing, he pushed past his fear to say the rest of the words. "Heck, *I* need you. I have no idea how to take care of an infant."

Worrying her bottom lip with her teeth, she wouldn't look at him. "If my being here endangers her, I wouldn't be able to live with myself," she said. "That intruder broke into *your* house, into *my* room. He was standing over Amelia's crib. How is it that you can even think my being here is safe for her?"

"We'll take every precaution to make sure it doesn't happen again. I promise." At least this was one promise he knew he could keep.

When she finally turned to look at him, her expression was troubled. "Why'd you kiss me?"

The simple question took him by surprise. In all his life, he didn't think a woman had ever asked him that question.

He had to think. He knew he could give her the glib answer, say something like *because I wanted to.* Which he had. But he figured he owed it to Ellie to give her the truth.

"When I saw him knock you to the ground, my heart stopped," he answered quietly. "I jumped him. If not for my damn injuries, I would have had him. You would have been safe and that piece of trash wouldn't have bothered you ever again. My blood was pumping, he got away and I let you down. When I saw you watching me, you looked scared and disappointed and..." He dragged his hand through his too-short hair. "I wish I was better with words. I'm not saying it right."

Her soft smile transformed her face. "That's okay. I get it. The adrenaline was flowing. And, Theo, you didn't disappoint me. I barely know you and I just started working here." She cleared her throat. "But I do need you to understand that's not part of the deal."

Realizing she meant sex, he managed to keep his expression neutral. "I never thought it was, Ellie. Look, I'm sorry I kissed you. It won't happen again."

"Thank you," she said. Her obvious relief made him feel even worse.

The security company truck was waiting in the driveway when they pulled up. Theo went to talk with the men while Ellie hurried to her room to check on Amelia and relieve Gemma. Theo told the security crew what he wanted and let them go to work. Headed toward Ellie's room, he was met by Gemma.

"We need to talk," she said, taking his arm and steering him back toward the kitchen. But when she saw the alarm people were installing there, she shook her head. "Where can we speak privately?"

"My office?" he suggested. Years ago, he'd turned a spare bedroom into a sort of trophy room slash office, though he rarely did any work there. Still, when he needed to get on the computer, he had one. As well as a great mahogany-wood desk Gemma had once found him at a flea market.

"Sure." She followed him down the hall.

Once inside, he quietly closed the door and turned to face her. "What's up?"

"We just had a second fatality from the virus," she said, trying to sound matter-of-fact but unable to hide her worry. "Old man Thomas. Remember, I told you he came in yesterday?"

"I remember. You also said you had two children who were sick. How are they?"

She sighed. "One is a six-year-old girl and the other a thirteen-year-old boy. They're still sick. Same symptoms. It doesn't look good. For anyone. Another woman, someone who was passing through and staying at the Holcombs' Bed-and-Breakfast, walked in saying she had the flu, and died while she was still in triage. More people are dying from this thing. I'm worried about Gram."

Theo swore. "How is she?"

"I checked with Dr. Rand, and he said her condition is stable." Gemma bit her lip. "I'll know more once I get to work and see her for myself."

"What makes it kill some people so fast and others seem to have it longer?"

"We don't know." Frustration plain on her face, she grimaced. "We don't know anything about it. How it spreads, what path it takes. All we know are the early symptoms. Even the people the CDC sent are stumped."

"I'm sorry. We've got our own weirdness going on." He told her what had happened in town and filled her in about Ellie's stalker.

"That's terrible!" Gemma exclaimed. "But if he stands out that much, Flint should have no problem locating him."

"Unless the dreads are a disguise." He shrugged. "He's white, with blue eyes. If they're a wig, once he removes it, he looks like any other rodeo drifter who might blow into town."

"I see your point." Gemma looked away, her expression troubled. "You know, if the CDC really does quarantine Dead River, everyone will be stuck here, including this stalker."

Theo waved off her concern. "Surely it won't come to that. Dr. Rand swore he'd figure it out. Plus, you have all those other doctors there at the clinic. If they put their heads together, they'll come up with something."

"Maybe." But Gemma looked doubtful. She glanced at her watch. "I've got to go to work. Oh, and don't forget. Molly's rehearsal dinner is Friday night."

He nodded. Their young cousin had fallen madly in love with Jimmy Johnson, a newcomer who'd arrived in Dead River a few months ago and taken a job at the auto body shop. After a whirlwind courtship, they'd gotten engaged and the wedding was to be held in two weeks.

"Maybe we should postpone it, because of the virus. That'd be a good excuse to drag things out, give Molly time to think this through. If you're asking me, she's rushing it."

"No one asked you. And I think a family get together is safe. Now, please, just remember, it's Friday."

"Got it. I still don't understand why anyone would want to get married so young."

Gemma laughed. "She's twenty-one. Not that young. And with all this craziness going on, maybe this wedding is just what we need to help distract us."

"Except Gram won't be able to come."

Gemma's smile disappeared, making Theo regret saying anything. "True. And she was so looking forward to it." Again she glanced at her watch. "I've really got to go."

"Thanks for coming and checking us out. Also, I really appreciate you watching Amelia."

"I enjoyed it." Her earnest expression said she meant it. "I might even do it again sometime." Then, with a wave, Gemma left.

Alone again, Theo went into the kitchen and grabbed a diet cola. Suppressing the urge to check on Amelia— since that would entail dealing with Ellie as well—he walked over to the window above the sink and stared out at the rolling hills of his family's land. He'd always wished he could feel some sort of bond with it, the way those ranchers did on TV and in books. But all Theo had ever wanted to do was get away from the place. Flint had been the same way.

He shrugged. He'd long ago come to peace with that part of himself. Now, despite at first feeling as if he had no choice, he realized he wanted to stay. He wanted to build a life here and get his breeding program going.

About time he started moving forward. First he'd need to set up a meeting with Slim George and make sure Theo's plans wouldn't interfere with the successful running of the ranch.

Decision made, he felt better. Like he had a purpose again.

His thoughts turned toward what had happened early today, in town.

When he'd seen the man come out of nowhere and launch himself at Ellie, Theo reacted purely by instinct. He'd managed to get the attacker off her, but he should have had the guy. The man he'd been before the accident wouldn't have had a problem. He'd been fast on his feet. He'd have had Ellie's stalker on the ground, arm twisted behind him, quicker than the kids took down those greased pigs at the county fair.

Now he couldn't move as well, couldn't twist around to save his life and the attacker had gotten away. What Theo would have given to be able to assure Ellie that her stalker wouldn't bother her ever again.

The morning had started out so nice. He'd felt good, taking Ellie into town, giving her a break from caring for the baby who'd been thrust unexpectedly at her.

After his haircut, he'd actually planned to take her to the café for a cup of coffee and a slice of pie. The stalker had ruined that idea.

And then there'd been the kiss. What the hell had he

been thinking? Ellie wasn't the type to go for a little recreational sex. Even so, he hadn't been prepared to realize his touch apparently repulsed her.

Though it sounded conceited, even to himself, Theo wasn't used to women turning him down. He didn't want to have sex with Ellie, or so he told himself, but she'd reacted to his kiss as if lips touching were a gateway drug to the rest of their bodies connecting.

Most women actually *wanted* him. The fact that Ellie clearly didn't rankled more than it should. Especially considering that she wasn't his type.

He couldn't help thinking this had something to do with his back injury. Maybe in her mind, he wasn't man enough for her. Normally, he would have found the idea laughable. He wasn't usually so insecure.

But now…he wasn't the man he'd always been. Truth of the matter was, he didn't know who he was anymore. Maybe getting his breeding program off the ground would help with that. Give him a purpose.

Rodeo had been more than his occupation. Riding broncs had been his life. Without that, he was like a foal cut loose from the herd and left to fend for himself in a field full of predators.

The analogy nearly made him smile. He realized he was taking this entire situation—at least the kissing part—way too seriously. Apparently his back injury had made him more sensitive and his feelings more easily wounded too. He grimaced. Time to get over that.

Still, he'd gone way too long without a woman. The injury, his long hospitalization and his return home as a veritable invalid for the first few months had made this virtually impossible. Now he'd suddenly become a father and a virus was threatening the town. Which meant nothing was likely to change.

One thing he knew for sure. Until he could get a handle on this strange attraction to Ellie Parker, he'd need to spend as little time with her as possible. After all, she had enough to worry about—dealing with her stalker and trying to hold down a double job here at the ranch.

Ellie couldn't stop thinking about the kiss. Though it hadn't lasted long—not nearly long enough, as far as she was concerned—the brief contact had melted her to a puddle of quivering desire.

Theo wasn't even her type. At all. She'd grown up around cowboys and had learned to avoid them and their swaggering, blustery self-confidence. But Theo was different. Sure, he practically bristled with masculinity, but he was kind too. She actually really liked him.

But the last thing she needed was a romantic entanglement to complicate things. Especially since she still planned to leave as soon as possible. Despite Theo's assurances and the newly installed alarm system, she simply couldn't take the chance that her stalker might somehow harm this precious infant.

Turning her gaze on baby Amelia, whom Gemma had fed and changed and who now slept, she smiled. No doubt Theo felt as uncomfortable about the entire thing as she did. Maybe it would be best to keep as low a profile as she could, until the incident was forgotten.

Getting back to work preparing food helped Ellie get her composure back. She just didn't have time to worry about it. For lunch, the ranch hands got sandwiches and chips, a lot of them. She used three entire loaves of bread and various containers of cold cuts and sliced cheese.

Once they'd devoured that and trooped back out the door, she sat down and had a quick bite herself, making an extra sandwich for Theo in case he got hungry later. Then she got busy preparing the evening meal. Within an hour, she had a huge pot of chicken stew simmering on the stove for dinner, and buttermilk biscuits ready to be popped into the oven.

A nice dinner for a Monday night.

Amelia woke crying and Ellie took care of getting her fed and changed. Finally, as the infant fell back asleep, Ellie was able to sit down for a moment before popping the biscuits in the oven.

Still no sign of Theo. She supposed that was for the best. At least while she'd been busy, she'd had time to think and to make up her mind.

She wouldn't leave Amelia without someone to care for her. She couldn't do that to the poor baby, or to Theo. She'd stay until everyone got adjusted and then as soon as she could, she'd leave. If she was lucky, she'd slip out of town without her stalker realizing.

Meanwhile, she'd save up every penny she could. And hope and pray no one around her came down with that mysterious virus. Especially this precious baby. Watching Amelia while she slept, she realized she'd need to guard her heart. Not just against Theo, but against Amelia, as well. It would be all too easy to become attached.

The next morning, Theo deactivated the alarm system and wandered into the kitchen for an early morning cup of coffee. As he'd expected, Ellie was already there, making massive stacks of pancakes, which she placed in the oven to keep warm. She didn't look at him when he entered, giving him the opportunity to study her slender, yet shapely form. She'd coiled her long hair in a bun on her head, highlighting her sensual neck. He wondered what she'd do if he went up behind her and slid his arm around her waist and put his mouth to that little bit of exposed skin. Amelia cooed from her little seat, distracting him from his thoughts. Theo swore her eyes latched on to him the moment he entered the room. Ignoring Ellie, he crossed to his daughter, and crouched down in front of her. "Well, good morning, sweetie," he said, doing his best impression of baby talk.

She rewarded him with a bright smile and gurgling sounds. His heart squeezed. He'd never really paid that much attention to babies, but Amelia was exceptionally cute. And bright.

"She only woke up twice last night," Ellie said. "And she fell back asleep as soon as I changed and fed her."

He got to his feet and turned to face her, frowning as he noticed the dark circles under her bright blue eyes. She looked even more delicate than usual, making him want fiercely to protect her.

"Are you feeling okay?" he asked sharply, thinking about the virus and feeling a stab of panic at the thought Ellie might be sick.

"I'm fine." Her dismissive smile didn't fool him. "Just tired. I have trouble falling back to sleep after getting up with Amelia, that's all. I'm sure once I settle into some sort of routine, I'll adjust."

Despite knowing better, he crossed the kitchen to be closer to her. "Ellie, my offer still stands. I don't mind hiring someone else to cook. Just say the word and I'll start looking."

"No." Despite appearing frazzled, she also looked determined. "I can handle this. Plus, like I said, I need the money."

This piqued his interest, but he didn't ask. It was none of his business.

The ranch hands filed in, cutting off any further discussion. Theo pitched in, pouring the hot maple syrup into dispensers and putting them on the table, along with butter. He also dished up the sausage patties that were staying warm in a large electric skillet. Meanwhile, Ellie removed several towering stacks of pancakes from the oven, placing them in the center of the table before turning back to make more.

Apparently ravenous, the men dug in. Theo poured himself a second cup of coffee and watched.

"Aren't you going to eat?" Ellie asked as she flipped the next round to cook the other side.

"I'll wait," he said, smiling easily. "I'll eat when you do."

With a shrug, she returned her attention to feeding his hands. They were a noisy bunch this morning; apparently the cold weather had energized them.

The talk was all about separating the cows. Theo listened, remembering the rare occasions when he'd been home and had gone along for the ride. Now he couldn't even climb up on one of the perfectly trained ranch horses.

Pushing the bitterness away, he took the towering platter from Ellie and carried it to the table.

When he turned around, he caught sight of Ellie, pushing a strand of hair that had escaped from her ponytail away from her eyes. Her shoulders sagged and she appeared exhausted. As she looked up and realized he watched her, she straightened and lifted her chin.

"Your breakfast is ready," she said, flashing a quick smile as she made two plates. "Get it while it's hot."

In the other room, the men were finishing up and making their way outside to get to work.

Theo retrieved one of the syrup containers and butter, carrying it over to the smaller kitchen table. "Here you go," he said, wishing desperately he and Ellie could get back on comfortable ground. He regretted that one impulsive kiss had messed things up. Despite the sharp tug of attraction he felt when around her, he valued the friendship they'd begun.

He waited until they'd both made short work of their pancakes before he leaned forward. "Ellie, maybe we need to talk," he began.

"Good morning!" Gemma's cheerful voice sang out. "Where's my little niece?" Wearing her maroon scrubs, she breezed into the kitchen, smiling. "That smells delicious," she said.

Ellie jumped to her feet. "I'd be happy to make you some," she said."

"Oh, no need." Gemma waved her back to her seat. "I've already eaten. Let me have a look at sweet baby Amelia." Without waiting for a response, she scooped Amelia up and held her close. "Ooh," she said, wrinkling her nose. "Someone has a poopy diaper."

"I'll get that." Ellie took the baby from Gemma and hurried away to get her cleaned and changed.

Gemma watched her go. "She looks tired," she commented. "Is she feeling all right?"

"I just asked her and she said she's fine. No signs of the virus." Theo started gathering up the dirty plates and silverware, carrying them to the sink. "For whatever reason, she doesn't want to give up her cooking job. She insists she can be both—Amelia's nanny and the ranch cook. I think it's too much."

"Maybe so." Gemma cocked her head, her green eyes curious. "I wonder why she's so bent on working herself so hard."

"She says she needs the money."

"Ah. That would explain things."

After squirting in dish soap, Theo began running hot water to fill the sink. "Yeah. So I'm trying to help out as much as I can."

Gemma touched his arm, making him look at her. "Maybe you should help more with the baby instead of the kitchen. Sooner or later, you're going to have to learn how to be a father."

He winced because she was correct, then shrugged. "I'm doing the best I can," he said, meaning it.

Gemma began helping him.

"What brings you out here so early anyway?" he asked.

"Since it's Tuesday, I have to be at the clinic at eight," she said. "Some of the doctors have been working all night, along with the CDC. Everyone is focused on figuring out how to cure this thing."

He nodded, rinsing off dishes and then putting them in the dishwasher. "That's two hours away. And you still didn't answer my question."

"I don't know," she finally admitted. "Little Amelia is like a breath of fresh air in all this sickness. I wanted to see her before I start my day. I also wanted to make sure no one out here is feeling ill."

"We're fine. And I promise to call you immediately if anyone so much as sneezes."

She smiled, though her eyes were still serious. "Flu-like symptoms, Theo. Fever, aches, chills, nausea."

"Got it." He reached around her for the skillets on the stove. "How's everything at the clinic?"

Grimacing, she looked away. "Things are so crazy I don't even want to think about work," Gemma said. "If I do, I might just start crying and never stop."

Awkwardly, he patted her shoulder. "I'm sorry. Hopefully it will get better soon."

Her expression told him she didn't think that was likely.

"At least you have Molly's rehearsal dinner to look forward to," he pointed out. "It sounds like you need this get together as much as Molly does."

"Maybe." Gemma gave him a sharp look. "What about you? I heard you're pretty much holed up at the ranch."

"I go to town." He tried not to sound too defensive.

"Yeah, now you do. To pick up diapers and formula or take Ellie. I'm talking about even before you found out you were a daddy. People were starting to call you the Colton Hermit. How long are you going to stay holed up here at the ranch?"

Refusing to let her needling bother him, he laughed. "Hey, give me a break. I already agreed to go to Molly's rehearsal dinner."

"And dress appropriately?"

By which she meant no jeans and boots. "You know I don't own a suit," Theo said.

Her skeptical look had him chuckling again. "Surely you at least own a pair of dress slacks."

"Yep." Crossing his arms, he waited, not willing to make it any easier on her.

"Button-down shirt, Western tie, dress slacks and your

best pair of boots," she ordered, doing her best Gram Dottie impersonation. Which cracked them both up.

"Fine." He rolled his eyes, exactly the way he'd used to when he was a thirteen-year-old handful. "Whatever."

Which only made them both laugh harder.

"Thank you for that," Gemma finally said, wiping her eyes. "I can't tell you how long it's been since I laughed."

He gave in to impulse and hugged her. "Me too, sis. Me too."

When she looked at him, she was still smiling. "Now, about the rehearsal dinner. We've settled what you're wearing. Do you have a date?"

Recoiling in mock horror, he shook his head. "Oh, hell no."

"Well, then, you might as well bring Ellie and Amelia," Gemma drawled. "God knows we could all use a distraction around here."

"I thought the rehearsal dinner and the wedding would be enough of a distraction," Theo said. "You know how everyone can gossip. Once they get a look at Amelia, the tongues will be wagging."

"Theo, they're already wagging. Everyone knows you have a daughter. If you hide her away, they'll think you're ashamed of her."

He straightened. "I didn't think of it that way. You know I'm not ashamed or anything like that. I'm just trying to adjust to being a father. It's come as a bit of a shock."

She shrugged. "So let the family meet her. Maybe some of them could help you out."

"What about the virus? You said I needed to keep her away from germs."

Gemma's face fell. "You're probably right." The resignation in her posture told him for a brief, glorious moment she'd allowed herself to forget about her job and the growing crisis as the virus spread. Now she'd come back to reality. "I don't want you to do anything that might endanger Amelia. Especially since we still don't know how the virus is spread."

Again, he voiced his doubts. "Is it even a good idea to have a party?"

She grimaced. "Life has to continue to go on. People still shop, go out to eat, to see movies. Our baby cousin is getting married! Molly is so happy and excited we can't deny her this."

"I guess you're right. But we need to tell anyone who's sick—even if it's just with a sniffle—to stay home."

"The CDC has printed up flyers." Her tone had gone back to brisk and efficient, what Theo thought of as her nurse voice. "They'll be distributed all over town on Wednesday. Plus, they're mailing them to every resident in town. Basic, commonsense stuff, like washing your hands often. Hopefully they'll do some good."

"Is the CDC still considering a quarantine?"

For the first time in as long as he could remember, his brave little sister looked scared. "I'm not supposed to tell anyone this, so you can't repeat it. The quarantine will go into effect on Friday. That will be in the flyers. So if you need to go out of town for any reason, do it before then. And make sure you're back by Thursday night."

Chapter 6

The enormity of what Gemma was saying stunned Theo. "Can they really do this? Is it even legal?"

"I don't know," she said simply. "They've been in talks with the mayor and the city council. I'm pretty sure Flint's been involved too, since he's the chief of police."

Theo nodded. "What about people coming from out of town for Molly's wedding?"

"We'll deal with that when we have to." She passed her hand across her eyes. "But I'm guessing they won't be able to come."

"Are you feeling all right?" he asked, suddenly concerned that Gemma herself might be coming down with the virus.

"I'm fine." She met his gaze. "Not sick, I promise you. At the risk of sounding like a broken record, I'm just so tired. And stressed. Everyone at the clinic is. We've been working around the clock. And more and more sick people are coming in. Pretty soon, we're going to have to increase our isolation area or we'll be out of room."

"How many more?" Staring at her in horror, Theo wondered how he'd managed to stay so aloof that he didn't even know what was going on in his own hometown.

Gemma looked as if she was about to cry. "Enough.

Look, I don't really want to talk about this anymore. Sometimes I just need to escape, get some time away." She glanced at her watch. "Let me have just this time before I have to head into town to go to work."

"I'm sorry, sis." Placing his hand on her shoulder, he gave a gentle squeeze of reassurance. "One more question, and then I'll drop it. Is Gram improving any?"

A shadow crossed her face. "No. But she's not getting any worse either. That's something."

"I'll take it." Deliberately, he turned the conversation back to the rehearsal dinner. "Too bad. I was going to bring Ellie as my date to Molly's thing. Guess I can't now, since we can't risk exposing Amelia."

As he'd known it would, the prospect of matchmaking provided distraction and brightened his sister's mood. "Sure you can. All we need to do is find a sitter for Amelia."

"A sitter? Why?" Ellie's voice had them both turning. She carried a freshly changed Amelia, though the baby had now fallen asleep.

Theo kept a smile on his face, but inwardly he wished she hadn't walked in on the conversation. Now he had no choice but to brazen it out. "My cousin Molly is getting married. Her rehearsal dinner is Friday night. I was hoping to bring you as my date."

Date might have been the wrong choice of word, Theo thought, as Ellie's face flushed pink.

"I'd rather not," she said, her voice strangled. "Plus, I don't know who else we could trust with an infant as young as Amelia."

"I've got several nurse friends who'd be perfect," Gemma put in promptly. "One or two of them are even pediatric nurses at Dr. Meyer's office downtown. I'll ask them if they can watch her for a few hours."

Theo almost felt sorry for Ellie. She appeared shell-shocked as she looked from him to Gemma. "I really can't," she said. "Sorry."

"Why not?" Gemma sounded perfectly reasonable. And also determined. Theo recognized that tone.

"Well, for starters, I don't have anything to wear."

"You've got time to purchase something. We have a couple of great boutiques in town."

Ellie's horrified expression begged Theo to help her out. He looked away, pretending not to notice. Though in the past, Theo went to parties alone, but rarely left alone, he wanted Ellie to meet people, put down some roots. That way, she might want to stay and he wouldn't lose his nanny. Also, the more people she knew, the more protected she'd be. Until her stalker was caught, he wanted to keep Ellie as safe as possible. He'd point that out to her later, once Gemma was gone.

"Come on, Ellie. It'll be fun." Gemma made it clear she wasn't giving up. "I'll even help you shop if you want."

"I'll think about it, okay?" Placing Amelia back in her bassinette, Ellie turned to face them. Her crossed arms spoke volumes. "That's the best I can do for right now."

Amused, Gemma nodded. "I'll let my brother convince you. I can't speak from experience, but I've heard he can be *very* persuasive when he wants to be."

Theo wouldn't have thought it possible, but Ellie's creamy complexion turned an even deeper shade of red. He grinned wickedly at her. "Should I test out my powers of persuasion?"

Sounding as if she were choking, Ellie muttered something about needing to freshen up and rushed away.

Theo couldn't help it, he laughed out loud.

"What the heck was that?" Gemma demanded. "Are you tormenting that poor girl?"

He reared back in mock offense. "Just teasing her. Come on, Gemma. You know how I am."

"I do." The way she pursed her lips told him she was debating whatever she might say next. Which meant he probably wasn't going to like it.

"Theo," she began. Yep, she used her scolding voice. He crossed his arms and waited her out.

"Ellie's not at all like the kind of women you normally hang around with. You can't—"

"What?" he interrupted, raising one eyebrow in fake outrage. "What are you implying? That my former lady friends are…what?"

Her gentle smile told him she wasn't buying it. "Come on. You know what I mean. Promise me you won't hurt her."

That was easy. "I promise." He didn't even hesitate. "She and I are getting to be friends, nothing more. I'm not going to sneak into her bedroom at night or whatever you think. She's not even my type."

"Okay, good." Gemma sounded relieved. "I guess I just imagined those sparks flying between you. Just make sure she understands the situation. She seemed awfully flustered a minute ago."

"Yes, ma'am." He gave her a salute. "But I'm pretty sure she gets it already."

About to walk back into the room after her embarrassingly fast exit, Ellie froze when she heard Theo say she wasn't his type. As her heart squeezed, she wondered what the heck was wrong with her. She already knew she wasn't Theo's type. Really, she did. So she didn't understand why hearing him say it out loud hurt so much.

Pasting a smile on her face, she squared her shoulders and sailed back into the room. "Gets what already?"

This time, it felt gratifying that Theo was the one who appeared ill at ease. "Nothing," he began.

Once again, Gemma cut him off. "Ellie, if Theo's teasing ever makes you uncomfortable, just let him know. Okay?"

Ellie managed a puzzled frown. "Okay, sure. But to be honest, he reminds me a lot of a pesky older brother. Though I never had one, my best friend did."

She looked up in time to see a look of horror on Theo's handsome face.

"Ouch," he said, wincing. "Pesky, huh?"

"Only sometimes," she said back, thinking she might be getting pretty good at this bantering thing. She just didn't know how long she could keep it up.

Baby Amelia let out a wail, saving Ellie from finding out. She hurried over and picked the baby up, making cooing sounds as she checked the diaper. "She's wet, again," she explained. "It's time for her bath anyway. I'll go do that and then feed her. Then I'll get started on the prep work for lunch."

"I've got to run," Gemma said. "Ellie, let me know if you want to go shopping."

"I will," Ellie said, even though was pretty sure she wouldn't. After all, she wouldn't be going; therefore she had no need to buy something to wear.

As Ellie turned to take gather up the supplies to bathe Amelia, Theo's touch on her shoulder stopped her.

"Would you mind showing me how?" he asked, his tone and expression serious.

"Show you how?" she repeated, drawing a blank as she tried not to drown in his amazing green gaze.

"To give her a bath." One corner of his sensual mouth lifted. "I'm thinking I need to learn how. You know, just in case."

Somehow she managed not to gape at him. "Sure," she said. "Of course." She swallowed. "I use the sink in the wet bar. It's the perfect size, and much easier to keep clean than the kitchen sink."

He nodded. "How often to you bathe her?"

"Not too often, at least until she's older. Once or twice a week is enough. Too much and her skin might dry out or she could get rashes."

She showed him how to test the water temperature and the correct level to fill the sink. Then, taking a deep breath, she handed him his daughter and the soft baby washcloth and took a step back.

His hands looked impossibly large and tanned as he gently handled his daughter. He washed and rinsed her, making soothing sounds. The melodic tone of his deep voice made Amelia chortle. Seeing this, Ellie knew Amelia would be all right. Little by little, Theo would learn his way. And she could leave with a clear conscience.

Weird how the thought made her chest ache.

After she'd handed him a towel and he'd dried Amelia off, Ellie showed him how to powder her little bottom and then put her in a clean Onesie. Baths always made Amelia drowsy, and her little eyes kept drifting half-closed.

He carried her back to the kitchen and placed her in the bassinette, before getting busy making her bottle. Ellie supervised, feeling both pleased and oddly bereft as she watched a tough cowboy become putty caring for his daughter. Still, from the frequent looks he gave Ellie, as if to ask if he was doing everything right, it was clear he didn't feel comfortable yet. She knew that would come with time and experience.

The house phone rang, making Ellie jump. Even Theo appeared startled, as he made no move to answer it.

"That's weird," he said. "The only one who still uses that phone is Gram Dottie. Everyone else just calls my cell."

He finally answered, listened for a second and then said, "Sure. Here she is." Turning, he faced Ellie and held out the phone. "It's my cousin Molly. Seems Gemma called her a minute ago and told her you need help shopping for a dress."

Not sure how to react, Ellie accepted the phone. "Hello?"

"Hi. Ellie, I hope you don't mind me calling, but Gemma said we'd like each other and I can use all the friends I can get, you know what I mean?" Molly's cheerful voice brought a smile to Ellie's face.

"Anyway," Molly rushed on. "I need another woman around my age to hang around with." She laughed, sounding slightly breathless. "I'm getting married really soon and it's at the point where I don't trust my own opinion."

Ellie wasn't sure how to respond, so she didn't. Molly didn't appear to notice. She continued talking. "So, what I guess I'm trying to say, is will you be my friend? We can meet for lunch on your day off. What do you say?"

Finally, she paused.

"On my day off?" was all Ellie could think of to say. "Um, I'm not sure I actually get a day off."

"No way," Molly squealed. "Find out."

"Hold on, let me ask." Ellie looked at Theo. "Do I? Get a day off, that is?"

"Sure," he said easily. "Once I know how to take care of Amelia. When do you want one?"

She shrugged, held up a finger and got back on the phone. "Molly, when do you want to meet for lunch?"

"The sooner the better." Molly barely paused for breath before continuing. "How about today? We can shop for a dress after."

Though the idea definitely appealed, Ellie couldn't help worrying about her stalker. "Um, can I call you back and let you know?"

"Sure. My number should be in your caller ID."

Feeling slightly dazed, Ellie pressed the off button and then just stood there staring at the phone. "Wow."

Theo chuckled. "Molly's a force of nature, isn't she?"

"I'll say. And while I'd love to meet her for lunch and then shop, I'm afraid. What if my stalker shows up? I can't put yet another innocent person at risk."

Theo considered her for a moment. "That's easy. Just tell Molly you want to go into Cheyenne. We're about forty minutes away from there. No way will the stalker know where you are."

She felt like jumping up and down with relief. Instead she simply nodded. "As long as I make sure we aren't followed."

"Exactly."

About to hit Redial on the phone, she paused and eyed him. "Are you up to watching Amelia this afternoon? I'll make sure lunch is prepared and dinner. All you'll have to do is heat it up and serve it."

"No problem." He didn't appear the least bit fazed by the prospect. "I can handle it."

Privately, she thought this would be a good thing for both Theo and Amelia. They could continue to bond, as a father and daughter should. Before he could change his mind, she called Molly back and made arrangements to meet. It turned out Molly had been planning to go into Cheyenne anyway.

"I'll pick you up in a couple of hours," Molly said, sounding as excited as if she'd just won the lottery.

Ellie barely got out an okay before Molly hung up.

When she looked up, she realized Theo was watching her, amusement making his eyes gleam. "Go." He waved her away. "Go and get ready. I've got Amelia."

Grateful, she nodded. "Thank you. I really appreciate this. I've got to get everything ready for the two meals."

"I can do that. You just worry about getting ready."

She stared, stunned. "Are you sure?"

"Of course." His grin contained a hint of wickedness. "But you know this means you have to go to the rehearsal dinner with me, right?"

He had her there. Slowly, she nodded. "I guess so."

The deep richness of his laugh made her grow warm. "You know," Theo said, his tone musing, "I think Molly will be good for you. She might help you loosen up, be less serious."

Serious? Stung, rather than replying, she ignored him and hurried off to her room to get ready.

Ninety minutes later, having done everything she could think of to fix herself up, Ellie returned to the living room. She had on her favorite pair of jeans, the low-heeled boots she'd only worn once and a dangly pair of silver earrings. She'd taken her hair out of it customary ponytail and used her flatiron to straighten it.

She thought she looked pretty good. Young and carefree, at least. Not serious at all.

When she walked into the living room, Theo whistled. "You clean up good," he said.

And of course, she blushed. Something she hated but had no control over. "Thanks," she managed.

A horn honking outside stifled whatever he'd been about to say.

Ellie rushed to the window, staring at the bright red, low-slung sports car idling in the driveway. "A Corvette? Your cousin drives a 'Vette?"

Theo cocked his head. "You don't like Corvettes?"

"I love them," she said. "I always wanted one someday." By which she meant when she was working somewhere where she made a lot more money.

"I bet if you ask Molly, she'll let you drive hers."

The thought made her smile. "I just might have to do that."

Molly looked like her voice. Her trademark Colton green eyes sparkled, and her red wavy hair tried to escape her loose braid.

The instant she caught sight of Ellie, she squealed and hugged her as if Ellie was a long-lost relative. Her infectious joy made Ellie feel as if she'd dropped a boulder that she hadn't even known she carried.

Molly chattered all the way to Cheyenne, which Ellie appreciated since her innate shyness made it difficult for her to find topics of conversation with people she didn't know. Molly clearly had no such problem.

But the time they reached the sign that welcomed them to Cheyenne, Ellie felt as if she'd known Molly all her life.

They visited a few boutiques.

"Surely, here, you'll find something you like." Molly smiled encouragingly.

"I've never really been a dressy person," Ellie confided. "Jeans in the winter, shorts in the summer and that's about it."

"I'll help you." Molly's confident smile reassured Ellie. "I know what kind of dresses will look fabulous on you."

Trailing along behind her new friend, Ellie accepted each dress Molly handed her while trying not to stress with figuring out how she was going to pay, as she hadn't gotten her first paycheck from Theo, yet. She had one credit card that she used only for emergencies, and she rapidly realized she'd have to consider this an emergency or face total and utter humiliation. She could only hope the prices weren't too bad—so far she'd been afraid to look.

"Okay, that should do it." Molly pointed toward the dressing room. "Go try them on. I want to see you in each one."

Resigned, Ellie did as she said.

The first four or five dresses didn't work. Ellie knew the moment she dropped each one over her head. Too tight, too loose, too long, the wrong cut for her long legs and long waist.

Molly giggled, winced, nodded and agreed.

Dress number six looked plain on its hanger compared to the others. Midnight blue, made of some clingy fabric Ellie couldn't identify, the dress didn't look like it'd be the one. Still, she might as well try it on. There were only two more after it, and if she didn't find a dress this go-round, she knew Molly would make her do it all over again.

To her surprise, she realized the instant she looked at herself in the mirror that this was *the* dress. Checking the price tag, she felt relieved to see the dress was under a hundred dollars.

Pushing open the dressing room door, she stepped out to see if Molly concurred.

"Wow." Molly's eyes went wide. "You look absolutely gorgeous. I don't think you should even try any of the others."

"Okay." Ellie looked down at her feet. Throwing caution to the wind, she liked the lighthearted feeling. "I'm going to need shoes to go with this too."

Once they finished their shopping, Molly drove them to a little Mexican restaurant tucked away on a back street near the mall. "I've been here before," she proclaimed. "And I promise it's good."

They talked all through lunch. Ellie learned about the whirlwind courtship Molly had enjoyed with her fiancé, Jimmy Johnson.

"I can't wait until you meet him," Molly gushed. "He's so cute! The first time I met him, the instant he smiled at me, I knew he was The One."

Finishing the last bite of chicken fajitas, Ellie pushed he plate away. "I take it that's the reason you two decided not to have a long engagement. You both knew and decided there was no reason to wait?"

"Yes." Molly's expression grew dreamy. "He proposed two weeks after we met."

Shocked, Ellie looked down to hide it. "How long ago was it that he proposed?"

"A month." Molly's wide smile invited Ellie to partake in her joy. "I know, I know." She fluttered her small hand dismissively when Ellie didn't comment. "It's not long enough. For most people. But for us, we can't wait to live together as husband and wife and get started on a family."

"You're very fortunate," Ellie said, meaning it. "Not everyone finds that kind of love."

"I know." Grinning good-naturedly, Molly grabbed the check from the waiter. "My treat. And don't you dare try to pay anything, not even the tip. You can treat next time."

More relieved than she cared to admit, Ellie nodded. She had no cash saved up. She hadn't exactly made a lot, working in the bookstore in Boulder. All she earned went for rent and food. Since coming here, she'd opened a bank account and planned to start saving her pay, eventually hoping to have enough to travel far, far away.

With that goal in mind, all she carried was that emergency credit card that now had a hundred and fifty dollars charged to it. She considered herself lucky she'd been able to talk Molly out of making Ellie purchase jewelry and a purse, as well.

Ellie had earrings and a few bracelets she figured would work. And she'd never been one to carry a purse.

After lunch, Molly took them to a nail salon and treated them both to mani-pedis, over Ellie's protests. Though Ellie loved feeling pampered, she knew she'd need to have a frank talk with Molly. If they were going to be friends, she needed to understand Ellie couldn't afford this kind of thing and refused to continually mooch.

Once they were on the road back toward Dead River, Ellie spoke up.

"I'm sorry." Instantly contrite, Molly looked as if she might cry. "I didn't even think. I just wanted to have a girl's day out and…I promise it won't happen again."

Ellie let out a sigh of relief. "I really like you," she

said. "And I think we might become good friends while I'm here. But I needed to put that out there, so you knew."

"I can afford it, you know." Molly smiled sadly. "I might work as a waitress, but my sister, Sarah, and I inherited my parents' life insurance when they were killed in a car accident three years ago."

Horrified, Ellie stared. "I'm sorry."

"It's all right." Unbelievably, Molly reached out and patted Ellie's shoulder, as though comforting *her*. "It's been long enough that I can talk about it."

Not sure how to respond, Ellie simply nodded.

"Anyway." Molly lifted her chin, smiling again as she made the turn that would lead them to the ranch. "This has been one of the best Tuesdays I've had in a long time. Tuesdays are my day off. Tuesdays and Fridays."

"I agree," She said, meaning it. Unbuckling her seat belt, Ellie asked, "Would you like to come and meet Amelia?"

"Ooh, Theo's baby?" Molly glanced at her watch and then frowned. "You know, I'd love to, but my sister has scheduled a caterer meeting in half an hour. She's making last-minute tweaks to the menu again. By the time I get home and freshen up...I simply don't have time."

"That's okay." Ellie swallowed her disappointment. She'd have enjoyed showing off Amelia to Molly. "Maybe another time."

"Definitely!" Molly leaned across the seat and hugged her. "See you on Friday!"

After Ellie got out of the car, she stood and watched Molly drive off before going back inside.

Theo was waiting in the living room, holding a sleeping Amelia in his arms. Ellie stopped, taking in the picture, marveling at the warm glow she felt as the sight of the rugged cowboy and the dainty baby.

Not hers, she reminded herself. For one brief moment, she'd had the absurd fantasy that this was her family, her man and child.

"Hey," she said, keeping her dress bag high so it wouldn't drag the floor. "How'd everything go?"

"Fine." He flashed a proud grin, which predictably turned Ellie's insides to mush. "Amelia and I managed. How about you? Did you have a good time?"

"Yes." Unable to keep from glancing at her watch, she realized it was nearly dinnertime. "Is there something ready for me to serve to the hands for their supper?"

"Yep. I cooked those baby back ribs you had thawing. And baked potatoes and black beans. I've got everything staying warm until it's time."

Exhaling with relief, she nodded. "Thank you."

"Why don't you go and put your dress—and whatever else you bought—up and then meet me in the kitchen?" His wink sent another stab of heat straight to her center. "You'll probably want to check up on my work and made sure I did everything I was supposed to."

Tongue-tied, she turned to do exactly that. Feeling his gaze burn into her back, she struggled not to react. Though she'd count it as a miracle if she made it to her room without stumbling.

Once she'd hung up the dress, she hurried into the kitchen. She saw that Theo had placed Amelia back in her little bassinette to continue to sleep.

"I really like your cousin," she said, opening the massive oven door to check on the ribs and potatoes. "Good. You used tinfoil."

Again he flashed that devastating grin. "This ain't my first rodeo, you know."

Quietly considering him while trying to ignore the way her nerve endings suddenly came awake, she shrugged. "No, I don't know. So you can cook? What's your specialty?"

"T-bones on the grill," he replied promptly. "But I don't cook those on a large-scale basis, for obvious reasons. I also can make a mean chicken enchilada casserole. Gram Dottie taught all three of us to cook."

Another surprise. Turning away to cover her confusion, she stirred the large pot of black beans simmering on the stove. She felt...relieved, actually. She hadn't realized how much her worry about her stalker making an appearance had made her tense. Back at the ranch, with Theo, she could relax. Feel safe. Almost.

"What about bread?" she asked. "We need rolls or corn bread or something."

"I got that covered." He pointed to three unopened loaves of Wonder bread. "Just bread. It goes great with ribs. They'll love it, I promise."

She decided to trust him on that one, mainly because she was too tired to whip something else up.

Everything was ready when the men, tired and hungry, began to file in for the last meal of the day.

The ribs looked perfectly done, restaurant quality. Judging from the comments of the ranch hands, they tasted as good as they looked.

"Aren't you going to eat?" she asked Theo.

"When you do." Pointing to Amelia, who managed to still sleep despite the boisterous group of ranch hands in the next room, he smiled. "Come on. Let's get our plates before they're all gone."

Enjoying the companionable feeling of sitting beside him in the kitchen, with the men chowing down in the other room, Ellie picked up a rib and bit in. Her mouth exploded with flavor. More than just barbecue sauce, she tasted a hint of jalapeño and something else. "What did you mix with the sauce?"

"Dr Pepper," he said.

She laughed. "You'll have to show me how to make it sometime."

After dinner, they worked side by side cleaning up while Amelia worked her pacifier in her bassinette. Ellie loved the feeling of working side by side with Theo, almost as if they were a couple.

Which they weren't, of course. Nor would they ever be. Shaking her head at her own foolishness, she finished stacking the last of the pan in the dishwasher, added soap and turned it on.

"You look happy," Theo observed, making her blush.

"You know, right this moment, I am. It's been a really good day."

He nodded, going to the fridge and grabbing a beer. "There's a John Wayne marathon on tonight. Do you want to watch with me?"

"I love John Wayne," she said, before she thought better of it. Best she remember her place. Spending her leisure time with Theo would only make her want more of what she couldn't have. "But I'm really tired. Amelia still isn't sleeping through the night. I think I'm going to go to my room and read a little."

Was that disappointment she saw in his rugged face? No, most likely a trick of the light. "Sleep well," he said, and left her standing in the kitchen, her foolish heart aching.

Chapter 7

Though he'd been expecting it, Theo still felt stunned the next morning when he found the flyer on his front door bright and early. Wednesday, just as Gemma had said. Everything his sister had warned him about was coming to pass, and it scared the hell out of him.

Carrying it inside, he read in the kitchen as he drank his first cup of coffee. More details were outlined in the flyer. It said the CDC would be announcing the quarantine using multiple media outlets. No doubt they were trying to make sure to reach everyone they could. They had also taken out a front-page ad in the *Dead River News,* put public service announcements to run every hour on the small radio station, mailed out flyers to every single resident and posted the same flyers in the window of every business downtown. They were nothing if not thorough. They'd even listed a toll-free number for people to call if they had questions.

Carefully folding the flyer, he stuck it in his shirt pocket and wondered if he should show it to Ellie or not. Part of him worried she'd leave town, before things got too buttoned down.

But he'd never been much of a liar and he didn't intend to start now. He'd have to take his chances.

Along with freshly brewed coffee, a scent that vaguely reminded him of Thanksgiving tickled his nose. Who knows, maybe Ellie had made pumpkin cinnamon rolls or something.

The kitchen was empty, though the wonderful scent had intensified, which meant Ellie had already gotten a head start on breakfast. Theo poured a second cup of coffee, took a seat at the table and pulled the flyer from his pocket.

He read it again and started over for the third time. His cell phone rang, disrupting his musings. "Did you get your flyer?" Gemma asked.

"I'm looking at it right now." With a sigh, he put the paper down. "You know, once everyone starts reading these, the town will be in an uproar."

"I'm thinking an immediate town hall meeting will be held," Gemma said.

"Probably."

"Are you going to go?" she asked him, her voice worried and weary. With all the craziness at the clinic, she often sounded that way these days.

"No." Sometimes short answers were the best. But of course, being his sister, she had to pry.

"Why not? This is your town too, Theo. I think you need to have an interest in what's going on."

He snorted, unable to help himself. "Thanks, sis. I'll keep that in mind."

Which they both knew meant he had no intention of participating.

"I don't understand." An undercurrent of disappointment had crept into his sister's voice. "You're a Colton. You have a responsibility to this town."

"Do I?" Privately, he doubted that. Anyway, his

brother, Flint, carried enough responsibility for all three of them. "Gemma, I already know how the townspeople are going to react to the quarantine. They aren't going to like it. Who would? They'll be angry, the meeting will consist in a lot of shouting and accusations and after a couple of hours of this, absolutely nothing will have changed. Going would be a complete waste of time."

"Fine," Gemma huffed. "I guess Flint will have to represent our part of the family. Like he always does, with no help from you."

Even though he'd just been thinking the exact same thing, Theo let that one pass. "Any other news? How's Gram doing?"

"She's holding steady. No improvement, but she's not worse either. That's what's so crazy about this virus. We don't understand why it takes one path with some people and another with others."

"I'm just glad Gram isn't worse. At her age…" He didn't have to finish. Gemma knew exactly what he meant.

"I've got to go." And she hung up.

Theo knew he was trying, by means of avoidance, to pretend the world around him hadn't gone crazy. In the space of a few short days, he'd gained a baby and turned his new cook into a nanny, and his Gram Dottie was sick with a mysterious virus that had the capability of killing her. Add the quarantine to that, and if he thought about it too long, he might start to wonder if he'd gone downright nuts. If he hadn't had the possibility of his future as a breeder of rodeo broncs to ground him, he didn't know what he'd do. The bad part was that he finally felt ready to get started, and now the town had been shut down.

So he got a third cup of coffee, sat down at the table

and read the flyer again. The reading didn't improve with time.

Ellie wandered into the kitchen shortly after Theo ended the call. With a cloth over her shoulder and burping Amelia, Ellie looked adorably disheveled. Just gazing at her made his mood a little better.

Before either could speak, Amelia let out a satisfied belch. "Ah, there we go." Ellie placed the baby in her bassinette, then headed for the coffeepot to pour herself a cup. Once she'd doctored it up the way she liked it and taken a deep sip, she turned to face Theo.

"Breakfast is already made." She did a double take, frowning as she peered at him.

"What's wrong?" she asked. "Why do you look like the world has just ended?"

For a split second, he again considered not telling her. But that wouldn't be fair to her, not after all she'd been through. He had to at least give her a choice.

"You might want to sit down."

Clearly not understanding, she pulled out a chair and sat.

Wordlessly, he handed her the flyer.

Ellie's frown deepened as she read. When she'd finished, and she raised her face to look at him, he recognized the flash of panic in her eyes. "I can't believe this is happening."

"I know." He swallowed. "Not only can no one leave town, but no one can come here either. It's like we're in a bubble."

He saw the moment she realized what this meant.

"My stalker is trapped here with me."

"You don't know that," he hastened to reassure her. "For all you know, the bastard might have gone into

Cheyenne to buy more black roses or something. Maybe he's stuck outside Dead River."

Though she nodded, he could tell she didn't really believe him.

"Think positive," he chided. "Gemma said everyone will try to call a town meeting."

"That's a good idea." She sat up straighter. "I think we should go."

He groaned. "You sound like my sister. I don't live in town, so I'm not going. Of course, you can if you want. I'll even watch the baby."

Considering, she finally shook her head. "I'd better not. For all I know, my stalker could be there."

Time to change the subject, before the entire morning was ruined. He eyed her. "What are you making the men for breakfast?"

"Oatmeal," she said promptly. "With pumpkin and brown sugar. It's been cooking in the Crock-Pots all night."

"Now I understand the smell. I thought you'd made pumpkin rolls or something."

"Nope. Oatmeal." She crossed the room and opened two huge Crock-Pots, giving the insides a good stir. "Healthy and perfect on a chilly October morning."

"It smells great." He inhaled appreciatively. "Though to be honest with you, it doesn't sound like something the hands will like."

One corner of her lush mouth tugged up into a smile. "Then maybe it's time they broadened their horizons."

Oddly enough, when the men trooped into the kitchen and were presented with steaming bowls of oatmeal, every single one of them cleaned his bowl. Theo didn't hear a single word of complaint.

"Here." Ellie slid some in front of Theo. "I added a little bit of milk. Try it. It's good."

She returned to the Crock-Pot and got her own full bowl, taking a seat across from him.

They ate in companionable silence, while baby Amelia cooed in her bassinette. As they finished, the men in the other room filled their own cups with coffee from the large urn and, smiling shyly at Ellie, made their way outside to begin their workday.

"They like you," he said.

She laughed. "You don't have to sound so surprised. They'd like anyone, as long as they were fed well."

While he wasn't so sure about that, he didn't comment.

To his surprise, his bowl was empty before he knew it. "That was really good. Thank you."

Again her laugh rang out, making him smile. "You don't have to thank me for doing my job."

"I know. But I do when you're doing it well. Which you are. You're a damn good cook, Ellie."

Again her porcelain skin turned pink. "Thank you," she said quietly.

Suddenly he wanted to kiss her. So much so that he nearly pushed himself to his feet to go to her. Stunned, he looked down at his coffee, took a deep breath and tried to get himself back under control.

Ellie didn't seem to notice. "I wonder how they're going to enforce it," she said. "Did they call in the National Guard or something? I know Dead River's police force isn't large enough to be up for the task."

The quarantine. He slid the flyer back in front of him and read it again, feeling as though he was trying to memorize the damn thing.

"Let's take a drive into town," he said. "All three of

us—you and me and Amelia. We can check it out ourselves."

Her frown made a tiny line appear between her perfectly shaped eyebrows. "I don't know. Is it safe?"

"We don't have to get out of the truck. I just want to see
how people are reacting." And to find out if armed guards
were now patrolling the town's perimeter, though he kept
that one to himself since he didn't want to frighten her.

After considering for a moment, she agreed. "We
might as well pick up more diapers and formula while
we're there."

"We just did that."

She laughed again, the sound tickling his nerve endings and making him smile. "Babies go through a lot of
diapers and formula. Believe me. We need to stock up. I
don't want to ever run out."

Right then and there he resolved to make Ellie laugh
as much as possible. She always looked pretty, but when
she laughed, she was downright beautiful. Not his type,
but gorgeous nonetheless.

"We'll go now," he decided. "Though the other stores
don't open until ten, Dead River Pharmacy opens at
eight."

Her blue eyes widened. "I need a few minutes to get
ready," she said. "If you don't mind keeping any eye on
the baby, I'll be back in a few."

"Go ahead." He waved her away. "Amelia and I have
some things to discuss anyway."

Once Ellie had gone, he crossed to the bassinette and
picked up his smiling daughter. "You're such a happy
baby," he said to her. She rewarded him with gurgles
and coos.

Lifting her up, he held her suspended, just above his

face. She went silent as they studied each other. And then she made a gurgling sound and spit up all over his face and shirt.

At first, Theo stood frozen, afraid to move. He tried to think back, to remember if Ellie had given him instruction on how to deal with baby spit-up. It smelled bad and felt worse.

Finally, he just put Amelia back in the bassinette, grabbed a few paper towels and wiped himself clean. Though he'd have to change his shirt, he felt proud that he'd survived.

Moistening a fresh paper towel, he went back to the baby and gently cleaned up her little face. Because of the way he'd been holding her—note to self, don't do that again—she hadn't gotten any spit-up on her clothes.

Sighing, he continued to drink his coffee, waiting for Ellie to return so he could go and change.

"What happened?" Eyeing his shirt and wrinkling her nose, Ellie glanced from him to the baby and back again. "Let me guess. Spit-up?"

He nodded. "Be right back."

Once he'd cleaned up properly and donned a new shirt, he returned. "I know Mimi brought a car seat when she brought Amelia. Her car is still here. Give me a minute to get it out of there and installed in my truck." He smiled, unable to keep from noticing how lovely she looked.

"Ok." She nodded, looking at him curiously. "Didn't Mimi have any family? I would think someone would have fetched the car by now."

"Good point. I don't know. I'll need to ask her ex, Dr. Rand. Meanwhile, it'll take me a bit to figure out how to do the car seat. I've never done this before."

She smiled. "I need to pack a diaper bag anyway."

At first glance, the infant car seat seemed a simple thing. After fiddling with it for a few minutes, he decided the infernal contraption had been invented by a sadist. He knew enough to be aware proper installation was of the utmost importance to Amelia's safety.

Finally, he felt satisfied he'd gotten it right.

When he returned to the house, Ellie and Amelia were waiting.

"It's done." He smiled, refusing to hang on to his frustration for any longer than necessary. "So, let's go."

A mile from downtown, he came upon traffic. Red taillights, stopped cars, reminiscent of rush hour in Cheyenne.

Braking, he tried to see what might be ahead. "This is really strange," he said. "Even if there was an accident or something that closed down the road, there's never this many cars heading into town at the same time."

"Maybe it has something to do with the quarantine," she suggested. "It's possible you're not the only one who wanted to go and check things out."

"Or they've already called a town hall meeting, and everyone is rushing to get there." He sighed. "We can turn around and go back home or sit here until things start moving again. Your call."

"We really need diapers."

"Then we'll wait."

Traffic slowly crept forward. It wasn't until they rounded the corner into town that Theo saw the roadblock. "What the…"

State police vehicles were parked on both sides of the road, stopping every car and checking ID.

When Theo finally reached the officer, he handed over his license. "What's going on?"

"Quarantine," the man said. "Miss, I'll need your ID too."

"Wait a second," Theo interrupted. "I thought the quarantine was at the city limits. You're simply blocking access into town proper."

"Sir." The trooper looked him directly in the eye. "We have two circles around this town. The National Guard is stationed on every road leading into or out of Dead River, including the rural areas. The state police are manning the roadblocks around the downtown area. Any other questions?"

Theo shook his head. "No, sir."

"Good." Turning his gaze on Ellie, the officer held out his hand. "ID please."

Ellie rooted in the diaper bag, withdrew her driver's license and passed it over.

"Colorado?" Mouth pursed as if he found the entire state distasteful, he handed it back. "You two are free to go. Please be aware you will have to stop at the checkpoint again should you wish to leave." He motioned at Theo to pull forward.

Once they'd moved away, Theo let out breath he hadn't even been aware he'd been holding. "That is just plain weird." He glanced at Ellie, who appeared a bit shell-shocked herself. "I think I need to stop in and talk to Flint before we go home."

"I agree." Looking back over her shoulder, she grimaced. "None of that makes any sense."

"And it's not what was outlined in the flyer."

They pulled up in front of the sheriff's department and parked. "Do you mind waiting here with Amelia?" Theo asked.

"Not at all."

"I'll be back in a few minutes," he said, unable to keep from noticing how the sunlight turned her reddish-brown hair to molten fire. She really was quite beautiful, though she appeared not to be aware of that fact.

Hurrying into the building, he noted the reception area seemed more crowded than normal. Both of the dispatchers were there, which was odd, as Glenda McDonald usually only worked the night shift.

Waving at Kendra so she could buzz him in, he hurried past the bull pen where the deputies had their desks.

Flint looked up when Theo appeared in his door. "Let me guess," he said, his voice weary. "You want to complain about the quarantine."

"Not really." Hooking his thumbs on his belt, Theo studied his brother, who seemed to have aged years the past few days. "I just wanted to ask about the barricades coming into and going out of town. I knew they'd be patrolling the city limits, but..."

"I don't know." Flint dragged his hand through his closely shorn hair. "I've been informed with no degree of uncertainty that the CDC and the National Guard are in charge of this entire operation. I'm not sure who called in the state police, but it wasn't me."

Theo couldn't believe what he was hearing. "They're keeping you out of the loop?"

Flint shrugged. "Right now, yes. I'm sure once things settle down a bit, they'll do a better job of keeping me informed. I'm actually kind of relieved. I've got enough problems, dealing with a bunch of irate citizens. We're having a town hall meeting later today."

"Gemma said that would happen."

"And I suppose you're not going." There was no censure in his brother's voice, more of a tired resignation.

"I'm not planning on it. I've got enough on my plate as it is. Any word on catching Ellie's stalker?"

"No. I've passed around the description to the National Guard and state police, so if he shows up at one of the checkpoints, they can nab him."

Theo stared at his brother in disbelief. "That's it? You're not actively searching?"

"I'm sorry. Right now, my guys are stretched so thin we haven't been able to do much. You need to keep some of your hands around to guard the house."

Bristling, Theo shook his head. "I can protect Ellie and Amelia just fine, thank you."

Now it was Flint's turn to stare. "Sorry. I didn't mean to imply that you couldn't."

The rush of protective determination he felt floored Theo, though he took care not to show it. "No problem. I guess being a father has made me a bit defensive."

Flint still watched him closely. "Understood. How are they doing?"

"Fine. As a matter of fact, they're both waiting for me outside in the truck if you'd like to come see for yourself."

"Any other time, I'd love to go out and talk to them." Flint sighed. "But as soon as I step out into the waiting area, I'll be mobbed. I know. I went out to get some breakfast at the diner. It wasn't pretty."

"Is there anything I can do to help?"

Flint gave him a considering look. "Not right now, but thanks for offering. Just keep my little niece safe, okay?"

"Will do." Saying his goodbyes, Theo hurried back outside to Ellie and Amelia.

Once they'd pulled back out into the street, Ellie spoke. "People are upset. While I was waiting for you, I couldn't help overhearing a couple of conversations. One group was even talking about organizing a riot."

"A riot?" He shot her a look. "Are you serious? Maybe they meant more like a demonstration?"

"Maybe." But she sounded doubtful and he made a mental note to call Flint later and let him know.

They stopped at the small market to pick up three more boxes of disposable diapers and another case of formula, Ellie apparently being of the belief it was necessary to stock up. Theo couldn't help noticing the way she stuck close to him, or how she constantly looked over her shoulder.

He hated this for her. If he could get his hands on her stalker right now, he'd make sure that idiot would never bother her again. Since he couldn't do that, he did his best to try to make her feel as safe as he could.

After he'd loaded the supplies in the back of his truck, instead of heading straight home, he decided to surprise her. He stopped at a little shop he'd spotted the other day when he got a haircut but forgotten to mention to her in all the excitement.

"What's this?" Ellie asked, peering at the brightly decorated window.

"A children's clothing store. Let's go buy Amelia some new outfits." He waited expectantly. If Ellie was like every other woman he'd known, she'd be delighted and would temporarily forget about her stalker.

"Seriously?" As a slow smile blossomed on her face, he wasn't disappointed.

Smiling back, he nodded. "I'll hang on to her so you can shop."

Amazing, he thought, grinning as he watched her bounce out of the truck, waiting with barely concealed impatience for him to get Amelia out of the car seat. She practically bounded into the store. Once inside, she headed right for the little girls' side.

Luckily, the shop owner had placed a couple of chairs around the room. Theo took a seat in one that gave him a perfect view of the door and sidewalk. Gently rocking a drowsy Amelia, he couldn't stop smiling as he watched Ellie flit from rack to rack, her excitement and joy both palpable and contagious.

After a few minutes, he realized he hadn't seen a single salesperson or cashier. In fact, the store seemed deserted.

Slightly alarmed, he got up and walked toward the back, where the checkout counter was. Beyond that, a door led to the back of the shop.

Unwilling to leave Ellie, he pushed open the door. "Hello?" he called. "Anyone here?"

Ellie hurried over, still flush with excitement. "What's wrong?"

About to tell her, he spun as someone appeared. A short, middle-aged woman came from the back. She wore a white, surgical-type mask.

"I'm sorry," she said, her words muffled by the mask. "With this epidemic, I'm trying to minimize contact with people. When you've made your selections, I'll be happy to ring them up, but I do ask that you keep your distance."

Just like that, Ellie's joy dissipated, reality smacking her in the face. Theo clenched his teeth and managed a terse nod at the woman. In truth, he really would have preferred just leaving without buying anything, but this was the only children's store in town. And since they couldn't drive to Cheyenne, if they wanted to buy Amelia new clothes, they had no choice.

Ellie made her remaining choices with a brusque efficiency. She placed everything on the counter, stepping back so the woman could ring up their purchase.

Once the total had been calculated—nearly three hundred dollars, which sort of shocked Theo, just a little—he fished his money clip out of his pocket, peeled off three bills and tossed them on the counter.

"Keep the change," he said while the clerk shoved the clothes into a bag. When he reached to take it, the woman moved back so fast she nearly stumbled over her own feet.

She didn't say thank you and neither did they. Theo handed the bag to Ellie so he could manage Amelia. Ellie climbed into the cab, her expression pensive. She didn't speak while he buckled Amelia in her car seat.

He didn't either. Backing out of the parking spot, he drove to the barricade, pleased that at least this time, the line was much shorter. A quick glance at Ellie's profile told him she was still internally processing what had just transpired in the store.

Once they'd made it through and were on the road heading back toward the ranch, Ellie finally spoke. "What happened back there really made what's going on with the virus hit home."

"She didn't have to act like that," he said, aching for the way the happiness had been leached out of the day. "She could have handled it differently."

"I don't know. I could understand her fear. She was only protecting herself."

"Then she shouldn't even have opened the store. Staying home would have been better than treating us like lepers."

Ellie's eyes widened. He supposed his vehemence

surprised her. He didn't care. He'd enjoyed making her happy, even if only for a little while.

And this realization might have been the most shocking of all. Since when did he try to make a woman happy, other than in the bedroom?

Glancing at her, he saw she'd turned to watch Amelia sleep in her car seat. Well, at least she didn't realize. He took solace in the knowledge that Ellie apparently remained oblivious.

He'd just have to make sure she stayed that way.

Once back at the ranch, Ellie took off with Amelia for her room. Ordinarily she would have spent some time playing with all the new outfits, spreading them out on the bed and looking at them again before hanging them in the closet.

Not now. The stark fear in the store clerk's eyes had made everything feel unclean. Even the pretty, brightly colored baby clothes. Ellie left them in the bag. She'd wash them in the morning before she put them up.

She got the evening meal ready, working on autopilot. Once the men were fed, she ate her own meal, trying to pretend that Theo's conspicuous absence didn't bother her.

After she'd cleaned up the kitchen, fed and changed Amelia and put her down for the night, she was so exhausted she crawled into bed and fell instantly asleep.

The next morning she woke refreshed, her mood once again sunny. Though it was Thursday, it felt like a weekend. After feeding the men—once again Theo was a no-show—and scarfing down her own breakfast, Ellie made a huge pot of spaghetti with meat sauce, which she let simmer all day, filling the house with a delicious aroma that kept her in a constant state of hungry anticipation all day.

By the time the noon meal had been served and there was still no sign of Theo, Ellie began to worry.

Carrying Amelia, since she unashamedly planned to use her as an excuse once she found him, Ellie searched the house. It didn't take long; though the main house seemed pretty large, the open concept design made it easy.

Even Theo's bedroom held no clue as to where he might be. Heart beating fast, Ellie stood in the doorway, wondering if she dared enter.

Finally deciding against it, she turned and went back to her own room.

That night, dishing up the spaghetti with her own mouth watering in anticipation, she gave a little jump when Theo appeared, carrying a notebook. Trying to pretend not to be bothered, she greeted him with what she hoped was a friendly smile and a quick wave.

"Smells like heaven," he said, cocking one eyebrow and leaning his hip against the counter. His windswept hair and outdoorsy appearance made him even more devastatingly handsome.

Her mouth went dry, and she took a sip of water to cover. "Pull up a chair and I'll make you a plate," she offered.

"Don't mind if I do." Again the dazzling smile.

Turning away, she frowned, wondering why he'd gone back to his impersonal, flirtatious attitude. As if they hadn't ever shared a kiss or become friends.

And maybe they hadn't. Become friends, that is. Maybe it was all in her mind.

Either way, she was tired of worrying about it. She was hungry. Damn hungry.

She fixed him a plate and took it to him, then made her own, standing at the kitchen counter to eat her dinner. Hunched over, making notes in his book, he didn't speak and she didn't even try to make him. She hated that somehow she felt guilty. For what, she had no idea.

Which wasn't even logical. And that pissed her off even more.

The hands had finished and were ready for dessert. She'd gone simple with this one—a huge pan of brownies, which she served with vanilla ice cream.

Of course they loved that. Their obvious enjoyment put a smile on her face, the first one of the day.

Only after she'd served them did she turn to see if Theo wanted dessert.

As she did, his cell phone rang. Answering it, he shot Ellie a distracted look and got up, leaving the room. After a momentary flash of disappointment, she made her own dessert and sat down in his spot.

It wasn't really snooping if he'd left the notebook open, right? Spooning ice cream into her mouth, she slid the paper closer and took a look.

He'd made some sort of list. Two words jumped out at her. *Rodeo* and *Bronc*. Her heart sank. Surely Theo wasn't so intent on living in the past that he'd try to resume his former life, despite his previous injuries. If he did, what would happen to Amelia? And to Ellie too, she wondered. Was Theo still the sort of man who'd disappear on his daughter without a second thought?

Chapter 8

Theo didn't know why he felt so angry at Ellie. He'd managed to avoid her the entire day, not liking the unfamiliar feelings she caused. He hated to admit he'd been happy watching her shop, which was weird in itself. Still, he'd felt the happiest he'd been since that damn bronc threw him.

He wasn't sure what to do with this new him. For sure he nearly didn't recognize the person he was on the verge of becoming. Father to the cutest baby girl on the planet. A man who felt protective toward a woman he wasn't even sleeping with, for Pete's sake.

Even worse, every damn time he even looked at Ellie, he got a hard-on so massive he could barely walk.

It wasn't her fault. Objectively, he knew this. She was a sweet, fairly innocent girl with baggage, and she clearly had no idea how she affected him.

When he'd shown up at dinner, tempted by the tantalizing aroma of her spaghetti, he noted her surprise and could tell his behavior had hurt her. While he'd hated that, he couldn't seem to help himself. It was either avoid her as much as possible or talk her into going to bed with him.

Which he did not want. Really. He couldn't afford to

run her off. And truth be told, he kind of liked having her around.

His cell phone rang. Gemma. Glad of a distraction, he answered.

"I was beginning to get worried about you," he said.

"Sorry. I've been working pretty much around the clock. No time for a life."

"It's not getting any better?"

"No," Gemma answered. "Not really."

"How's Gram?" Theo asked.

Gemma sighed. "She's hanging in there. No one has died in forty-eight hours. That's something."

"At least it's not getting any worse."

"I wouldn't go so far as to say that," Gemma replied. "We still have new cases coming in."

"What about a cure? Dr. Rand vowed he'd find one."

Her brittle laugh spoke of her exhaustion. "All the doctors are working on that, when they're not treating patients.

"The CDC has people retracing Mimi Rand's steps before she got sick, since everything points to the virus starting with her."

"If it did, I don't understand why Amelia didn't get sick," Theo pointed out. "Illnesses like that seem to be particularly hard on babies and the elderly."

"Believe me when I say they're puzzling over that too. They still haven't figured out a common denominator. If the virus originated with Mimi, how'd she transmit it to the others? And with more and more people becoming infected…"

Theo suddenly realized what she was trying not to say. "We could lose half the town."

"Or more."

"People are going to start panicking."

"I know." Gemma sounded grim. "That's why we're making as little as possible public. We can't afford to have a mass panic. Especially since we're on quarantine."

"People will get hurt." Theo knew what might happen. It would involve beer, and a dare, and a couple of guys in a pickup truck. "I wonder if Flint has enough police officers."

"Since the state police and the National Guard have taken over, I think Flint is out of the equation. You might call him and check."

"Will do. I might be able to make myself useful for once." He didn't mean to let so much bitterness leak out into his voice, especially since he knew his sister would pick up on it.

"Just remember, you're supposed to be recuperating," she gently reminded him. "I know you're still doing physical therapy, but you can't do too much, too soon. Even though I know you want to do more, you've got to take it easy, so you don't risk reinjuring yourself. And you're also a father now. Amelia needs you. Don't do anything to endanger yourself."

"Since we both know Flint wouldn't allow that, I don't think you have to worry."

Gemma laughed with the first real trace of humor in a long while. Flint had actually returned to Dead River to help care for Theo after the accident. And she'd certainly also done her share. Theo's two siblings had been so worried he'd die that they'd dropped everything to make sure he wouldn't.

Theo owed them both a debt he doubted he could ever repay.

* * *

Ellie thought she could easily get used to this life. She'd never lived on a ranch before, and she'd always enjoyed taking care of babies, even though she hadn't done so since the triplets. She found herself waking up each morning with a smile on her face, eager to start her day.

Except for one thing. Theo had been avoiding her. If she entered a room, he left it without speaking. Worse, he hadn't been ignoring just her, but baby Amelia. This bothered Ellie enough that she planned to confront him.

If she could find him, that is.

Sighing, she decided to speak to Molly about it. Since their shopping expedition, she and her new friend had spoken on the phone once already.

"Maybe he's scared," Molly suggested, after listening silently to Ellie's complaints.

"Scared? Of what?"

"He's the one who kissed you. Maybe he wants more."

Ellie snorted. "In my experience, that's not how men act when they want more."

"In your experience? How much of that do you have?"

"Probably as much as you," Ellie shot back. "I've had a couple of serious boyfriends and a few not so serious. And the one thing they had in common was they let me know when they wanted more."

Molly conceded the point. "Well, maybe Theo just likes you too much, that's what I'm trying to say."

Ignoring the way her heart skipped at beat at that thought, Ellie took a deep breath and tried not to sound too eager. "What do you mean?"

"Theo's the love-'em-and-leave-'em type. Even before he became a big deal at rodeo, he blazed a scorching path through the girls in this town."

"And once again, you're back to not making sense." Ellie let some of her frustration come through in her voice. "If Theo's truly like that, then he must not find me attractive at all. Otherwise he'd be—"

"Seriously?" Molly cut her off. "You have mirrors there, right? You're gorgeous, girl. Theo's not blind. I think it's just that he's afraid to ruin things."

Though Ellie wasn't buying it, she was intrigued enough to ask, "How so?"

"Think about it. Theo can't commit. He's a good-time guy. Women want more. This is a recipe for disaster. Women tend to get pissed off. Some even have been known to go all-out psycho. He can't lose you. Ergo, he's going to keep his distance."

"I'm going to ask him," Ellie decided, sounding way braver than she felt. "Next time I see him, which should be the evening meal, I'm not going to let him run off without talking to me."

Molly whistled. "You go, you. I'll be silently cheering you on from over here. Call me and let me know how it goes, okay?"

"Okay." After she hung up, Ellie smiled. The conversation had given her a needed boost of confidence. It had been a while since she had a friend. Her stalker had scared away her former best friend, Angela, back in Boulder. Ellie hadn't realized how much she'd missed the camaraderie. Even though she'd only just met Molly, she felt as if they'd known each other forever. Sometimes people just clicked.

She thought of Theo. She'd thought sometimes they had serious chemistry. Too bad it was apparently completely one-sided.

Ellie began preparing dinner with mixed feelings of

anticipation and dread. Good thing the previous cook had stocked up with a major expedition to Sam's Club in Cheyenne before leaving. Ellie had been slow-cooking three huge beef briskets all day, and had a large pot of pinto beans simmering on the stove. She also used five pounds of potatoes to make a potato salad, along with several loaves of sourdough bread.

Instead of homemade barbecue sauce, she had the bottled kind, but she didn't think anyone would mind. And for dessert, she'd made a huge pan of peach cobbler.

The entire meal smelled wonderful. Her stomach growled, reminding her the dinner hour had grown closer.

As the men filed in, she dished up the food at their long table in the dining area. Theo arrived, his expression distant. He filled a plate and sat down to eat at the smaller table in the kitchen. After a moment's hesitation, she did the same.

She ate silently, trying to avoid locking gazes with Theo, but ready in case he tried yet again to slip out of the room without speaking.

The men were loudly appreciative of the meal. Two of them even jokingly proposed marriage, which made her smile. A quick glance at Theo revealed a thunderous frown.

Finally, everyone had eaten until they could hold no more. Amid a chorus of thanks, the ranch hands filed back outside, to head back either to their bunkhouse for the night or to their homes in town.

Theo pushed to his feet and turned to go.

Heart thundering in her chest, Ellie moved to intercept him. "Do you have a minute?" she asked.

He sighed. "Sure. What's going on?"

Now she met his gaze, quelling an immediate stab

of longing. "Why are you avoiding me? Is it because of the kiss?"

"Ellie, I—"

"Don't." Suspecting she knew what was coming, she waved away what sounded like the beginning of a feeble attempt at an excuse. "I certainly don't need to be treated as if I have the plague—or the virus."

"You're right." Theo sat down heavily. "I admit, I've been avoiding you for exactly this reason. I didn't want to talk about the kiss. But you're right, we should. So let me begin by promising you it won't happen again."

Stunned, she didn't know how to respond. "Okay," she said, even though it was anything but. "I don't understand why you kissed me to begin with."

Now he flashed a bit of his grin. "Fishing for a compliment?"

"Not at all." Her face flamed at the suggestion. "But clearly you regret it, so I wonder why you even…"

The grin vanished. Expression serious, he leaned across the table. "You might not realize how beautiful you are, but I do. And by now I'm sure you've heard enough about me to realize I'm not the settling-down kind."

Dumbfounded, she could only stare. Right into his sexy-as-hell, bright green eyes. "That's what you think I want?"

"Isn't it?"

Drawing herself up with dignity, she shook her head. "Theo, when all of this is over and I've saved up enough money, I plan to travel. I've always wanted to go to Australia."

Now it was his turn to do a double take. "You want to do what? Do you realize that's on the other side of the equator and the seasons are opposite of ours?"

"Of course I do." Making a face, she crossed to the sink and began loading dishes into the dishwasher. "Not everyone wants to try to tame the wild stallion."

As jokes went, it came out sounding sort of lame, but she saw the moment Theo got the humor. He shook his head and chuckled. "Point taken. So just to make sure we're clear, we can be friends but no more."

Glad she'd just turned back to the sink, she took a moment to compose her expression. "Sure," she said, sounding both casual and lighthearted, even though she felt the opposite.

"Great." Now the sexy grin came back, turning her insides to mush. "You should know, I've never been friends with an employee before."

And just like that, without even trying, he put her in her place. The truth had the effect of killing her libido. And the talk she'd planned to have with him about spending more time with Amelia? Well, she'd have to try again another time.

Somehow she managed to keep busy cleaning up the kitchen, thanked him politely for his time and gathered up Amelia to get her ready for bed.

She planned to spend the rest of the night in her room, hopefully with a pint of ice cream, trying to cheer herself up.

In truth, she thought she'd have been better off leaving things alone. Now she'd be the one avoiding Theo, at least until she could get over her hurt feelings.

Changing and powdering sweet baby Amelia took her mind off things for a little while. Once she had the baby fed and down for the night, Ellie went in search of that ice cream and a spoon.

As luck would have it, Theo walked into the kitchen just as she was leaving.

"Hey," he said, eyeing her ice cream. "Do you want to share?"

"Nope." She managed a smile to take the sting off her words. "I'm planning on hanging out in my room and eating this while I watch a chick flick." Words guaranteed to send any man running.

"Really? What movie?"

Crap. She hadn't thought that far ahead. She didn't even know what was on. "I'm not sure yet," she said, deciding to go with the truth.

"Do you mind if I watch it with you?"

She froze, not sure how to answer. While it was the last thing she wanted to do at this exact moment in time, if she declined he'd begin to suspect that maybe his words had hurt her. And she had way too much pride to let him figure that out.

"I've already put Amelia in her crib," she said, stalling.

"So? Just bring her bassinette to the living room. She'll be fine."

Before their little talk, she would have jumped at the opportunity to spend alone time with him. But now all she wanted to do was go lick her wounds.

"Okay," she finally agreed. "But I'm not sharing my ice cream with you."

Which made him laugh. Setting her ice cream down, she hurried away to get Amelia with the rich sound of his amusement making her chest hurt.

When she returned a few minutes later, he'd divided the pint into two bowls. "I thought we could share," he told her, sounding completely unrepentant.

"Of course." She glared at him in mock outrage. "I suppose next you're going to want to pick the movie."

Since he'd just shoveled a large spoonful of ice cream into his mouth, he didn't immediately respond. After he'd swallowed, he shrugged. "Nope. I don't care. I just need to relax and escape reality for a little while. You choose."

Relieved, she grabbed her dish of ice cream and plopped onto the couch. "Let's see..." Perusing the on-screen guide, she found one of her favorite movies of all time—*Sleepless in Seattle*. "I haven't watched that one in a while. It starts in five minutes."

Theo sat down next to her. "Sounds good. I've never seen it."

Now it was her turn to be shocked. "You've never watched *Sleepless in Seattle?* It's a classic."

"Maybe for you. My tastes for classics tend to lean toward *Die Hard* or *Fast and Furious*."

"Which are good flicks," she allowed. "But not what I'm in the mood for tonight."

When he didn't reply, she realized her words had unintentionally sounded seductive. Of course her face heated, though she tried to act as if she didn't realize.

The movie came on, to her immense relief. They watched it in silence—awkward at first, but as she began to relax, she thought it became companionable. And nice. With sex off the table, she tried to turn off her über-awareness of him and focus on the movie—and her ice cream. Although she had the strongest compulsion to scoot over next to him and cuddle on the couch. Imagining his reaction to that kept her in place.

When the closing music came on one and a half–plus hours later, she stirred and looked over to see Theo shaking his head in disbelief.

"What?" she asked. "Didn't you like it?"

"That was…ridiculous. People don't really act like that."

Since she liked nothing better than a good movie debate, she grinned, mentally accepting the challenge. "Oh yeah? And do you think people really act like Bruce Willis in *Die Hard?*"

"That's an action adventure flick. It's deliberately over-the-top."

She laughed. "And this is a romance. It too, is deliberately over-the-top."

Arms crossed, he exhaled. "Well, it's stupid. I couldn't buy in to it. Not even for one minute."

"It can happen. You just never know what life has in store for you. That's the whole reason I love this movie. It's optimistic, full of hope."

"Full of nonsense, you mean," he grumbled. "Maybe women think a guy is going to act like that, but I can tell you right now, they don't. That entire ending scenario would never have happened."

"Really?" Animated, loving the exchange and secretly marveling at the way this new "friendship" status made her feel more at ease, she grimaced. "You're telling me you wouldn't have taken a chance to meet the love of your life?"

"Don't you mean my soul mate?" he mocked. "I don't know about you, but I don't know very many men who believe in that crap. It's complete and utter nonsense."

"Wow." Amazed, she gaped at him. "I had no idea you didn't even believe in love."

He stared at her, his green eyes dark and unfathomable. "That's not what I said. At all. I said I don't believe—"

"That every person out there has someone special, waiting for him or her," she interrupted. "I agree, maybe that's a bunch of romantic drivel, but it gives people hope. I don't see anything wrong with that."

Theo groaned. His gaze dropped to her mouth, and then he turned his head and swallowed. "Let's just agree to disagree."

Disappointed, she bravely leaned over and touched his shoulder, making him look at her. "Okay, but I still think—"

She didn't get to finish the sentence. He muttered what sounded like a curse, before his lips captured hers, demanding. After the first initial shock, she returned the kiss with wild recklessness.

His tongue explored her mouth, sending shivers of pure lust exploding in her. For a split second, her emotions whirled, and then she gave in to the pleasure.

Curling her body into his as his hands moved possessively down the length of her back, she dared to caress his muscular shoulders, thrilling at the hard feel of them.

Thoroughly aroused, she squirmed against him, desperately wanting more. Instead he broke off the kiss and pushed himself away, off the couch and to his feet.

"My apologies," he growled, looking an odd combination of furious and aroused.

Confused, she could only stare at him, lips burning and feeling lost, aware her heart shone in her eyes. "What…" Her attempt to speak came out little more than a rasp.

"I promised you that wouldn't happen again." He drew himself up, inhaling sharply. She couldn't help noticing the proof of his arousal, which made her ache.

"Looks like you were wrong." Her weak attempt at

humor had no effect on his stony expression. She had the oddest impulse to comfort him. "It's all right, Theo."

"It's not all right," he snarled, turning away from her. "Obviously I need to work on my self-control."

Jumping up, she went to him, touching his shoulder. "What if I don't want you to?" she asked, her heart pounding like a trip-hammer in her chest.

He went absolutely still. "Ellie," he rasped, sounding like a man in torment. "You don't know what you're saying."

And then, before she could respond, he turned away and left the room. A moment later, she heard the sharp sound of his door closing.

Theo tossed and turned all night, furious with himself. He had more self-control than that. He shouldn't have kissed her. Even worse, he shouldn't have enjoyed it so much.

In his life, he'd kissed a lot of women. And each and every one of them had been different. He didn't know why or how, but the instant his lips touched Ellie's, it felt as if electricity had turned his blood to lava.

Thinking that, he shook his head. Listen to him, getting all poetic.

Ellie was a sweet, kindhearted girl. Almost a true innocent. She wasn't used to the kind of erotic playing he used to do. She'd get hurt, he'd feel like an ass and he'd lose the best cook he'd ever had. Not to mention Amelia's nanny, the only one besides Gemma he trusted to watch his daughter.

What a cluster mess his life had become. He wanted to saddle up a horse and just ride aimlessly. Doing that had always helped him think. But he couldn't even ride. With his type of back injury, doctors had specifically cautioned him against getting on a horse again, any horse, ever.

So here he was, a rancher who couldn't ride, a boss who took advantage of his best employee and a really horrible friend besides. Ellie had enough problems with her stalker; she didn't need a sex-starved ex-rodeo cowboy complicating her life.

"But what if I don't want you to stop?" Ellie's words replayed in his mind, over and over, tantalizing him, tormenting him. He closed his eyes and groaned. He had to figure out a way to make it past this craziness and get back on friendly footing.

Watching the movie with her had been a mistake. But after avoiding her for the better part of a day, he'd been missing her company, quite frankly. And when she confronted him, he'd felt comfortable enough to suggest hanging out together.

He hadn't anticipated how every move, every rustle of her clothing, every sigh, would skittle along his nerve endings.

Whatever it was about Ellie that affected him so strongly, he needed to get over it, like yesterday.

But no more avoiding her. That was the coward's way, and Theo had never been a coward.

Ellie had already begun serving breakfast when he walked into the kitchen. The men were dishing their own plates from a huge pan of scrambled eggs and sausage. Another pan contained toast and bagels, and a third bacon.

"Looks good," Theo said, keeping his tone light and cheerful.

Her back to him, Ellie stiffened. Then, turning slowly, she gave him a tentative smile. "Go ahead and fix a plate."

Nodding, he smiled back and did as she'd suggested. Hope flared. Maybe they could regain their casual footing; maybe things could go back to normal after all.

He grabbed a cup of coffee and sat at the smaller table to have his meal. After checking on Amelia, who cooed and squirmed in her bassinette, Ellie made her own plate and sat down across from him.

She avoided making eye contact with him while she ate, which he could understand.

In the other room, the ranch hands ate and talked and laughed. They were a boisterous bunch at meals, but especially in the morning when they hadn't yet expended all their energy at their work.

"I love that sound," Ellie said softly, almost as if she'd read Theo's mind. "It makes me happy."

Again he felt that flush of desire, the tightening of his body. Doing his best to ignore that, he nodded. "When they're happy, the ranch runs better. I've heard nothing but compliments about your cooking."

She blushed prettily and told him thank you. Theo knew he had to get out of there, but he also knew he needed to reassure her that they could interact as friends. Without the crazy passion.

Finishing the food on his plate, he pushed to his feet and carried his plate over to the sink. He refilled his mug with coffee and then gave Ellie a friendly wink and a wave before leaving the kitchen.

Once out of there, he took a deep breath, relieved to see his hands weren't shaking. Around her, he felt like an addict in need of a fix. Good thing he had something to occupy his mind this morning.

The ranch hands were sorting calves today, and while Theo couldn't actually participate, he planned to watch.

They were his cattle, after all. Even though the mama cows didn't take kindly to the brief separation from their babies, branding and castrating had to be done. It was a well-organized event, and everyone had their roles to play.

Ellie had been told to make sandwiches for lunch and one of his men would pick them up and bring them out to the corrals.

The day passed quickly. By the time the calves had been reunited with their anxious mamas, Theo was covered with grit and sweat. Still, he felt happy and alive.

Back at the house, he showered for a second time and put on clean clothes.

His cell phone rang. Flint. Maybe his brother could provide a welcome distraction.

"Can you meet me in town?" Flint sounded exhausted. And pissed. Theo knew his brother well enough to recognize that tone.

"Is there a problem?" he asked, wary despite feeling secure that he personally wasn't responsible for Flint's foul mood.

"Yes, there is, but I'd rather not discuss this over the phone. I'm off duty at three, and I'd love a beer. Or two."

"Okay." Theo checked his watch. A little after two, which meant he had plenty of time to get cleaned up and make his way to town. "Um, you do remember that tonight is Molly's rehearsal dinner, right?"

"That's why I'm leaving work early. It's also part of what I want to talk to you about." Now Flint sounded even more furious. Which meant things had gone from bad to awful. Theo figured it probably had something to do with the virus.

"I'll meet you there at three," Theo said. The Dead

River Bar was a couple of blocks from the police station. It wouldn't take Flint long to get there.

"Sounds good," Flint replied, and ended the call.

Theo supposed he ought to tell Ellie he was going out. After all, she'd agreed to accompany him to the rehearsal dinner.

Halfway toward her room, he stopped. Since when did he need to start checking in with a woman who worked for him? Shaking his head, wondering what had just almost happened, he turned on his heel and went the other way.

Theo hadn't visited the Dead River Bar since before he left town to live out on the road, chasing the rodeo circuit. Unlike other sports, rodeo season was year-round, now that there were so many indoor arenas. He hadn't been home much, before his accident. If he remembered right, the place packed them in on Friday and Saturday nights, when there was a live band, drink specials and appetizers for half off until nine.

Lucky for him, not many people stopped in for a drink so early in the day. All the stools at the bar were empty.

Sally Jean Mabry, part owner and sometime bartender, hurried over. "Long time, no see," she drawled. "Heard you were beat up pretty bad." She raked her gaze up and down him, then gave him a slow smile. "You look pretty good to me."

He laughed. Easily old enough to be his mother, Sally Jean had always been a flirt. Some people even called her a cougar, but Theo had never been one to judge. After all, it took two to tango.

"Flint's meeting me in a few minutes," he said. "While I'm waiting, how about a nice, cold beer." He didn't have to specify what kind. Everyone in his family drank Coors.

Flint arrived a few minutes later. Sally Jean took one look at his face and poured him a tall one, sliding it over to him. She hurried away without an effusive greeting.

Theo sipped his beer and waited, giving Flint a chance to decompress. Gripping his glass with both hands, Flint took a long drink, before wiping his mouth with the back of his hand. "I needed that," he said. "Christ, this has been a day."

Theo nodded, aware that if he waited it out, Flint would eventually unload. Plus, he knew from experience that it could be dangerous to speak when his brother was like this.

The two men sat side by side, not talking at first. Theo took the opportunity to check out the rest of the bar, to see if it had changed any since he'd been there last.

He was pleased to note it had not. Red pleather booths, the wooden tables scarred and worn. Of course the old Western bar, which had supposedly been brought in from a saloon up in Deadwood, South Dakota, was still in place, the dark wood polished and solemn looking.

Only one other patron was inside the place, and he sat in a booth by himself, back where the lighting created pockets of shadows. Narrowing his eyes, Theo checked him out. He didn't recognize the guy, but there were no dreadlocks at least.

Still, he considered going over and trying to make small talk with the stranger. If Flint hadn't been in such a black mood, Theo would ask him to do it. Even though Flint no longer wore a uniform, he no doubt still had his badge somewhere on him.

"Molly's wedding is off," Theo finally said, his voice little more than a growl. "She's really upset."

Chapter 9

"Off?" Privately, Theo thought his cousin must have finally come to her senses. She was too young to be getting married. "What happened?"

"Her piece-of-crap fiancé cleaned out her bank account." Flint shot Theo a dark look. "For whatever reason, she put his name on it. Now her money is all gone. I'd like to find the son of a bitch and punch him in the face. She's brokenhearted."

"Jimmy Johnson?" Despite having the same name as a famous football coach, Jimmy had seemed a nice enough guy. Theo had met him a few times. What he lacked in height, he made up for in personality. Outgoing and talkative, he'd seemed better suited to have been a salesman than a guy doing auto work in a body shop.

"Are you sure?" Theo asked when Flint didn't respond. "He doesn't seem the type. Plus, he really appeared to love Molly."

"The first thing I learned when I became a cop is nine times out of ten, appearances are deceiving." As he stared morosely into his beer, a muscle worked in Flint's jaw. "I've got men looking for him now."

"Well, he can't have gone far," Theo pointed out. "With the quarantine and all."

"True." Flint took another long drink, before turning to face his brother. "Who runs off with a quarantine in place? He never was the sharpest tool in the toolbox."

"Maybe he thinks he can figure a way to sneak out."

"Maybe." Flint sighed. "There are others who apparently think the same way. But those CDC people aren't messing around. I know you saw the National Guard the other day. They've set up even more roadblocks and barricades. They're determined no one is leaving this town."

Theo winced. "Which means Ellie's stalker is also stuck here." He couldn't help glancing back toward the guy in the booth. The booth was empty. The stranger had gone. Only thing, to get out he would have had to walk past the bar. Theo would have noticed him.

"Hey, Sally Jean," Theo called, making Flint wince.

"Ready for another?" she asked, gliding around behind the bar.

"Not yet," Theo said. "Hey, did you happen to see where that guy went? The one who was in the last booth?"

Sally cursed. "No. That turd better not have left without paying his tab." She practically flew toward the empty booth. "Ah, good. He left enough to cover his beer and a generous tip. That's what I get for thinking the worst."

Theo waited until she'd returned and put the cash in the till. "Sally, I didn't see him leave. Did you guys put in another door that I don't know about?"

She frowned. "No. The only other exit is if you go through the kitchen, and there's a sign on the door that plainly states Employees Only."

"And we know how everyone pays attention to signs, don't we?" Theo didn't bother to hide his sarcasm. "Obviously the guy didn't want to be seen. It wasn't Jimmy Johnson, was it?"

"No, of course not. That boy doesn't drink."

"Really? How sure of that are you? He's twenty-two years old and every time I've been around him, he acted like the life of the party."

Her mouth twisted in an admiring smile. "You got me there. I should have said he didn't drink in here." She shrugged. "For all I know, he could've been pounding down a twelve-pack every day."

"Okay, thanks." Flint turned his attention on the rest of his beer, which was dwindling fast.

"Anyway," Sally continued, as if she didn't notice his still-black mood. "Won't you be seeing him tonight at the rehearsal dinner?"

Theo watched his brother carefully, curious to see what he'd do. He knew, like everyone else in Dead River, if Flint told anything to Sally Jean, everyone in town would know about it within hours.

Instead of answering, Flint drained his beer. "Speaking of that, I think we'd better go." He slapped a five and two ones on the counter. "This is on me," he said to Theo. "Thanks, Sally Jean. We'll see you around."

"No problem." Scooping up the money, Sally Jean nodded at him coolly, though her intent gaze followed Flint as he moved toward the door.

"You coming, Hot Shot?" Without waiting for an answer, Flint crammed his battered cowboy hat on his head.

Grimacing, Theo gulped down the rest of his beer and followed.

Once outside, where Flint waited for him, Theo motioned toward his truck. "Do you want to ride out to the ranch with me?"

"Let's walk first. I need to think." Flint had always

gone for a walk when he was trying to puzzle something out.

Theo glanced at his watch. "You also need to start making some calls. Everyone's going to be arriving at the Blue Bear Restaurant in a couple of hours."

"I know." Flint grimaced again. "Gemma already knows. She can't leave work, but someone needs to be with Molly, helping to calm her down."

"Let me check with Ellie when I get home."

"Ellie?"

"Yes. She and Molly hung out the other day. Went shopping, had lunch, got their nails done—all that kind of stuff women do."

"That would be awesome." For the first time, Flint sounded relieved. "Head on home and see if Ellie minds going over there. From what I hear, Molly's locked herself in her house and refused to talk to anyone, even her sister."

Especially her sister. Both brothers knew how Sarah could get. The woman always had to be right. No doubt one of the first things she'd said when hearing the news was "I told you so."

Flint and Theo parted ways and Theo drove home. Though he usually took his time, barely driving the speed limit, this time he broke every speed limit.

When he walked in the front door, Ellie greeted him, clearly agitated. "Molly called," she began. "And my car still isn't running right. I haven't had the time—or the money—to take it in and get it fixed yet. And Molly really needs me."

"I know." He squeezed her shoulder, fighting the urge to let his hand linger. "I'll take you over there. The car seat is still in the backseat of my truck."

Ellie nodded. "I don't mind taking her with me. It might distract Molly to have a baby to fuss over."

Though he'd actually planned on watching Amelia while Ellie and Molly visited, Ellie's idea had merit. "That's a really good idea."

"Unless you think it'd be better for her to stay home."

They both spoke at the same time. Ellie smiled self-consciously, wearing her sadness for Molly like a scarf. Theo smiled. "Your choice. You decide what you think would be best." He liked that she could care so much for his cousin, a woman she'd only just met.

Though she'd only known Molly a day, hearing the anguish in her new friend's voice had Ellie holding back tears. She'd promised to be there as soon as she could. Molly had even offered to pick her up, but Ellie didn't want her driving in her condition. Poor thing couldn't even speak a complete sentence without breaking down and sobbing.

When Theo had arrived back home, Ellie was prepared to plead her case. She'd missed both the lunch and dinner for the hands once already, when she'd gone shopping with Molly, and now she would be leaving the cooking to Theo once again. On the bonus side, after hearing him talk about his chicken enchiladas, she'd cooked several chickens that morning and put them aside. She'd planned to ask Theo to show her how to make the dish.

Once she had the diaper bag packed, she hurried to the kitchen, where she'd made up several bottles. Putting those in a small, soft-sided ice chest, she double-checked to make sure she had everything before picking up Amelia and wrapping her securely in a warm blanket.

"We need to pick her up some more clothes next time

we go to town," she told Theo when he returned. "She'll need a coat, and some little shoes."

"I'll give you my credit card and you and Molly can do that, if that's okay with you," he replied as they walked outside. "Go today. That might help Molly cheer up."

"Not today." She sighed. "Molly is really broken up. I'll see if she wants to make plans to do that on my next day off."

"It won't be a day off if you're taking Amelia shopping." He took the baby from her and buckled her securely into the infant car seat. "Consider it part of your job."

Once again, if she did that, she wouldn't be cooking. She pondered this as she climbed up into the cab and buckled herself in. Maybe Theo was right and she did need to rethink her plan of holding on to both jobs.

Except she really needed the money. Not only to fix her car, but to save for her grand escape.

"I'll do it on my day off," she said firmly. "That way, it won't make me miss cooking any meals."

He sighed but didn't respond.

At first, the bouncing of the big pickup had Amelia squealing. But once they left the dirt road and hit pavement, the motion lulled her to sleep. Ellie couldn't keep from smiling as she turned to check on her small charge.

"She's beautiful, isn't she?" Theo said, pride and something that sounded an awful lot like affection coloring his deep voice.

"She certainly is. And a really easy baby too, I think. At least, she seems that way, compared to caring for the triplets."

"You're way ahead of me." He gave her a rueful smile. "There are no babies at all on the rodeo circuit."

"What was that like?" she asked, hoping the question didn't make him shut down. "I know there's a lot of driving involved."

"I never minded that. I got to see a lot of new towns, though I never stayed in one very long. But there's an adrenaline rush I can't really describe." His pensive expression seemed wistful. "I had my routine and I really enjoyed it. It really bothers me to think it's all still going on and I'm not a part of it."

Though Ellie nodded as if she understood, she didn't really. She'd never felt that passionate about anything. She'd taken a few classes at CU after high school, but since she didn't know where to focus, she soon lost interest and stopped going. She'd worked at a bookstore on Pearl Street, and part-time as a waitress in an Irish pub in the same area. But to find a job that meant everything… that was something she'd figured was for other people.

The idea of traveling to a place with sandy beaches, a turquoise ocean and year-round warm temperatures was about the only thing that even came close.

They pulled up to a neighborhood flanked by adobe walls. Inside, the houses seemed larger and more ornate, though the yards were incredibly small.

"Once of the first things Molly did once she got over the shock of losing her parents was pay cash to build a new home," Theo said. "Security has always been important to her. Though now that Jimmy cleaned out her bank account, I don't know how she'll pay the insurance and taxes. She doesn't make that much as a waitress."

"Cleaned her out?" Aware her mouth was open, Ellie closed it. "Are you saying her fiancé stole from her?"

"His name was on the bank account, so not technically. But yes. What he did was wrong. And when we catch up with him, we're going to make him pay back whatever he hasn't spent."

Molly hadn't mentioned this. All she'd said was the wedding was off, that Jimmy had broken up with her.

"That's terrible," Ellie mused. "What kind of man does this?"

"Not a good one, that's for sure."

They parked in front of a beige adobe house, with a red tile roof and matching front door. "Wow," she said, impressed. "What a great house."

"Yeah. I heard she fixed it up real nice too." Theo jumped out, went around to Ellie's side and opened the door, just as he had when they went shopping. Again unable to hide her surprise, she thanked him, which earned her a startled look. Just because most of the men she knew didn't know how to be a gentleman, didn't mean it was unusual to someone like Theo.

"You know what?" he said when she went to get Amelia out of the car seat. "I'll keep her. You comfort Molly."

Ellie froze. "But you still have to get supper on the table for the men. I can't ask you to watch the baby too."

"You didn't ask. I insist. I need to spend more time with my daughter."

Put like that, how could Ellie refuse?

"Thank you," she said. "You're a good man, Theo Colton."

He flushed, whether from pleasure or embarrassment, she couldn't tell.

"I'll call you when I'm ready to come home," she said, resisting the urge to kiss him on the cheek. Then she blushed too, realizing she'd used the word *home*.

"See you," she said, turning away to cover her discomfort. As she walked the last few feet up to the front door, she heard the truck drive away.

Molly flung the door open just as Ellie was reaching for the doorbell. Her puffy face was streaked with tears.

"Thank goodness you're here," she exclaimed, pulling Ellie inside. "I was just about to do a shot of tequila. You can join me."

Ellie considered telling her she didn't do shots, but seeing the pile of used tissue on the coffee table, she decided maybe she'd do just one. Later.

"Before you do that," Ellie said, dropping onto the sofa and patting the spot next to her. "I want you to tell me everything that's happened."

Swallowing hard, Molly promptly burst into tears.

It took the better part of an hour to get the entire story. Molly hadn't known Jimmy long, true. But she'd believed him when he'd claimed to recognize her instantly as The One.

"It was so romantic, you know," Molly said, then blew her nose and added another tissue to the pile. "He wanted to save for a ring, but I'd always wanted to wear my great-great-grandmother's ring. It's a family heirloom. And it's gone," she wailed. "I haven't told anyone in the family yet."

"Gone?" Ellie glanced at Molly's ringless hands. "Wouldn't you be wearing it?"

This question brought on another bout of weeping. Once Molly got herself back under control, she grabbed the bottle of tequila, poured a shot and downed it. Wiping her mouth on the back of her hand, she exhaled. "It needed to be sized. We were going to go this morning and have that done. The rehearsal dinner was supposed to be tonight, for pity's sake." And then she began weeping again.

Ellie patted her back, her heart aching for her friend. "I wish there was something I could do to help you."

"Yeah." Molly raised her red, puffy eyes. "The only good thing is he's got to be around here somewhere. With the quarantine, he can't leave town. Flint will find him. And then I want him to look me in the eye and tell me why he did this."

Privately, Ellie thought the reason was clear—greed. This Jimmy Johnson had seen a golden opportunity and had taken advantage of a trusting young woman.

"True," Ellie said. "I hope he hasn't sold your ring or spent all your money."

"That too." Molly poured another shot and held it out to Ellie. "Here."

"I don't think—" Ellie began, then caught sight of Molly's pleading expression. Sighing, she accepted the glass and took a deep breath before downing it. Immediately she shuddered, scrunching up her face at the taste. "There." She placed the glass back on the table. "I did it."

"Good." Molly took one more. "I want to drink enough to forget. Or get angry. Angry's good. Better than pain."

"Yes, it is. But..." Ellie took a deep breath. "I'm not sure getting drunk is the answer."

"Seriously?" Molly shot her a look of disbelief. "This is killing me. I've got to do something."

Ellie nodded, conceding the point. "Whatever you want. I'm here for you."

"Good. Then drink up." Molly poured and handed Ellie another shot.

"I don't think I want this," Ellie began.

"Drink with me," Molly said, her large green eyes

filling with tears, which she defiantly wiped away. "Distract me. Tell me stories. What's life like, living out at the ranch?"

"Normal. I'm taking care of the baby and trying to keep my first job as ranch cook. So far, it's not going well." She studied the shot glass, narrow-eyed, before downing it. The alcohol seared a path down her throat.

"At least living out there, you're not dealing with the constant fear of everyone who lives in town." Molly grimaced. "A lot of people are scared to leave their houses."

"Oh, I'm afraid too," Ellie said, after setting down her shot glass. She held up her hand when Molly went to pour her another. What was this, three? Or four? Ellie couldn't remember. "No more. I don't want to get sick."

Molly nodded, wincing. "The room's spinning. Maybe we should take a break." She sighed. "What are you afraid of? Your stalker?"

"So many things. Including him." Ellie tried not to sound maudlin, but on the rare occasions she drank, her emotions and innermost feelings always seemed to bubble to the surface. She sighed, then managed a wobbly smile. "This virus has me pretty terrified too."

"Yeah." Molly picked up the tequila bottle, examined it and put it back down. "So many people are sick and dying. Poor Gemma is working herself to the bone."

"I pray every day that Amelia won't catch it," Ellie confessed. "And I'm worried about Theo's grandmother. He clearly loves her."

"She's a strong woman. She's hanging in there. What about you?" Molly regarded her curiously. "For a day or two, I was paranoid that every little ache or pain might be a symptom. Mimi Rand was young and healthy, and she died. I'm not ready to die."

Ellie stared at her new friend. "Me either." She considered the tequila bottle, then decided what the hell? "Pour me one more shot."

After she'd downed it, she sat back and shook her head. "That would suck, to die this young."

"I'd want some warning myself." Following suit, Molly took another shot, as well. "Because at least if I knew, I could try to do some of the stuff I needed to do before I died."

"Me too," Ellie said, a bit too enthusiastically. "And there's one thing I definitely would want to do before I left this earth." Then, realizing who she was speaking to, she clapped her hand over her mouth. "Never mind."

"Oh, no. You're not getting off that easily." Like a bloodhound on the scent, Molly leaned in. "What is it? What's the one thing you'd do that you don't want me to know about?"

"I can only tell you if you swear to me you won't tell another soul."

"Tell anyone?" Molly waved her arms dramatically. "Who am I gonna tell? You're my best friend. If anyone's going to get dished the latest dirt, it'd be you."

Ellie giggled, which surprised her. She never giggled. Well, hardly ever. But she had just drunk four— or more, she'd lost track—shots of tequila. "Okay," she said, vaguely wondering if this was a good idea. "If I found out I was going to die, I wouldn't want to go until I'd made love with Theo."

"Theo?" Molly gasped. "Seriously?"

Ellie nodded, feeling her face heat. "I know he's your cousin and everything, but he's…" She closed her eyes, wishing she'd kept her mouth shut. "Never mind."

"Oh, no, you don't." Molly touched her arm. "I can

see the appeal. Heck, Theo's had every female in town fawning over him."

This caught Ellie's interest. "Really? I hadn't noticed."

"Well, not so much these days." Molly shrugged. "But before, when he was a big rodeo star. He always had a bunch of women throwing themselves at him. Like Mimi Rand."

Amelia's mother. Ellie wished the thought would magically sober her up. "I didn't intend on getting drunk," she sighed.

Molly shrugged. "You're not driving, so why not? Theo will understand."

"Maybe." The thought of facing Theo while tipsy made Ellie wince. "He keeps kissing me, then getting mad about it. I just hope I don't do something stupid, like jump his bones."

As soon as she spoke, she knew she'd had way too much to drink. "I won't, of course."

"I know you won't." Molly wagged her finger. "That's your problem. You're too afraid."

"Maybe. But I think I know Theo well enough now to know he won't take advantage of an inebriated woman."

For some reason Molly seemed to find this hilarious. "Fine, then," she said when she finally stopped laughing. "You can seduce him another time, when you're sober."

"Seduce him?" Horrified, Ellie started to shake her head, stopping when the room began to spin. "Oh no. I don't plan on doing that."

"Why not?"

Ellie shrugged. "For one thing, I don't know how. I've never seduced anyone in my life."

Molly stared at her, her eyes going wide. "You're not a…"

"A what?"

"A virgin." Molly whispered the words.

That cracked Ellie up. She laughed and laughed until tears ran down her face. "Oh, heck, no. I've had a boyfriend or two. But I never had to seduce anyone. I wouldn't even know how."

"I can teach you," Molly said solemnly, though her eyes twinkled. "As a matter of fact, you can be my pet project."

"No, no, no." Feeling dizzy, Ellie waved her away. "No, we're not going to do that."

"You have to." Batting her eyelashes, Molly pouted. "How can you take away the one thing that can distract me after my fiancé dumped me right before the wedding?"

Put like that, Ellie knew she had no choice. Molly gave her a wobbly grin. "Then you're in?"

Reluctantly, Ellie nodded. "I'm in." And wondered what she'd just gotten herself into.

"Yay!" Molly clapped and jumped to her feet. Or tried to. But her feet tangled and she fell back onto the sofa. "Maybe I'd better make us some coffee and try to sober up."

"Food would be better." Suddenly ravenous, Ellie attempted to stand. "Do you have anything to eat?"

"Sure." Molly waved her question away. "First, I want to try to figure out a plan for your seduction of Theo."

This time, Ellie knew better than to argue. She figured she'd let Molly talk, agree with everything and Molly would have totally forgotten about it by morning.

"We're going to buy you some sexy lingerie," Molly declared, her smile not quite banishing the shadows behind her bright green eyes.

"No. We're not." Ellie shook her head for added emphasis. "If I go into one of the shops in Dead River, everyone will not only know, but rumors will start flying around town. It'd be different if we could leave and go to Cheyenne."

"Fine." Molly thought for a moment, then snapped her fingers. "I know. We'll buy it on the internet."

Ellie thought of her one credit card and grimaced. "Not too expensive, okay?"

"Sure." Molly grabbed her laptop. With a few expert clicks, she navigated to a website. "Here you go. Take a look."

Ellie studied the page of negligees and shook her head. "Not these."

"Really?" Molly's perfectly shaped eyebrows rose. "What exactly did you have in mind?"

"Well, if I'm really going to do this, I need something that's the opposite of my personality. Something daring." She thought for a moment. "None of these pastel colors. I want red or black."

Molly laughed. "Wow. You surprise me." She jumped to her feet. "Just a second. Wait right here."

A moment later she returned, carrying a box from a popular store. "I had a bridal shower a couple of weeks ago," she said, her voice wavering before she cleared her throat and bravely lifted her chin. "I got this as one of my gifts. Clearly, I'm not going to be using it. I think it might be exactly what you're looking for."

"Oh no. I couldn't do that."

"Why not?" Molly squinted at her. "What am I going to do with it? Might as well put it to good use."

Ellie used the only excuse she could think of. "We're not the same size. I'm taller than you."

Hearing that, Molly laughed. "Open the box. It's sort of one size fits all."

With trepidation, Ellie did. After she parted the pink-striped tissue paper, she lifted the two scraps of red cloth and stared in disbelief. "Um." Not sure what to say, she could feel her face heating with embarrassment.

Which only made Molly laugh harder. Doubled over, she laughed until tears streamed down her cheeks and she couldn't catch her breath. Finally, she wiped her eyes and tried to rearrange her features into a pseudo solemn expression.

"Ellie, just take it home with you. Try it on. If you don't like it, throw it away. But I can guarantee you if you're serious about making Theo lose his mind, then this outfit will do it."

Ellie finally nodded. Wrapping the wisps of sheer material in the tissue paper, she returned it to the box and put it in her purse.

"Now about that food," she said.

They feasted on frozen pizza and carrots and hummus. And odd combination, but satisfying anyway. With this, they drank ginger ale, as the fizzy drink sounded better than coffee or water.

After she got some food in her, Ellie felt much better. Still a bit dizzy, but no longer on the verge of getting sick.

"Want to do more shots?" Molly asked, grinning. "Just kidding," she said, laughing in reaction to the shocked look Ellie gave her. A moment later, she weaved across the room and enveloped Ellie in a hug. "Thank you."

"For what?" Ellie asked, stunned.

"Cheering me up. You really helped."

"I aim to please."

Ellie glanced at her watched, stunned to see it was

nearly midnight. "I'd better call Theo to come pick me up. I didn't realize it was so late."

"Just spend the night," Molly suggested. "He can pick you up in the morning. I have a lovely guest room."

Shaking her head, Ellie gave her new friend a rueful smile. "As great as that sounds, I'd better not. Theo's already had to step in and make a couple of the meals for the ranch hands."

"So? He needs to do something. Better than sitting around feeling sorry for himself." As soon as she spoke, Molly clapped her hand over her mouth, eyes wide. "Oh, jeez. Don't tell him I said that. It's the tequila talking."

"I won't." Regarding Molly with open curiosity, Ellie knew she had to ask. "Is that what people think?"

Molly sighed. "I wish I'd kept my big mouth shut."

"I told you, I'm not going to repeat anything. I just wonder. It seems like Theo went through a lot."

"He did, he did," Molly hastened to reassure her. "I was being snarky. Mainly because he gave me a hard time for continuing to work as a waitress even though I had the trust fund. But I knew that money wouldn't last forever. So I paid cash for my house and my car and banked the rest. I don't make a lot waiting tables, but I enjoy my job."

"I've worked as a waitress." Ellie grimaced. "And a barista in a coffee shop, a salesclerk in a bookstore and now a ranch cook and nanny. Experience makes life richer."

"Exactly!" Beaming approval, Molly sighed. "I knew there was a reason we hit it off so well. We think alike." And then she sat down, leaned against the back of the couch and fell asleep.

Ellie could do nothing but envy her. More than anything, she wished she could claim the overstuffed armchair and do the same. Instead she got out her cell phone and punched in Theo's number.

Chapter 10

Ellie and Molly must have had a good time, despite Molly's crisis. When Ellie called him a little past midnight, she'd spoken with a slight slur to her words. He'd told her he was on his way. Carrying a sleeping Amelia out to his truck, he buckled her in her car seat, careful not to wake her.

When he pulled up in front of the house, Ellie hurried outside, a little unsteady on her feet. She opened the passenger-side door and jumped up into the cab.

"Hey," she said, a bit too brightly. "Thanks for picking me up."

He smiled and nodded, able to smell the liquor. "Did you manage to help make Molly feel better?"

"I think so. Between me and the shots of tequila, she wasn't feeling any pain."

He laughed with genuine enjoyment. As he watched her blink, apparently struggling to stay awake, he realized he hadn't laughed much at all until she'd come to work for him. Since then, even with all the craziness going on around them, he'd found himself smiling or amused at least once a day.

"Shots, huh?" he asked as they pulled away from the

house. "I wouldn't have pegged you for a shot-drinking kind of girl."

"I'm not. At all. But Molly insisted, and she was so miserable..." Her words trailed off and she yawned. "But in the end, we had a good time. Luckily, she had some munchies, so I could lessen the effect of all the alcohol."

"Was she still crying over that low-life fiancé of hers?"

"Not by the end of the night. She barely even talked about him."

"What did you talk about?" he asked, more to make conversation than anything else.

Ellie didn't respond. When he glanced over at her to see why, he realized she'd fallen asleep with her head pillowed against the doorjamb. Just like Amelia, who hadn't woken up once in her car seat.

Chuckling, he turned the radio up and hummed along to the music all the way home.

Once they'd left the pavement for the rutted dirt road leading to his ranch, the bouncing and swaying of the truck shook Ellie awake.

"Theo?" Voice husky, she sounded confused. And sexy as hell. Lust stabbed him instantly. He decided to try to ignore that.

"Um-hmm?"

"Are we almost home?"

"In a minute or two, darlin'." Slipping into the easy endearment he used with most women—at least those who weren't his employees—he turned to look at her. She looked befuddled, as if everything was slightly out of focus. "I bet you're dying to get in your own bed and sleep it off."

"Well, actually no. I don't feel good. I think I'm going

to get sick." And then she leaned forward and violently vomited all over the floorboard of his truck.

Hangovers were a fate worse than death, Ellie learned. The next morning when Amelia's hungry cries woke her, Ellie felt as if her skull might crack open. Her headache pulsed with every angry beat of her heart. She pushed herself out of bed, rushing to brush her teeth immediately, hoping to banish that awful taste in her mouth.

That done, she changed Amelia and staggered to the kitchen to make her a bottle. Luckily, the baby girl stopped crying the instant Ellie lifted her. Ellie didn't know how she would have survived if she hadn't.

Finally, with Amelia sucking eagerly on her bottle, Ellie sat down. What on earth had happened last night? She remembered leaving Molly's house with Theo, and then...

Oh no. Her stomach rolled as she realized she'd gotten sick inside Theo's truck.

When the coffee finished, she poured herself a cup and contemplated the stove. She had to make something for the men to eat for breakfast. Not an easy task when even the thought of food made her feel queasy.

That said, she made an executive decision that today would be a cold cereal and fruit day. They might complain, but they'd have to make do. That was the best she could manage.

Once everything had been set out, she took Amelia and headed back to her room. She needed to lie down for a little while. Hopefully when she next woke, she'd feel better.

One thing for sure—she was never going to drink that much again. Ever.

Somehow she made it through the day. Napping for a few hours helped settle her stomach and restore her appetite, and when she got up again and changed Amelia, she headed to the kitchen to make herself a sandwich.

She'd just sat down and taken a bite when Theo sauntered in, grinning, and looking sexy as sin. "How are you feeling today?" he asked. "I'm going to guess not great, since I saw you put out cornflakes for the guys this morning."

Swallowing, she took a sip of her ginger ale and managed a weak smile back. "Did they complain much?"

"Not after I told them what you did yesterday. Then they understood."

"You didn't," she protested, even though she knew he had.

He crossed to the bassinette and picked up a happy, gurgling Amelia. "Gemma said to tell you to make sure and drink lots of water today."

Gemma. Ellie closed her eyes. "You told her?"

"She called." He didn't sound worried. "She's glad you spent time with Molly."

"About last night," Ellie began.

"How much of it do you remember?" he teased, a devilish sparkle in his green eyes.

"Enough." With a groan, she took another sip of her ginger ale. "I'm sorry about your truck."

"Yeah, I am too. I left it for you to clean up today."

At the thought, her stomach rebelled. She swallowed, eyeing her barely eaten sandwich, and then pushed away the plate.

Unable to tell if he was serious, or still teasing, she sighed. "Really?"

"No." Rocking Amelia gently, he looked a study in

contrast. Rugged, devil-may-care cowboy combined with tender, loving father. Ellie found the combination darn near irresistible. Which made it even harder to understand if he really wanted to leave and go back to the rodeo.

"Eat your sandwich," he urged. "And I'll help with the preparations for lunch."

Grateful, she nodded, then winced at the stab of pain. "I need some ibuprofen," she said. Theo crossed the room without a word, opened a cabinet and brought her a bottle. After she'd swallowed a couple of pills, she got busy finishing her lunch.

Theo watched her silently while she ate, which made her want to squirm. Luckily, he alternated his attention between his baby girl and Ellie, so she was able to manage to choke down the rest of her food.

"So, how is Molly taking this?"

She sighed. "She seems more mad than brokenhearted, though she's hurt. She's more worried about the ring than the missing money."

He went still. "What ring?"

Cursing her slip of the tongue, she knew there was no help for it but to go on. "She hasn't told anyone in the family yet. It's her great-grandmother's ring or something."

"More like great-great-grandmother's." Theo sounded grim. "That thing's been in the family for generations."

"Is it valuable?"

"Very." He shook his head. "But there's no way he can even attempt to pawn it here in Dead River. Everyone in town knows who it belongs to. No doubt he intended to skip town and take it with him. I guess he thought he could somehow leave despite the quarantine."

Ellie got up and carried her plate to the sink. She felt a little bit better having eaten. "Well, Molly is broken up about him taking it."

"I imagine she is. How did he get a hold of it?"

"They were taking it to get resized. I'm guessing she left it lying around and he took it." Ellie sighed. "What kind of person does something like that? It's bad enough that he's dumping her practically at the altar, but to *steal* from his own fiancée?"

"He's a piece of work, that's for sure," Theo agreed, keeping his tone mild for Amelia's sake. "I knew she was rushing into things, but everyone else insisted she was in love."

Not sure how to respond, Ellie simply nodded.

"We need to let Flint know about the ring," Theo said. "I'm sure he's already looking for the SOB, since him jilting our cousin is a slap in the face to our family. Stealing the ring is him giving us the finger. Colton pride and all that."

Though his tone sounded a bit mocking, Ellie judged from his expression he meant what he said. "About Flint," she began. "I think I need to call Molly and tell her what I've done. She should be the one to tell Flint, don't you agree?"

He shrugged. "Either way, Flint needs to know." Glancing at his watch, he stood, still expertly holding Amelia. "I'll put her down and then let's figure out what you want to serve for lunch. Flint's supposed to stop by around noon."

In the end, Ellie ended up directing Theo in the browning of a large quantity of hamburger meat. They were making sloppy joes and would be serving them on hamburger buns, along with potato chips and pickles, for lunch. She took care to stand a fair distance from the stove, as even the smell of the frying meat made her feel nauseated again.

After the meat had browned and the grease drained off, she supervised Theo mixing up the tomato paste and seasonings. Even watching the fine hairs on his muscular arms as he cooked made her feel dizzy with longing.

Once he'd stirred that in and everything was simmering, she slipped away to phone Molly and let her know what she'd done.

"How are you feeling today?" Molly asked, sounding none the worse for wear. "You were pretty far gone when you left."

"I know." Ellie grimaced. "I'm not used to drinking. I got sick in Theo's truck."

"You did what?" Molly squealed, making Ellie wince in pain. "Oh no, I bet he was livid."

"I don't remember," Ellie admitted. "And I've felt horrible all day. Theo's even cooking the ranch hands' lunch for me."

"Is he? Now, that's true love."

Despite knowing Molly was teasing, Ellie felt her face heating. "Anyway, I messed up. In talking to Theo a little while ago, I slipped and told him about the missing ring."

"Crap." Molly went silent. When she spoke again, she sounded a bit stressed. "That means I need to call Flint. I've been dreading doing that. He's sure to lecture me." She grimaced. "Even though he's my cousin, he likes to act like a big brother. Maybe because I don't have any brothers. Who knows."

Seeing a chance to make amends, Ellie smiled. "Actually, Flint is supposed to be here for lunch. I can tell him for you, if you'd like."

"Really?" The infectious energy was back, just like that. "You'd do that for me?"

"Of course."

"Doesn't he scare you?"

"Flint?" Puzzled, Ellie glanced at Theo, still stirring the meat and not making any effort to hide his eavesdropping. "No, Flint doesn't frighten me. He seems like a nice guy."

"Ha." Molly snorted. "Sure, if you don't mind telling him, have at it. And when he calls me to gripe, I just won't answer the phone."

"Whatever makes you happy," Ellie said, smiling. "I'll take care of it."

"That was a weird conversation," Theo said.

Ellie shrugged. "Flint intimidates her."

"Seriously? That's weird. He's her cousin."

"Who apparently is fond of delivering lectures on how she should live her life."

Theo laughed, the rich masculine sound caressing her insides and turning her knees to water. "He's good at that. He only does it because he cares."

"Only does what because he cares?" Flint strode into the kitchen. "Damn, that smells good."

"Theo made it," Ellie said. "It's a big pot of sloppy joes."

Removing his cowboy hat, Flint looked from Ellie to Theo and whistled. "About time somebody taught this boy how to cook."

Theo laughed again. "It's not exactly French cuisine."

The men arrived then, interrupting whatever response Flint had been about to make. Ellie got busy serving them, amazed at the way Theo stood right by her side and helped. Flint stayed out of everyone's way and watched them, his face expressionless. "If anyone has questions about the quarantine," he announced, "I'll try to answer them as best I can after you eat."

Once all the ranch hands had their plates, Ellie gestured to Flint. "Come on, and I'll make you a plate."

The three of them ate at the small kitchen table. The easy camaraderie of the men in the other room buoyed Ellie's mood. "They sure are a happy bunch," she mused, pitching her voice low enough so that only Flint and Theo could hear.

The two brothers exchanged a glance. "They should be," Theo said. "I take care of my guys."

Ellie figured now would be as good a time as any to tell Flint about the ring. "Um, I talked to Molly," she began.

Theo looked down. From the way his shoulders were shaking, she figured he was trying to hide laughter. Ignoring him, she went on. "Anyway, she's pretty broken up about her fiancé running off right before the wedding."

"And cleaning out her bank account," Flint put in, exactly as she'd guessed he might.

"About that…"

Theo guffawed, trying to cover it with a cough. She gave Flint a nervous smile, wondering what Theo found so funny. "Anyway," she continued, bracing herself just in case. "Molly's more worried about the ring."

Flint froze, exactly the way Theo had done when she'd told him. "That jerk stole Molly's ring?" His voice had gone deadly calm.

Ellie nodded. "She wants it back."

"You're damn right she does." Judging from his clenched jaw, Flint was as angry as Molly had predicted. "We all do. I wish I'd known it was missing. I've got men watching for him, but I'm about to get into my car and go try to spot him myself. That ring has been in the family for generations."

Before Ellie could reply, he turned to eye Theo. "Mind telling me what you find so funny about this?"

Theo shook his head, not the least bit intimidated. "Sorry. It's just that Molly told Ellie you frighten her. Because of that, Ellie got a bit nervous to tell you. I think she thought you were going to start yelling or maybe throwing things."

Flint frowned, clearly puzzled. "I scare Molly? Why?"

Ellie looked down, wishing Theo hadn't started this line of conversation. Taking a deep breath, she raised her gaze, looking from one brother to the other. "You don't scare her, really. She even said you act more like a big brother than a cousin."

Ignoring Flint's grin, she continued, "Look, it's already bad enough that I slipped up and told you about the ring. She told me that in confidence. I had to call her and tell her what I'd done. Then Theo here listened in, and that's why he's saying she's afraid of you."

"Oh, really?" Crossing his arms, Flint looked from her to Theo and back again. "So there might be the possibility he made this up."

"Definitely." She glared at Theo, daring him to contradict her. Grinning back, he kept his mouth shut.

In the other room, the ranch hands had finished eating and were making their way out. Several of them stopped to exchange a few words with Flint, asking questions about when he thought the quarantine would be lifted. As the sheriff, Flint did a good job reassuring everyone, while not giving any concrete answers.

When they'd finished with Flint, they exchanged a

few words with Theo, and waved at Ellie on their way out, thanking her for the grub.

Once they were all gone, Ellie hurried in to gather up the dishes. To her surprise, Theo came and helped. They worked side by side in companionable silence while Flint sat sipping his cola and watched.

"Thank you for the meal," Flint said, once they'd finished. "I actually came by to discuss the progress—or lack thereof—the doctors are making on determining how and where Mimi contracted the virus. So far they seem to be in agreement that she was ground zero—where it all started."

"Nothing, huh?" Disappointment colored Theo's tone. "The CDC came by and took her car yesterday. I guess I was hoping they'd have some answers by now."

"If they do, they haven't passed them on."

"What about her family?" Ellie asked. "Surely they need to know what's going on."

Theo and Flint exchanged a glance. "Mimi was an only child, according to Lucas Rand. Her parents divorced when she was a teenager. Her mom married some wealthy guy from England and moved to London. And her father has been living on the beach in Mexico for years. As far as I can tell, Mimi rarely spoke to them."

Theo shrugged. "That's what I figured. If they cared, I would have had them calling to ask about Amelia by now." He looked at his brother. "Speaking of the CDC, have they been successful in determining what it is and how it's spread?"

A muscle worked in Flint's jaw as he eyed them.

Ellie waited with bated breath to see if he would answer.

"No. As unsatisfactory as this might be. They aren't

any further along, except for one thing. They think it might be man-made. A human-engineered virus."

Stunned, Ellie didn't know what to say. She looked at Theo, who appeared equally shocked.

"Like a terrorist?" he asked. "But why would someone like that pick Dead River to start a biological attack? We're just a small town in Wyoming."

"Whoa." Flint held up his hand in warning. "You're getting way ahead of yourself. No one said anything about terrorists or biological warfare. Just that this virus might have been created in a lab. If so, in all likelihood, it probably escaped by accident."

"If someone created it, then there must be an antidote," Ellie put in. "Though I'm sure all those medical types already realize this."

"I'm sure they do. Anyway, the quarantine still stands. There have been no reports of the virus anywhere else in Wyoming or any other state, for that matter."

Ellie's heart sank. "That's good, but not for us."

"Yes." Flint's expression briefly looked bleak, before he schooled it back. He met Ellie's gaze. "I take it you and Molly have become friends?"

Slowly she nodded, not sure where he was heading with this line of conversation. "I think so, yes."

"Good." He smiled and then winked, reminding her of Theo. "She needs a good friend. Someone she can trust."

Blushing, Ellie nodded. She looked up to find Theo watching her, his extraordinary eyes blazing. They locked gazes, and she shivered with a hunger so visceral it felt physical.

Flint cleared his throat. "I'll be going now," he said. "I'll keep you posted if we make any progress on finding Jimmy Johnson."

Theo looked away, breaking their locked gaze. "Theo, if you need any help, I'll be glad to assist. Just give me a holler."

"Will do." Flint grabbed his hat and let himself out.

Theo crossed the room and began going through the mail, which had been left on the counter.

Alone with him, Ellie found herself inexplicably tongue-tied. His broad shoulders and narrow waist made her ache to touch him. Not to mention his sexy, jean-clad behind. She wondered what he'd do if she went behind him and slipped her arms around him. Just the thought heated her blood.

Turning, he eyed her, making her wonder what was going on inside his mind. "You've got mail," he said, holding up a letter.

Puzzled, she moved closer. "From who?"

"It doesn't say. It's got a Dead River postmark."

Just like that, she knew. "Let me see it."

Silently, he handed her the envelope and a letter opener.

Willing her hands not to shake, she slit an opening. Inside, a single sheet of lined notebook paper had been folded three times, perfectly even.

"I'm almost afraid to look," she confided.

"Do you want me to do it?"

"No." She shook her head. "But thanks for asking."

Heart pounding, she unfolded the paper. For all its outwardly neat appearance, the writing inside was the antithesis. A single sentence, scrawled in what appeared to be black crayon, slanted across the lines.

"'You're mine—until death do us part.'" She read it out loud, fear stabbing her heart. And anger too. "This needs to stop," she said.

"I agree. I think it's time we figure out who your stalker actually is," Theo announced, sounding a hell of a lot more confident than she felt at the prospect.

Still, the idea of doing something, no matter how fruitless, sounded better than nothing.

Getting up to feed Amelia her midday bottle, Ellie looked at him, both intrigued and doubtful. "Oh yeah? How are we going to do that, exactly? The police in Boulder have already tried."

"Then they didn't try hard enough."

"They did, though at first they didn't take me seriously. I've been over this with them and on my own, as well. A hundred times."

He pulled out a chair and straddled it. "Hear me out. We need to go through people you've known in the past. He might be a bad blind date, or maybe someone who asked you out and who you turned down."

Ellie shook her head. "I don't know about that."

He eyed her, head tilted, looking so cocky and sexy it took every ounce of willpower she possessed to keep from crossing the room and planting a kiss on his sensual mouth. Ever since the night they'd kissed, she'd been battling the urge to see if he wanted to do it again, to do more. Only knowing Theo as she did, she knew if he really did, he'd have been in her room long before now. While this hurt, she'd decided he would have to be the one to make the next move.

Assuming there was one.

"Please," he said, the deep rasp of his sexy voice turning her insides to mush. "Let me at least try."

"Fine." Amelia had finished her bottle, so Ellie lifted the baby to her shoulder and began burping her. "Let me finish with her. Once I put her down, we can discuss this."

He nodded, continuing to watch her. Her heart skipped a beat as she tried to pretend not to be bothered by the intent way he stared.

Once Amelia was settled, Ellie returned to the table. Theo had a pad of paper and a pen.

He'd returned the letter to the envelope. "I want to show it to Flint," Theo said.

"Ok."

"Are you ready?"

She shrugged. "I guess. But I promise you, it will be a really short list."

"We'll see. Where did you go to high school?"

"Boulder High. And most of my classmates went on to college."

"At CU?"

"Yes. Since they were still there in town, a few of us continued to hang out together."

"But you didn't go to college."

Another one of her regrets. Keeping it light, she nodded. "I couldn't. After I turned eighteen, the family I'd been living with asked me to leave. I was too busy trying to support myself to go to school. The only kinds of jobs for people like me are working in the food industry, or retail. I did both."

"Can you think of any coworkers, bosses even, who might have been fixated on you?"

Ellie laughed. "No."

Despite her response, Theo pressed her. "Come on, Ellie. Think. Surely someone asked you out, even if it was in a kidding sort of way."

"I once had a manager who I had to report for sexual

harassment," she admitted, feeling reluctant. "But he quit and moved away. I'm pretty sure he's not my stalker."

Pen poised, Theo nodded. "Still, let's write him down. What's his name?"

"I can't remember. And I'm telling you the truth. Tom or Tim, maybe?"

"Fine. Let's move on. Ellie?"

She blinked, focusing her attention back on the task at hand. She'd die before she'd admit that she'd been eyeing the way the muscles on his arm flexed when he wrote.

Cleary, she didn't affect him the same way he affected her.

"I'm thinking," she said. "High school, there might have been a couple of people I turned down for a date. But very few. And the only job I had where I had to constantly fight off inebriated men was when I worked as a waitress on the graveyard shift. All the drunks came in to eat after the bars closed."

"There you go." Pen poised, Theo waited, clearly expecting her to name names.

"I didn't know them," she pointed out. "And while there were a few regulars for sure, I never got more than a first name."

"Can you list them?"

"Theo." She rolled her eyes. "No, I can't. Believe me, I've tried. I have no idea who my stalker might be."

"Have you given up?"

Stunned, she froze. Had she? "No," she answered. "At least I don't think so. I loved living in Boulder. I loved my life. But I was at my wits' end, so I fled, aware that I might not ever be able to return. I felt hopeless, and desperate. I can't tell you how many times I've gone over this in my mind, trying to figure out who might be stalking me, and why."

"Bear with me, okay?" He dragged his hand through his hair, giving him a rakish look. Just sitting across from him made her insides tingle. "Give me the names of anyone who might have made you feel uncomfortable."

Without even thinking, she rattled off a list of names. "The Boulder police have already checked them out." She watched as he wrote them down anyway.

"Do you know where any of them are now?" he asked.

"No. But I'm guessing you could look on Facebook."

He nodded and made another notation. "And the guy in the hoodie who jumped you, did his body size and shape match up with any of these men you listed?"

"Not that I could tell. But to be honest, that was the first time I've even seen him. Normally, he just leaves weird, depressing poetry and those damn black roses."

"He broke in here," Theo pointed out. "And next he tried to jump you in town."

"He seems to be getting more aggressive since I came here. I don't know why."

Theo gave her a long look. "My guess would be he feels threatened. You almost got away from him, and now you're starting a completely new life."

"Maybe so."

He folded the paper and got up. "At least we've made a start. I'll pass this list along to Flint and have him check them out. At the very least, we should be able to tell if any of them have left Boulder."

"Thank you." She smiled, even though she didn't have much hope her stalker would be on that list. And with everything going on in Dead River with the quarantine and Molly's ex-fiancé, she figured Flint and his men had too much on their plate already.

Right now she'd settle for protection. If Theo could just keep her stalker away from her and baby Amelia until the quarantine was lifted, she'd leave town.

Though the possibility of spending the rest of her life looking over her shoulder seemed a bleaker one than it had when she'd left Boulder. She didn't want to think why.

Chapter 11

The rest of the week passed calmly. Ellie cooked, Amelia continued to thrive and Theo continued to charm Ellie. Several times she felt so content she caught herself dreaming of what it would be like to have this life forever.

Dangerous thinking, that.

Still, alone in her room at night, her body throbbed and ached for Theo. The kiss they'd shared had only ignited a desire for more.

Friday afternoon, Molly called. Ellie answered eagerly, glad to hear from her new friend.

"Meet me in town," Molly said, sounding excited. "We'll stop at the diner for dinner and then head to the bar for drinks and dancing."

"Oh, that sounds lovely." Glancing at Amelia still sleeping soundly in her crib, Ellie knew she'd have to decline. "But I can't. I don't have anyone to watch the baby."

"Get Theo to do it. She's his daughter."

Ellie snorted. "He's not here. I haven't seen him all afternoon."

"Being a nanny isn't 24/7."

"I know." Glancing around to make sure she wasn't overheard, Ellie confided in her friend. "I think Theo is afraid he can't take care of her. Plus, I'm not sure he wants to. I found a notebook he was writing in. I believe he intends to go back to the rodeo."

Molly gasped. "He can't. The doctors told him if he jostles his spine, he could be paralyzed permanently."

"Maybe he just doesn't want to believe it."

"No." Molly sounded thoughtful. "Theo's an intelligent man. You must have misunderstood."

"Maybe."

"Then ask him to watch her."

Ellie sighed. "I'll think about it. He really does need to spend more time with her. He actually is pretty good at it."

"There you go. You know, maybe he is trying to make you think he's incapable, so you'll stay."

For an instant, hope slammed into her, making it difficult to breathe. But reality reared its head. "No. Theo's not like that. The one thing he's always been is honest. If he really wanted to make sure I'd stay, he'd just ask."

"Okay. But still, you can't be on call every second of your day. You're allowed time off."

"True." Ellie smiled at the belligerence in her friend's voice.

"Good. Then you're coming with me. How about a sitter? Gemma was just saying the other day she wanted to spend more time with her niece."

"I'm tempted, but..."

"But what?"

"I have a stalker, remember? What if I run into him?"

"You won't." Molly sounded determined. "I promise to make sure you're never alone. Nothing's going to happen. I'll get a hold of Gemma. Let me call you back." And she ended the call before Ellie could protest.

Ellie's first thought was to worry about what Theo

would think. Her second was to remember his promise about her having time off. If she waited to go until the evening meal had been served and all the hands were taken care of, then he wouldn't have room to complain.

Two minutes later, her phone rang again.

"Guess what?" Molly said. "Gemma would adore watching over little Amelia. She said she really needs a break from bad stuff, and a baby would be just the ticket."

"I can't go until seven or eight," Ellie said, beginning to get excited herself. "I've got to feed the hands and then change and put on makeup."

"Perfect! Do you want me to pick you up or would you rather meet me there?"

Ellie winced. "I still haven't gotten my car fixed. And I haven't seen Theo at all today, so I can't ask to borrow his truck." As if she would.

"I'll pick you up," Molly chirped. "That way I can pop in and say hello to the baby while I'm there."

"Sounds great. See you later."

Humming happily, Ellie hurried over to her closet to decide what to wear. Thanks to Molly, she suddenly felt happy and young again. Even better, she paid off her credit card bills from before and could afford to spend a little on a girls' night out. She made a mental note to use her next paycheck and see about getting her car repaired.

Theo or no Theo, Ellie decided she'd have a darn good time. As long as she didn't run into her stalker. No. She was done letting him ruin her life. She'd take precautions to stay safe, but she refused to let him destroy her night.

Gemma arrived just as Ellie had finished cleaning up the kitchen. The dark circles under Gemma's eyes attested to the amount of time she'd spent working at the clinic.

For the first time since Molly had come up with the plan, Ellie felt a twinge of guilt. "Maybe this isn't a good idea," she said.

"No worries." Gemma waved her off. "What I need more than anything is to breathe the sweet scent of baby and let Amelia's pure innocence remind me of better times."

"Are you sure?" Ellie shifted her weight from foot to foot.

Fixing Ellie with her Colton green eyes, Gemma smiled. "Positive. Now go get ready."

Still, Ellie didn't move. "She's already been changed and she's due another feeding around nine o'clock. We've got plenty of diapers, and she's had a bit of diaper rash, so I've been putting ointment on."

"Got it." Gemma waved her hand, shooing her from the room. "She'll be fine. Don't worry."

Worry? The word galvanized Ellie into action. Turning on her heel, she hurried off to her room. What was wrong with her? Amelia wasn't her baby, just her charge. Yet here she was, feeling like an overprotective mother, afraid to leave her baby and go out for an evening.

Shaking off her misgivings, she jumped into the shower to begin the preparations for her night out.

An hour later, she stood in front of her dresser mirror. Skintight jeans, cowboy boots and a Western shirt tucked in. She almost didn't recognize herself. Not only did she have on makeup, but she'd straightened her long hair and wore it down, something she rarely did since accepting the job here. A pair of dangly silver earrings and five or six bracelets completed her outfit.

Squinting, she finally decided she looked okay. Turning, the heels of her boots clunking on the wooden floor, she grabbed her purse, and headed out to wait for Molly.

For some reason she'd thought Theo would make an appearance while she waited. Oh, who was she kidding? She'd hoped to run into him, just so he could see what she looked like when she was all fixed up.

Of course he didn't show. Mildly angry at herself for feeling so disappointed, she went back into the den, where Gemma sat on the couch playing with Amelia.

"Wow," Gemma said, clearly impressed. "You look nice."

"Thank you." Trying not to sound too glum, Ellie sat in the chair. "Have you talked to Theo lately?"

Could she have been any more obvious? Blushing, Ellie tried to act as if her question had no hidden meaning.

Unfortunately, Gemma apparently could see right through her. "Are you two fighting?"

"Fighting?" Ellie shook her head. "That would imply a relationship. He's my employer."

Gemma studied her for a moment. "Then why'd you ask?"

Feeling her face heat an even deeper shade of red, Ellie looked away. "I just haven't seen him at all today. Usually he at least comes to see his daughter, but his truck's been gone since early this morning."

And there, she put it right back where it belonged. The father-daughter relationship.

"He's probably helping Flint with something," Gemma said. "I'm sure he'll pop in and see this precious girl tonight."

Which would be fine with Ellie.

The doorbell chimed.

"That will be Molly," Ellie said, hurrying to answer.

"Hey! Don't you look fabulous!" Molly hugged her, hard and fast, before breezing inside. The instant she caught sight of Amelia, Molly squealed. Simultaneously, Gemma winced and Amelia jumped, letting out a wail and starting to cry.

Ellie rushed over, barely stopping herself from snatching Amelia out of Gemma's arms to comfort her.

"Shhh, it's all right," Gemma soothed, rocking Amelia expertly. Almost immediately, the baby's sobs became hiccups, then quieted.

"You're really good with her," Ellie said, trying not to sound jealous.

"Thanks." Gemma smiled. "I work with a lot of infants at the clinic."

"She's adorable," Molly chimed in, appearing not the least abashed at all the ruckus she'd caused. Spinning, she grabbed Ellie's arm. "Are you ready?"

Glancing one final time at Gemma and Amelia, Ellie nodded. "Sure. Let's go."

Molly chattered nonstop all the way to town. Ellie didn't see any sign of the brokenhearted, jilted bride, and she was glad. Apparently Molly was resilient. Either that or she'd mastered the art of hiding her emotions.

They pulled up in front of a brick building with a neon sign proclaiming it as the Dead River Bar.

"What about the diner?" Ellie asked.

"It's just a block away. I'd rather park here and walk there and back. Neither of us has on heels. Is that okay with you?"

Glancing down the street, Ellie shrugged. "It seems well lit and there are enough people out and about, it should be safe."

"Of course it's safe." Molly stared at her a moment, before comprehension dawned. "You're worried about your stalker, aren't you?"

"Yes. If he was here when the quarantine came down, he's trapped here with us."

"It'll be okay." Molly squeezed her shoulder. "I've got your back."

Getting out of the car, Ellie tried to shake off her apprehension.

"Hey." Molly took her arm as they walked side by side. "Don't let him ruin your night. No one should have that much power over someone else."

Easier said than done. Ellie smiled and tried to act nonchalant, but she couldn't help checking behind them and keeping a constant eye on their surroundings.

They made it to the diner without incident. "See?" Molly said, letting go of her arm and grinning. "No problem."

Inside, the place smelled like bacon and burgers. There were red booths circling the place, with tables in the center. At one side was an old-fashioned counter with stools.

"Where do you want to sit?" Molly said. "I like the booths myself."

"Sounds good." Ellie pointed to one that was not in full view of the outside window. "How about there? And I'm sorry, but I've got to sit where I can see the door."

Though Molly sighed, she didn't comment.

Once they were seated and the waitress had brought menus, Molly put hers down and touched the back of Ellie's hand. "I hope for your sake, he's caught soon."

"Me too." Molly sighed. "Now, let's not talk about him again. I'm here to have a good time."

After their meal, they walked back to the bar. The

sidewalks had gotten even more crowded, which seemed unusual in such a small town at night, and Ellie said so.

"Oh, that's because one of our local bands is playing tonight," Molly said, grinning with excitement. "The Dead River Diamonds."

"Makes sense, I guess." Ellie had never heard of them, but that didn't matter. The townspeople were showing their support. Pretty nice, as far as she was concerned.

The bar charged a five-dollar cover, something Molly told her was unusual. "But this is a special night."

Inside, the place had begun to fill up. Molly made a beeline to a bar table on the edge of the dance floor. "Killer seats!" she crowed. "I can't believe we lucked out and got these."

Glancing over her shoulder, Ellie made a point of checking out all the exits, a habit she'd gotten into after her stalker had shown up one too many times. They were on a direct path from the front door, but once the bar got crowded, she wouldn't have a great view of anyone entering.

They'd barely gotten seated when a tall, angular waiter with multiple piercings stopped to take their orders.

"Hey, Chad!" Molly greeted him happily. "I didn't know you still worked here."

"Just on special occasions," he replied, smiling back. "What can I get you ladies to drink?"

"This seems like a beer night," she said, winking at Ellie. "What do you think, Ellie?"

"Sure." Ellie didn't care what she drank. She wasn't planning on having a lot of it, whatever it was. Out in public like this, she couldn't afford to let her guard down.

They sat and sipped their beers as the bar filled up. Men began carrying in instruments and getting them set up on a raised wooden stage. According to Molly, the band would start at nine. Which wasn't too far away now.

Molly's excitement must have been contagious, as Ellie began to get antsy. Why not? She loved music, enjoyed dancing and the place had not gotten so crowded that her stalker could try anything here. And it wasn't as if anyone had known she'd be here either. She might as well relax and have a good time.

Promptly at nine, five guys with shaggy hair and beards strolled out. The crowd greeted them with thunderous applause and whistles, which they acknowledged with waves and grins.

The first chords filled the room. Expression rapt, Molly leaned forward. Stunned, Ellie began tapping her foot along to the beat. No wonder half the town had come to hear this band play. They were really good.

A few seconds into the first song, and people began appearing on the dance floor. Ellie watched with enjoyment, sipping her beer and rocking along on her bar stool. The sound was a catchy combination of country and rock, entirely danceable and the kind of music she would sing along with in the car if she knew the words.

A tall man with a bushy mustache and a brown cowboy hat touched her arm and asked her to dance. She glanced at Molly, who was chatting away with Chad, and then agreed.

Out on the dance floor, she let her body sway to the music, smiling up at her partner. As he spun her, she got a good view of the crowd through the smoky haze. Her heart skipped a beat as a familiar face caught her eye.

Theo. Her heart sank—for no good reason—as she realized he was with a woman. Mortified, she turned her back to him, praying he didn't recognize her.

The song ended. The man—she thought he said his name was Sam—wanted to dance again to the next one, but she declined. Hurrying back to her seat, she took a long drink of her beer, startled to realize she'd nearly finished it. Weird, as she wasn't overly fond of beer.

Still talking to Molly, Chad noticed and hurried off to bring them another round.

Molly caught sight of her face. "What's wrong?"

"Theo's here." Ellie swallowed, aware her friend wouldn't get her distress. "With a date."

"So?" Raising an eyebrow, Molly drained her own mug. "What's the big deal? It's not like you're dating, are you?" Then, before Ellie could answer, Molly's mouth formed a shocked, round O. "Oh. Em. Gee. Did you use that negligee?" she asked, looking stunned. "Have you two done the nasty?"

"No. Absolutely not." Ellie shook her head. "And the only reason I'm sort of unhappy to see him is that he doesn't know I took the night off." Okay, this was a bald-faced lie, but this wasn't the time or place to tell Molly how distant Theo had been.

"Pshaw." Waving her hand, Molly glanced toward the crowd, apparently trying to spot him. "He won't care. Especially since Gemma is taking care of Amelia."

"He's on a date." Ellie tried not to sound miserable, and she prayed the music drowned out her feeble attempt to act as if she didn't care.

"Really?" Now Molly stood on the bottom rung of her chair, scanning the hazy room. "Who with?"

"Some redhead."

The band announced they'd be taking a short break. Canned music began to play over the speaker system, the volume much lower.

"I see them. Hey, I know her." Molly waved. "Theo! Over here."

Great. Ellie wanted to crawl under the table. She considered excusing herself and rushing away to the ladies room, but Theo had already spotted them.

Frowning, he made his way through the crowd toward their table, his date tagging along behind him.

"Hey, you two." He smiled, but his green eyes were cold as he looked at Ellie. "I'm surprised to see you here. Where's Amelia?"

"Gemma's babysitting her," Ellie said, resisting the urge to apologize or explain.

"Lucy!" Jumping up, Molly hugged the redheaded woman. "I didn't know you and Theo were seeing each other."

"We're not," Theo said. "I came to hear the band and Lucy here decided to befriend me." The layered sarcasm in his tone left no doubt how he felt about that. Ellie squirmed for the other woman.

"Now, Theo, you know we have some catching up to do," Lucy drawled, apparently oblivious. "We might as well have some fun while we're at it. Buy me a drink, and I'll find us a table."

"I think that's going to have to happen another time," Molly put in smoothly, clearly deciding to be Theo's wingman. "My cousin, Theo, was supposed to be meeting us here tonight. Sorry. I guess you can catch up with him later."

Pouting, Lucy gave Theo one last lingering look of longing. When he didn't respond, she sighed and sashayed away. Ellie silently watched her go, wondering why she didn't feel sorry for her.

"Thanks," Theo said, grabbing a chair from another

table and pulling it up between Molly and Ellie. His black cowboy hat shadowed his face, and he wore a fashionable button-down white shirt with a gray-and-black swirling design around his broad shoulders. He looked dangerous and sexy as hell. "I'll buy the next round," he said.

As far as Ellie was concerned, there'd be no next round. She tried to figure out a way to talk Molly into leaving. But when Chad showed up and plunked her mug of beer in front of her, she took a sip just to have something to do.

"Having fun?" Theo asked. His aloof expression had vanished, replaced by the friendly, flirty Theo she'd come to know.

Still uncertain, she nodded. "The band is really great."

"I saw you dancing," he said, the teasing sparkle in his eyes inviting her to smile along with him. Instead she looked down, her insides churning with a confusing mix of emotions.

He leaned closer, speaking in a voice pitched low enough that only she could hear. "You look beautiful," he told her, his husky tone making a mess of her insides.

How should she respond to that? "So do you," she blurted, mortified when he laughed. She decided she'd go hide in the ladies' room. But before she could jump up, Molly announced she was going to the restroom. "You wait here with Theo and hold the table," she told Ellie, grinning mischievously to let Ellie know she was disappearing on purpose. With a quick wave, Molly disappeared into the crowd.

"You could have held the table," Ellie muttered at Theo.

He shrugged. "I can, if you want to go with her."

Sorely tempted, instead she found herself unable to move, as if her legs had grown roots. "I can wait."

"So, how have you been?" he asked kindly, his expression full of polite interest. As if they didn't live in the same house.

"Fine." Her impersonal response told him what she thought of that. "Thank you for asking."

Some of her frustration must have come through in her voice. "What's wrong?" he asked, sounding concerned.

Taking a deep breath, she decided to tell him. "Well, for starters, where have you been? You just kind of vanished."

"Missing me, were you?" Again the flash and teasing grin, which made her stomach lurch in instant response.

"Amelia has," she countered, proud of herself for the quick comeback. "She needs her daddy."

Just like that, his smile vanished. The sharp pang of guilt she felt nearly made her apologize, but for once she managed to hold her tongue.

"I'll always be there for her," he said, his expression serious, his green gaze intent. "You know that. It's just been crazy around town and I had to help out with a few things."

His ruggedness and masculinity made him the most attractive man in a sea of cowboy hats. Damn, he looked good. Mouth suddenly dry, she nodded and took a gulp of her beer.

"The band's coming back," Molly pointed out as she slid into her seat. Seeing her opportunity, Ellie excused herself and pushed through the crowd toward the ladies' room.

Once there, she eyed herself in the mirror. With her

heightened color, she thought she looked like a woman in heat. Trying to shake it off, she headed into a stall.

When she emerged and washed her hands, she appeared a bit calmer. Taking a deep breath, she sucked it up and headed back toward the table.

Halfway there, a man stepped in front of her, blocking her way. "Hey, darlin'," he slurred.

"Excuse me," she said firmly, stepping around him.

"Wait a second." His hand shot out, grabbing her arms so hard she stumbled backward, into him. "Now, that's much better."

His hands were everywhere while he turned her to face him. Acting purely on instinct, she brought her knee up, slamming it into his groin.

Immediately he let go and doubled over, his face contorted as he flung a stream of curses at her. Heart pounding, she tripped over her own two feet, trying to move away.

When she looked up, Theo was there. He hauled her up against him and then stepped in between her and the other man. "You got a problem, buddy?"

Still gasping for air and trying to recover, her assailant took a look at all six foot two of Theo and began backing away while shaking his head.

Relieved, Ellie sagged against Theo.

"Are you all right?" he asked, holding her close enough for her to feel every muscle in his body.

"Yes." Her answer was more to keep him from going after the other man. If Theo got in a bar fight, she figured there'd be all kinds of trouble. "No harm, no foul."

Though he appeared unconvinced, he finally nodded and, keeping his hand in the small of her back—possessively, she thought—followed her back to the table.

Molly and Chad were deep in conversation and Ellie figured her friend had missed the entire thing. Which was good, as all Ellie wanted to do was forget about it.

The band started playing a slow song just as Theo began to pull out Ellie's chair.

"Let's dance," he said, pushing her chair back under the table.

Though Ellie wasn't 100 percent sure her legs would hold up, she wanted nothing more than to dance with Theo, so she nodded.

He pulled her into his arms and she thought she'd died and gone to heaven. They began to move around the dance floor, gliding really, as she followed his lead.

She'd never been with a man like him. Never. Muscular and tall, a man who made his Wranglers look like designer jeans. He moved with a sexy, masculine confidence that was addictive. She fought the urge to dance closer, rubbing herself all up on him like one of his groupies, or a cat in heat.

Despite reminding herself that he was her boss, aware he was something she could never have, she felt dizzy with craving him.

Finally, the song—and the slow torture—ended. Breathless, she hurried back to the table. The instant she took her seat, Molly jumped up and dragged Chad out onto the dance floor.

"She doesn't seem to be hurting too badly," Theo observed.

"I think she's keeping busy so she doesn't have to think about it," she said, suddenly thirsty. She took a couple of gulps of her beer, wishing for water.

"Just a second." Theo got up, went to the bar and returned with a tall glass of ice water, which he slid over to her.

"How'd you know?" she asked, amazed.

"Because I can tell by your face that you're not a beer drinker." He smiled, watching as she gulped down the water.

"Thank you," she said when she'd nearly drained the glass.

"You're welcome." Arm over the back of Molly's empty chair, he surveyed the room. "Are you ready to go home?"

Longing swept her, but she shook her head. "I can't. I came with Molly."

He glanced at Molly, dancing up a storm on the dance floor. "I don't think she'd mind."

Ellie blushed as she realized what he meant. "Do you really think Molly and Chad…?"

Though he gave a mild shrug, his eyes sparkled. "We all do what we have to in order to distract ourselves."

Feeling hot all over for no good reason, Ellie resisted the urge to fan herself.

"I'll have to check with her." She already knew if Molly thought there was even the most remote chance Theo and Ellie would get together, she'd merrily send them on their way with a wink and a shove. Not to mention two wispy scraps of cloth.

Ellie tried to calm her racing heartbeat and focus on something else. Like finishing her water and then taking teeny-tiny sips of what remained of her beer.

When Molly finally returned, out of breath from dancing and sans Chad, who apparently had to go back to waiting tables, she eyed the two of them. "What's up?"

"Nothing," Ellie said, aware she was blushing again.

Luckily, Theo didn't appear to notice. "I asked Ellie if she wanted to catch a ride home with me," he said.

Molly grinned. "Rrrreally?" she purred.

"But not just yet. I'm not ready to leave right now," Ellie put in, sounding more breathless than she'd intended.

Both Molly and Theo laughed.

"Fine," Theo said. "I'll stay until you're ready to leave, and then I'll take you home. There's no reason Molly should have to drive all the way out to the ranch when I'm right here."

Looking from one to the other, Molly continued grinning like a madwoman. "True. He has a point."

"Whatever." Pretending to be supremely disinterested, Ellie kept her gaze firmly fixed on the band.

"Actually, Ellie…" Molly leaned over, appearing sheepish. "Chad gets off work at midnight. He and I were thinking about going to a private party at his brother's house. Of course you're welcome to come, but you won't know anybody. It's your call."

What Molly had just described might have been fun, on any other night, for any other person. But Ellie wanted to go home—or back to the ranch. She seriously missed Amelia, which confounded her. And she'd never been a big partier.

"I'll just ride home with Theo," she said. "But I want you to promise me you won't drive drunk."

"I won't." Molly held out her hand. "Pinky-swear." They locked pinkies, which felt both childish and fun. "Worse comes to worst, I'll just stay over there and go home in the morning."

"Then it's settled?" Theo touched Ellie's shoulder, making her jump. "Ellie's coming with me?"

"Yep." Molly still sounded way too cheerful, making Ellie eye her. Was she matchmaking again?

Her next statement confirmed it. "Hey, Ellie, don't forget that little present I gave you, okay?"

By which she meant the sexy negligee.

If possible, Ellie's face turned even redder.

"What present?" Theo asked, which made Molly dissolve in a fit of giggles. Theo looked from one to the other, his eyebrows raised.

"Never mind." Ellie's voice came out sharper than she'd intended. "It's a private joke."

"Whatever." He cocked his head. "Just let me know when you're ready to leave."

Suddenly, Ellie wanted to leave right now. Ignoring the knowing way Molly eyed her, she stood. "Let's go."

Hand on the small of her back, Theo urged her toward the door. Just then, the band began to play a slow, romantic ballad that had been popular a few years ago.

Theo stopped. "Do you want to dance one last time before we head out?"

Did she? She made the mistake of glancing at him. He exuded masculinity. Sexuality and self-confidence. No wonder women threw themselves at him everywhere he went.

Her heart skipped a beat. Sweet torture. She wasn't sure she could endure going body to body with him again, without doing something she definitely would regret.

"No, thanks," she managed. "I'm pretty tired." Her words sounded like a lie, even to herself.

His gaze searching her face, he finally nodded. "All right."

This time, when he settled his hand in the small of her

back to guide her toward the door, she felt the heat of his touch burning through her shirt.

Outside, the night air contained a chill, helping cool her overheated body. She breathed in, glad Theo had found her. Being with him made her feel protected and safe.

She felt almost giddy as she climbed into his truck. For just one instant, she let herself pretend they were escaping the bar for a romantic rendezvous. Even imagining the things they might do if that were the case made her mouth go dry and her body wet.

She didn't think she'd ever wanted a man as much as she wanted him.

And that alone was reason enough to try to have him.

Again, Molly's words came back to tease her.

It might have been the alcohol giving her false bravery, but she thought she just might give that little negligee a try.

Chapter 12

As they approached the barricade, Ellie sat up straight. She didn't want whatever officer was manning the checkpoint to think she was intoxicated, though she imagined that might be the least of their worries right now. No one had been informed what purpose exactly the barricades served. It was one thing to keep people from leaving Dead River. But entering too? She didn't understand what they were trying to keep out.

Since there were few vehicles out this late, they pulled up, spoke, and after a quick glance inside the truck, they were waved through. Ellie relaxed, feeling sleepy.

A few seconds later, Theo glanced at his rearview mirror. "That's weird," he said, almost to himself. "A minute ago, we were the only ones out. Now another car just went through the checkpoint and is behind us."

Mildly concerned, she turned to see. Two headlights, about three car lengths behind them. "Hopefully it's just someone else going home for the night."

"Yeah, maybe." Theo gave her a reassuring smile. But she couldn't help noticing his white-knuckled grip on the steering wheel.

Praying it wasn't her stalker, she tried not to over-react. Still, she had to force herself to take deep, calming breaths.

Theo smiled reassuringly. "I'm sure it's nothing."

She nodded.

They continued to drive a steady speed. Theo made the turn from the highway onto the two-lane paved road. They were in familiar territory. The gravel road that led to the ranch was about two miles away.

"Damn it." The curse exploded from Theo. "They're gaining on us. I'd think they were just wanting to pass, but I've been doing close to eighty miles an hour."

"What is it?" she asked, twisting to try and see. "A car or truck?"

"It's another truck, about the same size as ours."

Heart pounding, she gasped as she saw the headlights growing closer until they were right on their rear bumper. "Oh, I hope he just wants to pass."

Jaw grim, Theo accelerated. "If so, there's certainly been plenty of opportunity to do so. They've been hanging back until now."

Panic clawing at her, Ellie couldn't look anymore. Turning to face front, she checked her seat belt and watched the speedometer inch past eighty-five, ninety, before she looked away. Awfully fast. She found herself clutching the door handle, her teeth clenched, praying it would turn out to be nothing.

"He's keeping up with us." Theo had barely gotten the words out when *bam!* The truck slammed into their rear bumper.

Ellie gasped. Her seat belt held, cutting into her chest and making her cry out.

"What the hell…" Theo stomped on the accelerator. "This is crazy."

And then she knew. "It's my stalker, isn't it?" she rasped. "He followed us."

"Could be." Theo's grim expression confirmed her fears. "I think the sick son of a bitch is trying to run us off the road."

Though she knew she shouldn't, she peered at the accelerator. They were pushing ninety-five.

"If we wreck at this speed…" She didn't have to finish the sentence. They both knew what would happen.

"Hang on," Theo said. "I'm going past our road and taking the turn that leads back to the main highway. I'm going to have to slow down. There's no way we can make a turn at this speed."

She nodded, bracing her hands against the dash. "I'm ready."

"Here we go." Gradually easing off the accelerator, he slowed them down, also using the brake. "The turn is coming up."

He cursed. "That son of a bitch is going to ram us again."

The words had barely left his mouth when the other truck slammed into them. This time, it hit them hard, sending them spinning out of control.

"Hang on," Theo shouted. "And pray."

Ellie closed her eyes, terror threatening to strangle her. They were going to wreck. Wreck badly.

Everything seemed to slow down, time suspended in measured motion. Theo. Oddly enough, Ellie's first concern was for him. He still hadn't fully healed from his rodeo accident. She didn't know what kind of damage a crash like this might do.

"Damn him."

Spinning, spinning. Cursing, Theo fought to keep them on the road. The other truck hit them again, this time on the right front wheel well, just before the passenger door. That impact was just enough to send them tumbling into a roll.

Ellie screamed. She closed her eyes as Theo's truck turned over with a sickening crunch of metal. The windows shattered, shards of glass raining on them. She shrieked again and again, an endless voicing of her terror and pain.

"Ellie!" Theo shouted, his voice harsh and raw.

The sickening crunch of metal and shattered glass seemed deafening. Miraculously, they rolled all the way over and came back up, wheels on the ground, roof crumpled, windows broken, the engine quiet. Stopped.

Shards of glass covered her, along with a lot of cuts. Stunned, she tried to process what had just happened. One, she didn't hurt at all. Yet. Dimly, she realized she was most likely in shock.

"Are you all right?" Theo asked. Dazed, she could only nod. Something wet obscured her vision, and when she used her hand to wipe it off her eyes, her hand came away red with blood.

She screamed again, then choked it off midstream, hyperventilating as she clutched at Theo's arm.

"You're fine," Theo soothed, his deep voice unbelievable steady. "Ellie, please try not to panic."

Exhaling sharply, he took a deep, shaky breath. "As far as I can tell, neither one of us is seriously hurt." He reached out and turned the key, even though the engine was already dead. "Just in case," he said. "Ellie, honey. Please. Look at me."

Blinking, she managed to close her mouth, though involuntary whimpers escaped her in a continual stream. Struggling to focus she locked gazes with him.

"Now breathe," he told her. "Just breathe."

In. Out. As she did, everything came back into focus.

"Now," Theo continued. "We need to get out of here. Just in case. Can you do that?"

"I think so. But the guy who hit us," she managed, her numb fingers fumbling to unhook her seat belt. "Where is he?"

"I don't know." Theo struggled to open his door. He cursed when he couldn't. "It's too damaged," he said. Instead he used his elbow to push out the rest of the glass in his window.

Theo had cuts too, she belatedly realized. A lot of them. In addition, one of his eyes was black and blue and beginning to swell.

But they were alive. That's what mattered.

"See if you can open your door," he said. "If not, once I'm out, I'll come around to your side and try to free you."

"Or else I can crawl after you," she said, feeling more like herself. "I don't think anything is broken." Of course, for all she knew she could have bones poking out of her skin. She'd read when people went into shock, they didn't feel pain.

She guessed she'd now learn if that was actually true.

"Let's give it a try." Twisting in his seat, Theo grimaced. He opened his mouth to speak, but before he could, a face appeared at Ellie's window.

Jumping, she squawked a strangled scream, recoiling back against Theo.

"You belong to me," the apparition snarled. Ellie squinted, and then realized he was wearing a mask, the kind of thing someone would don on Halloween. Deliberately trying to frighten them.

"Remember that. No one else can have you." Then, just as she was starting to wonder if she'd begun hallucinating or something, he tossed a single black rose on her lap. Her stalker.

"Next time, he dies. Maybe you too."

"What do you want?" Ellie cried. But he turned away and didn't answer. And then he was gone.

Theo cursed, trying again to push his door open. Once more, he failed. A moment later, they heard the sound of a truck taking off and roaring away into the distance.

Shaken, Ellie stared down at the black rose amid the glass shards. "He nearly killed us," she said, her voice sounding weak and trembling. "What he's doing makes no sense."

Theo reached out and plucked the rose from her lap and tossed it out his window. "He's here in town. With the quarantine, he won't be able to leave. And now his truck is damaged too. It shouldn't be too hard to find him."

Still feeling kind of numb, she didn't immediately respond. When she moved again, it was to wipe more blood from her eyes. "Where is this coming from?" she asked, frustrated and scared.

"You have a head wound." He opened the glove box and rummaged around, emerging with some fast food napkins. "Here. Use these." He pressed one to her face, right above her temple. "Press and hold. Head wounds bleed a lot, but you need to stop the bleeding."

Glad to have someone telling her what to do, Ellie did as he said. "Thank you," she murmured. "What now?"

"Well, since he's gone, let's see if this truck will start. If it does, I want to try and drive it back to the ranch."

She nodded, sending shooting pain through her head, and winced.

The engine caught on the first turn of the key.

"Starts just like nothing happened," Theo said, sounding amazed. Ellie tried to focus on that, but her vision blurred.

"Ellie? Are you all right?"

Feeling as if she'd separated from her body, Ellie tried to smile, but her lips felt cracked and she couldn't. "Maybe. Maybe not. Right now I can't tell. I think so. But just in case, maybe we should see if Gemma can check us out before she goes home. You know, just to make sure nothing is broken."

"We will." He reached out to squeeze her shoulder, then stopped himself. "I don't want to hurt you."

Though she nodded, Ellie could think of one thing. "What if Amelia had been with us? She could have been killed."

"She wasn't," he said firmly. "And until that bastard is caught, she won't be going anywhere with either of us. Right now try not to worry about what might have happened, okay? Focus on what did. We're safe, we're okay. Can you do that for me?"

About to nod again, Ellie thought better of it and settled for a sigh. "I'll try."

Theo kept his fury hidden—Ellie had already been through enough because of her psycho stalker. Now not only had she nearly been killed, but he knew she'd spend a lot of time worrying about what had happened to him and his truck, blaming herself. When none of this was her fault, at all. So help him, if he could get his hands on that guy...

What kind of crazy fool did stuff like that? He'd known the guy wasn't right in the head; he was a stalker after all. But to profess undying love and then nearly kill the object of his affections? The guy was a psychopath, and his behavior had escalated. Now he was much more dangerous than Theo had originally believed.

Theo knew one thing. He had to protect Ellie. He'd enlist Flint's help, but with or without his assistance, Theo planned to hunt the creep down.

Ellie drifted in and out of consciousness as they limped home. He worried she had a concussion or some other, more serious injury, but he couldn't do anything about that. They'd never make it back to town, and the clinic was closed anyway. No, Gemma was their best option.

As for himself, Theo felt reasonably sure he had a few cuts and bruises, nothing serious. Maybe a bruised rib or two. He'd had worse. Of course, he hadn't actually tried walking yet.

When they finally pulled into the ranch drive, he parked in front of the house and cut the engine. Breathing a sigh of relief, he tried one more time to open his door. It still wouldn't open, apparently too badly damaged.

Glancing at Ellie, he knew she'd need his help getting out. He'd have to go out his window and risk getting cut on any remaining pieces of glass. Just as he'd started hefting himself up and out, Ellie opened her eyes and looked blearily at him. "Are we home?"

Home. Hearing her say the word like that brought a tightness to his chest. "Yes, honey. We're home."

If she caught the use of the endearment, she didn't react. Instead she tried her own door handle, exclaiming when she was able to wedge it open, not fully, but enough.

"Can you get out on your own?" he asked. "If so, hold on to the truck until I can help you. I'll be right over there." And he pushed himself the rest of the way out his window, dropping to the ground and stifling a grunt of pain.

Testing his legs, he held on to the door. He needed to see if his legs would support his weight. Once he knew they would, he kept one hand on the truck for support and hurried over to her side. Her door still sat partly open.

"Take my hand and let me help you," he said. "Do you think you can do it?"

"I think so." Taking his hand, she managed to slide into the open space and out.

"Can you walk?"

"I don't know." Taking his arm, she took a tentative step forward. "It appears that I can."

She held on to him all the way into the house. Once inside, he sat her down at the kitchen table. "Let me call Flint. Then I'll go wake up Gemma and we'll see about getting you cleaned up."

"What about you?" she asked. "You're all cut up too."

Not as badly as her, though he kept that information to himself. "I'll clean up after you."

He dialed Flint, not liking the way his hands shook. Delayed reaction, he guessed. His brother picked up on the second ring.

"What's up?"

Speaking tersely, Theo relayed what had just happened.

"Thank God Amelia wasn't with you. He's escalating," Flint said. "And if he wasn't dangerous enough before, I now consider him extremely so now. We'll charge him with vehicular assault."

"Good," Theo said. He suddenly realized he ached in places he hadn't even realized he'd hurt.

"Are you and Ellie all right?"

"I think so. We're home now, but we're both pretty banged up. I need you to have your guys look for a white pickup, a Dodge Ram, I think. It'll have some front end damage."

"Do you want me to come over and take a statement?"

"Not tonight," Theo said, trying his damnedest to sound calm and composed. "She's pretty shook up. You can come talk to both of us tomorrow, okay?"

"Fine. What about medical treatment?"

"Gemma's here. She babysat Amelia for Ellie, though she's most likely asleep. I'll wake her up and have her check us out." Despite his best efforts, Theo knew he sounded shaky—hell, he *was* shaky.

"I just can't believe the SOB tried to kill you." Even Flint, seasoned lawman as he was, sounded traumatized.

"Well." Theo took a deep breath. "If you want the honest truth, I think he just wanted to scare the crap out of us. He could have kept ramming us, and done even more damage. He could have shot us, assuming he had a gun."

Flint swore. "What he did was bad enough. We need to find him and get him locked up. Until then, I want you and Ellie both to take extra precautions."

"We will." Theo hung up. A moment later, Ellie emerged from the bathroom, swaying slightly. Theo hurried over and helped her to the couch. "Wait here. I'm going to wake Gemma and have her check you out."

"You too." Ellie stared up at him. The dark hollows under her eyes made him ache to comfort her.

Instead he did the wise thing and hurried to fetch his sister.

* * *

The next morning, Ellie came awake with a gasp. Bad dream. She stretched and winced, hurting all over. And then she realized it hadn't been a nightmare after all.

Her stalker now wanted to kill her. For what reason, she had no idea, but then she'd never understood what motivated him to follow her around and leave black roses and weird messages.

Clearly, he thought he owned her. The thought made her shudder, as she could see how he'd think if he couldn't have her, no one could.

He planned to kill her. Never more had she felt the panicked urge to flee, to take everything she had and sneak out in the middle of the night. If not for the quarantine, she might. Not only had she become far too attached to sweet Amelia, but she couldn't risk endangering the precious newborn.

And Theo. He'd almost been killed, merely because he'd given her a ride home.

She shuddered, fighting back waves of panic. She'd die before she let anything happen to him or his perfect daughter. Since she knew she couldn't leave, at least not while the National Guard patrolled the town's borders, she'd have to figure out a way to fight back.

Though she'd wanted only to flee, that was no longer an option. Plus, her stalker had now tried to hurt someone she cared about. She had no choice now. No matter what, she wasn't going to let her stalker win.

The next morning, Flint came out to take both Ellie's and Theo's statements. For whatever reason, Ellie started shaking as she recounted the events of the night before.

To her surprise and relief, Theo came and put his arm around her shoulders, offering his strength and comfort.

Flint narrowed his eyes as he looked from one to the other, but he didn't comment. He'd just about finished writing everything up when his cell phone rang.

"Excuse me a moment," he said. "I need to take this." Answering the call, he left the room.

Glad of the respite, Ellie turned to Theo. "Thank you," she said quietly. "I'm still pretty raw."

"I know and that's understandable." He winked, grinning at her instant blush. "You're going to be fine. Flint will catch that guy. He's really good at what he does."

She nodded, so distracted by the warmth in his green eyes that she couldn't speak.

"Damn it." Flint returned, his eyebrows drawn together in an agonized expression. "I've got to go. There's been an emergency."

"What happened?" Theo asked.

"I left my rookie deputy, Mike Barnes, alone in the station, guarding Hank Bittard."

"That guy you arrested for murder?" Theo asked.

Grim-faced, Flint nodded. "Yes. I had him there awaiting transfer to the county jail. I'm not sure how, but Hank attacked Mike and escaped. He left Mike for dead. One of my other deputies found him and called the paramedics. They took Mike in to the clinic, so that's where I'm headed."

Ellie gasped. "Oh no. How badly is he hurt?"

Jamming his cowboy hat on his head, Flint met her gaze and then shook his head. "It's going to be touch-and-go. I've got to go check on him before I can round up men to search for Bittard."

"Do you need any help?" Theo asked, clearly wanting to go with his brother. Ellie wondered why he didn't.

"Not right now. I will need you to help me organize some search parties later, okay?"

"No problem."

Halfway to the door, Flint stopped and turned. "Listen, you need to be extra vigilant. This property is on the outskirts of town and near the woods. Bittard will probably keep a low profile. He'll want to slip out of town quietly the instant the quarantine is lifted."

Ellie glanced at Theo, who nodded. "I understand," he said. "We'll watch for any signs of him."

"Just be careful." Flint left.

"Thank goodness you installed that alarm," Ellie said. "I'm not sure which scares me more—an escaped murderer or my stalker."

"I think they're both about equal," he replied. "I want you to try to rest up, and try not to think about any of this."

She grimaced. "Easier said than done."

"You'll have ample opportunity to heal," he said. "I've asked one of the ranch hands' wives to fill in as cook for a couple of days."

About to protest, Ellie decided not to. Even though nothing had been broken when the truck rolled over, she had several nasty cuts and bruises. Plus, her entire body felt as if she'd served as a punching bag for a particularly angry boxer.

She did prefer staying busy, though, so that she didn't have time to dwell on things. Like her growing attachment to both Amelia and Theo. She really would have preferred not to think about that, or the fact that her stalker presented a danger to both of them.

So she took care of the baby, acted polite to Theo and anyone else she came in contact with and mostly kept to herself to lick her wounds. She took her meals in her room, noting with a bit of perverse satisfaction that her temporary replacement wasn't nearly as good a cook as she was.

Theo checked on her, but his visits were brief and perfunctory, letting her know he battled his own demons.

Finally, after three days of self-imposed isolation, she felt good enough to resume her life. She gathered up a happy, gurgling Amelia and went in search of Theo. She found him in his office, intent on something he was reading on his computer screen.

"Absolutely not," he said, when she told him she wanted to resume her cooking duties.

Pride warred with common sense, but she finally gave him the truth. "I really need the money."

"Fine, I'll double your nanny salary. But until you're all healed, I don't want you cooking."

Shaking her head, secretly pleased at his coddling, she smiled. "Have you tasted the meals lately?"

One corner of his mouth quirked in response. "Of course I have. But you'll be cooking soon enough. I just want you at 100 percent."

"Fine," she huffed. "But what am I supposed to do with myself?"

His smile widened and for a second she thought he might actually flirt with her. Instead he held out his arms for Amelia. Once she'd transferred the baby, she watched with her heart in her throat as this beautiful, rugged cowboy cooed and spoke baby talk tenderly to his daughter.

In a flash it hit her. She loved him.

Stunned, Ellie took a step back. How had this happened? What on earth was wrong with her?

Somehow she found her voice. "Do you mind watching her for a few minutes? I've got something I need to do."

He barely looked up as he agreed.

And she fled.

Instead of going back to her room, she stepped outside, breathing in great gulps of fresh air. Had she completely lost her mind? All her life, she'd pictured the type of man she'd eventually love, and Theo was about as far from her imaginary lover as a man could be.

Worse, he'd told her up front, he wasn't the settling-down kind.

Still, she loved him. And she needed to wrap her mind around that.

Absorbed in the beauty of his little girl's tiny hands and perfect button nose, Theo remained conscious of Ellie watching him interact with the infant. He often wondered if she thought he was doing it right.

And when she'd gotten that strange expression on her face and rushed off, he was pretty damn sure he wasn't.

A good thirty minutes passed before she returned. Amelia had dozed off to sleep in his arms.

"Do you want me to take her?" Ellie asked softly.

He searched her face. She seemed normal now, back to her usual competent and beautiful self. "Sure."

Once he'd transferred the baby, he decided to voice his doubts. "Sometimes I wonder if I'm any good at this. I have no idea what I'm doing."

"You're going to be fine," Ellie said, her smile patient and so lovely it tugged at his insides. "Just give it time."

Something about the softness of that smile made him want to tell her the truth.

"I have no idea how to be a father," he told Ellie, his

voice cracking. "After my mom died, my dad picked up the bottle and never looked back. Some parents are strong and know they have to take over raising the family with the other one gone. Not my father. He dumped us off on Gram Dottie and took off. He only showed up often enough to make an ass of himself and embarrass us. Like the time he came to my senior prom stone-cold drunk. He stormed out on the dance floor and humiliated my date."

"And you," she said softly, wincing. "I can't even imagine."

"Yeah." He knew his expression was bleak, but he didn't see any need in pretending his life had been something it wasn't. "He's the reason both Flint and I got out of town as soon as we could."

"And now you're both back."

He shrugged. "That's life. Sometimes it just does a one eighty from what you had planned."

"Did Gram used to live here on the ranch?"

"Yes. But she moved to town a few years ago. Slim George has kept the place running ever since I can remember."

The tenderness in her gaze had him wanting to kiss her. To distract himself, he forced a half smile. "What about you? What are your parents like? I imagine they've been beside themselves trying to help you deal with that crazy stalker."

She made a sound low in her throat that sounded like harrumph, but he couldn't be sure. For a brief second, he thought she was going to stonewall him and retreat into her own private world.

Finally, she made a face and answered, "My parents are the opposite of what your father is like, at least to all outward appearances. They're missionaries, devoted to spreading their religion to all parts of the world. When I was really small, they made an effort to try to be parents, and took me with them. But after I contracted malaria in Africa, they dumped me off in Boulder with friends from their church."

The raw pain in her voice had him clenching his hands into fists to keep from touching her.

Unaware, she continued. "They didn't even bother to come back for holidays, like Christmas, or for my birthday. The family that I stayed with said I needed to understand the gospel came first."

He winced. "I take it you had no desire to follow in their footsteps?"

"Oh, hell no." Her eyes widened. She seemed shocked that he'd even suggested such a thing. "I understand having convictions, but if they didn't want to be parents, why'd they even bother having a child. Even if I was an accident, which I'm pretty sure I was, being a parent is a responsibility and a privilege. I spent my entire childhood wondering what I'd done to make my parents not love me anymore."

Her words both moved him and stunned him. "That's terrible," he said. "I'd never do anything like that to my child."

"Which proves you're going to be fine."

"I don't know. Since I can't rodeo anymore—"

"Hush." Ellie stomped her foot. "No matter how badly you might want to, you can't go back to rodeo. For a man who has so much, you act like you have nothing. You're alive, you have family who loves you, a productive and profitable ranch and a beautiful baby girl. What more do you want?"

He started to respond, then thought better of it.

"You don't know, do you?"

Slowly, he shook his head. "No. I don't."

"Look at you," she continued, her expression fierce. "You say you don't know how to be a father, but you've already owned up to the responsibility and are doing your best. You understand Amelia has no one else."

Her praise made him feel worse. "I'm worried I won't do right by her. I'm bound to make mistakes."

She gripped his hand, sending a shock wave through him. "You're human, Theo. We all make mistakes. As long as you love her and are there for her, everything will be fine."

He curled his fingers around hers, holding on as though for dear life. "You don't know how badly I hope you're right."

Chapter 13

Ellie didn't know what to think about the tender moment she and Theo had just shared. Even later, after she'd headed to her room for the night, she knew the image of his tanned fingers wrapped around hers would be burned in her mind.

He would make a fine father. *And a wonderful husband,* part of her mind whispered.

The thought surprised her. She'd never even considered marriage. To anyone, not just Theo. The fact that she even was thinking about it now scared her, so she tried to push it from her mind.

Despite everything, or maybe because of it, she fell asleep almost as soon as her head hit the pillow.

With only Amelia to take care of, Ellie's body healed. She slept well, and even if she preferred to eat food she'd cooked herself, she had to admit it was nice not to have to head down to the kitchen at the crack of dawn to cook for the ranch hands.

She completely forgot about the negligee until she spied the fancy box poking out from under her bed a few days later. She pulled it out slowly, glancing at the open door to make sure no one was there. Opening the box, she lifted the tiny scraps of material and tried to figure out where they went. Even the thought of appearing like this in front of Theo made her entire body heat.

Not going to happen. This so wasn't her. She started to put the negligee back into the tissue paper, intending to slide the box back under her bed. Then, taking a deep breath, she changed her mind.

She wanted to try it on. She'd never in her life purchased or even tried on anything like this. Never even imagined how she'd look in one.

Might as well see.

A quick glance assured her Amelia still slept soundly in her crib.

Before she lost her nerve, she closed the door and kicked off her shoes and unzipped her jeans, stepping out of them as well as her panties. She pulled her shirt over her head and discarded her bra.

Then she picked up the little wispy creation and tried to arrange it on her body.

To her surprise, it settled over her and clung to her shape as if it had been made just for her.

Ellie almost didn't recognize the woman she saw in the mirror. Just for fun, she struck a pose. Hip cocked, breasts out and up.

Fun.

A sharp tap sounded on her closed bedroom door. "Ellie?"

Theo. Just like that, her heart began beating a rapid tattoo in her chest. She eyed herself in the mirror, an almost unrecognizable version of the Ellie she faced every day.

Could she do it? Did she dare?

"Ellie? Are you in there?"

"Just a moment," she called. She could open the door,

and finally see his reaction to the negligee. Or...she could ask him to wait while she got dressed. Her choice.

Quivering, she pressed her hands to her stomach. It would be so worth it if she risked it all, and won. And so humiliating if he didn't react at all.

She needed to know. If he truly didn't want her, the time had come to find out and stop mooning over a man she couldn't have. For once in her life, she wanted to go for the gusto. Take a chance. Be brave.

As soon as she realized she'd made her choice, she began trembling. No matter. Crossing the room to the door, she cracked it a little and peered out, hoping she could do this.

Theo stood in the hall, his expression a combination of impatient and concerned. "Are you all right?"

Oh, wow. Ellie thought her heart might just pound right out of her chest. She inhaled, swallowed and then opened the door wide, revealing her entire body. "Come in."

Instead he froze. He locked gazes with her, his pupils dilated, before his gaze slowly slid downward.

"What?" He sounded weak. "Are you doing?"

"Oh, this?" She made herself spin, fighting the urge to cover herself with her hands. Her nipples were so achingly hard even the tiny scraps of cloth rubbing against them felt supercharged. "Molly gave it to me, so I thought I'd try it on. What do you think?"

Still he didn't move. Had she gone too far? If he resisted even this, her blatant, albeit inexperienced, attempt to seduce him, then she might as well give up. Forever.

He took a step toward her, reaching out to touch her, his expression almost reverent. "You look," he rasped, sounding like a man in torment, "amazing."

Hope warring with desire, she smiled. At the smoldering fire in his gaze, a tingle of excitement gave her the courage to pull him into the room.

"No fair," he protested, though it sounded like a token attempt at best, especially since he reached for her at the same time.

He slid his hand across the exposed skin on her belly, making her shudder with delighted need. Caressing her breasts, he lingered over the sensitive nipples. When he bent his head to take one in his mouth, she gasped.

Her body throbbed as she arched her back. Theo used his lips and tongue to sear a path up her throat, until he claimed her mouth and kissed her.

And then she was lost.

He shed his clothes and gently lowered her to the bed while she struggled not to claw at him, to urge him to just take her, for heaven's sake.

Instead, he touched her lightly, teasingly, which felt almost painful, making her whimper as she curled herself into his body, pulling him over her. Needing more. So much more.

Slowly, maddeningly, he explored her thighs, with a feather-light touch. She groaned as she felt the swollen hardness of his arousal pressing against her stomach. Reaching blindly, she cupped her hand around the length of him, thrilling to the touch.

Theo groaned as she began to move her hand up and down. "Don't," he said. "Not yet."

But she was done with slow and steady. Her insides were melting. "I want you inside me," she said, arcing against the magic touch of his fingers as he explored.

"All in good time," he gritted, his arousal jerking against her touch. She shifted, moving her body so the tip of him pressed against her, and undulating so the engorged tip of him rubbed against her slick woman parts.

Theo groaned again and then, with a muttered curse, gave in and pushed into her.

Pleasure—pure, explosive and powerful—ripped through her as he began to move.

Mindless with need, she wouldn't let him go slow, though he tried. She moved and rode him from underneath, her body trembling just on the edge of ecstasy.

With a cry, she came apart, shattering in a wave of soul-drenching, perfect and sweet agony.

Her spasms of joy brought Theo to his own release shortly after, his body throbbing as he emptied himself into her.

Nestling against him while he held her, their slick bodies cooling, Ellie realized she could stay there forever.

And for that reason alone, she knew she had to get away as soon as she could.

Furious with himself, Theo had to notice the irony of the emotion. The man he'd once been, the popular rodeo star and ladies' man, would have celebrated his victory and mentally carved another notch in his bedpost.

For whatever reason, he was no longer that man. In fact, despite the way he missed bronc riding, he never wanted to be that way again.

The bad thing about all of this was he knew Ellie would end up hurt. And he cared about her, maybe too damn much.

He managed to avoid her at breakfast, sneaking down into the kitchen for a bagel and coffee half an hour before the new cook would be there to start making breakfast for the ranch hands.

Bad thing was, he knew he couldn't dodge her for too long. Actually, he didn't want to. He just needed to come up with a way to explain that what had happened between them was an aberration and wouldn't happen again. It couldn't happen again. The more and more she gave of herself to him, the deeper their connection, their attachment.

And despite the growing realization that he wished he could be the kind of man she needed, he wasn't. He doubted he could ever, no matter how hard he tried, change enough to be that man.

Poor Ellie had run to Dead River to escape danger, but it had followed her. And now things had gone from bad to worse, with the virus essentially shutting down the town.

In addition to that, now they not only needed to worry about a stalker, but about an escaped murderer. Hank Bittard had nearly killed the rookie deputy, and Theo had no doubts the man wouldn't hesitate to kill again.

Sometimes he felt as if his life had become a soap opera. Once everyone was occupied with breakfast, he figured he'd slip out of the house and head to town.

A sharp tapping on his bedroom door jolted Theo out of his thoughts. He turned, about to ask who was there, when he heard Amelia begin crying right outside the door. This cry sounded different. More of a shriek, as though she was in pain.

Heart pounding, he barreled to the door and threw it open. A disheveled and worried-looking Ellie stood in the hall, rocking a wailing baby.

"She's sick," Ellie said, sounding on the verge of tears. "Burning up. I took her temperature rectally, and it's a little over 101. I looked online and read that I shouldn't give her baby Tylenol without talking to a doctor. Can you call Gemma or one of the doctors at the clinic?"

He spun and grabbed his phone. Since he had Gemma's cell phone number stored, he punched it. A second later, she answered, sounding groggy.

"Amelia's got a fever. Ellie needs to know if we can give her infant Tylenol."

"A fever? What temperature?" Just like that, Gemma came instantly awake.

"One hundred and one. Ellie took it rectally."

Gemma swore. "A fever that high in such a young infant would warrant a sepsis work up in an E.R. One hundred and one is extremely worrisome in a newborn because her immune system is immature. What else is wrong? Any vomiting or diarrhea?"

He asked Ellie, who told him no, fear making her voice quiver. He knew the feeling.

"Right now we need to get her temperature down. Go ahead and give her infant Tylenol, along with a luke-warm bath."

Gemma waited while he relayed the information to Ellie. Meanwhile, the unspoken word hovered between them.

Virus.

All three of them knew how deadly a virus like the one that'd killed Mimi Rand could be to a tiny infant.

"It's not the virus," Theo said finally, determined not to give that particular terror power over him. "It's not."

"It can't be," Ellie agreed with him. "It's been too long since she was exposed."

Only Gemma was silent. Theo hadn't realized how desperately he needed her to agree until she spoke.

"Let's hope not. But since Amelia's mother died from it, we've got to go with the assumption that it is."

Theo glanced at Ellie and realized she was silently crying, tears streamed a silver path down her cheeks.

His throat closed up. "I can't lose her, Gemma," he said, his voice rough. "We can't lose her."

"And we won't." Gemma had gone back to her brisk, efficient nurse voice. "Get started on the bath and the infant Tylenol immediately. Take her temperature again in thirty minutes and call me back. Understand?"

Murmuring his assent, Theo ended the call and hurried after Ellie, who was already on her way to the bathroom.

Her hands shook as she handed him the Tylenol to open. Once he'd filled the dropper, he gave it back to her, watching as Ellie squeezed the recommended amount in Amelia's open mouth. This infuriated her, and she scrunched up her tiny red face, gearing up to let out a good screech. Ellie tried to soothe her, managing to get her quieted down somewhat, though it was clear Amelia didn't feel well.

Ellie sighed, still rocking the snuffling baby. She met his gaze, her own steady. "Will you hold her while I run her bath?"

For an answer, he held out his arms. The instant she placed the restless infant in them, he could feel the heat radiating from Amelia's tiny body. "She's really warm," he commented, his chest tight.

"She is." Ellie raised her head to look at him. "I really hope the medicine and this bath help."

"We have to believe it will." He let his determination fill his voice, aware that he had to be strong for all their sakes. "I don't want to have to take her in to the clinic. Right now, that's no place for a baby."

Ellie turned back to the bathwater, checking and double-checking the temperature. "I have to make it the perfect temperature," she said. "Definitely not too warm or too cold. Just lukewarm, enough to get her body temperature down."

Once she was satisfied she had it right, she took Amelia from him and divested her of her clothes. Briefly hesitating, she inhaled. "Get ready. I suspect she's not going to like this."

And Ellie lowered Amelia into the water.

After the first initial shock, Amelia began squirming and wailing in protest. "Shhh, baby girl," Ellie soothed, continually pouring water over her. "We're only trying to help you."

After a few minutes of this, Ellie gently lifted Amelia out of the water and toweled her off. "In a few minutes, we'll take her temperature again."

Watching Ellie taking such tender care of his daughter, he thought his heart would explode. Amelia had to be all right. She couldn't have caught the virus. In that instant, he realized he'd gladly trade places with his baby. He'd lay down his life if it meant saving her.

For the first time since he'd been a young boy and Gram Dottie had dragged him to church on a regular basis, Theo lowered his head and began to pray.

"All right," Ellie said briskly, startling him. "I think it's been long enough. Let's see if we were successful in getting her fever down."

She moved with cool efficiency, as though already certain of their success. He recognized this as a way to keep terror at bay.

Watching as she inserted the rectal thermometer, managing to keep a squirming Amelia in place, she watched the clock. The second hand seemed to creep around as she counted off one minute, then two and finally three.

"Here we go." She held up the thermometer and squinted at it in the light. "Oh, Theo." And her eyes filled with tears.

"What? Is it bad?" he asked, reaching for it to see for himself.

"No. It's normal again." She gave him a watery smile. "We just need to keep an eye on her and make sure it doesn't climb back up again. As long as she has no other symptoms, I think we can safely say it's not the virus."

Theo's knees felt weak. He leaned over and gave his still-fussy daughter a kiss on the forehead. "Thank God," he said and rose and kissed Ellie for good measure.

She blushed but barely paused a beat as she diapered and redressed Amelia. "I'm going to go rock her in the rocking chair for a while," she said, ducking her head shyly. "If you don't mind, will you call Gemma back and let her know?"

He thought she'd never looked so beautiful and nearly said so but managed to keep quiet. "Sure. I'll call her in a minute."

Watching as she carried Amelia out of the room, he wondered what the hell he was going to do. He'd gone from having nothing to having an almost family. And all of a sudden, he realized he might be able to have it all, if he was willing to take a chance and try.

After making a quick phone call to Gemma, he went out to the barn to brush a few horses, maybe even take one or two out and lunge them for exercise in the round pen. Anything to make him feel like himself again. He couldn't even look at breeding stock until the quarantine was lifted.

Theo needed to find his equilibrium and needed to do so soon. Only then could he think clearly, and figure out what he truly wanted.

That night, after dinner had been eaten and the dishes put away, Ellie brought Amelia into the den to watch television. Though Theo knew such a simple act would feel far too intimate, he'd also been compulsively checking on his daughter throughout the afternoon, fearful her fever would return. Ellie seemed to understand this, no doubt because she had similar fears of her own.

They settled on the couch, Amelia on a blanket between them, and watched a singing talent competition. Theo couldn't have cared less about the show, but he needed somewhere to park his gaze so he wouldn't feel compelled to study every nuance of Ellie's expression.

Amelia seemed normal, wide awake and happy with her pacifier. As she grew, she became more and more beautiful, and even without the DNA test, Theo believed with all his heart she was his. Not only did she have the Colton green eyes, but she had his chin.

When he finally allowed himself to relax, contentment stole over him. He could get used to this, quiet evenings with the family.

The instant the thought occurred to him, he wondered why he didn't feel the familiar urge to bolt. Then, not wanting to ruin a perfectly good evening by overanalyzing things, he pretended to watch the show.

Ellie took Amelia's temperature again before putting her to bed. Theo watched, willing it to be normal. And it was.

"I think we're over the hump," Ellie said, beaming. "But I'll keep watch on her tonight."

He wanted to tell her to try to get some sleep, but since he knew she wouldn't, he settled for asking her to promise to wake him if anything was wrong.

"I will," she said softly. Then she leaned over and kissed him on the cheek. "Good night, Theo."

Stunned, he murmured the same in response and left her room. Only when he'd closed the door to his own room did he allow his hand to touch his cheek.

He went to sleep smiling.

And when he woke in the morning, his mood annoyingly cheerful, he realized he was in deep trouble.

After grabbing breakfast and checking on Amelia, who Ellie informed him was completely back to normal, he headed outside to check on his hands. They were bringing cattle down from the summer pastures, a task that had always been one of Theo's favorites when he was growing up. He longed to go, despite knowing it was not possible.

Most of the hands had already ridden out, and the few that remained were about to go. After being assured that everything was under control, Theo returned to the house.

At loose ends, he decided to go into town, even though he realized it was another way of avoiding his growing feelings for Ellie. Just as he couldn't yet consider he'd eventually have to deal with them, or he'd lose her.

He just had to figure out what he wanted. While his ranch continued to be prosperous, he wasn't sure Ellie would want a broken rodeo cowboy like him. Even if he did eventually have a successful breeding program.

Just as he picked up his keys off the dresser, Flint

called. Seeing his brother's name on the caller ID, Theo figured it was time to talk about organizing a search party.

"What's up?" Theo asked.

"Gemma called me. How's Amelia?"

"She slept through the night." He sighed. "Ellie's watching her like a hawk. I'm about to head into town myself. I want to make sure we have plenty of infant first aid supplies."

"Can't you have one of your guys do that? I really need to meet up with you."

Instantly alert, Theo froze. "Sure. What's going on?"

"The whole town's gone freaking crazy." Hoarse, Flint didn't sound like himself.

Theo felt a stab of fear, wondering if his brother had taken sick.

"Are you okay, man?" Theo asked. "Any fever, body aches?"

"Of course not." Flint sounded offended that he'd even asked. "More than anyone, I'm aware of the need to check in at the clinic at the first sign of the virus."

Relieved, Theo exhaled. "Then what's happening?"

"You mean beyond the fact that the National Guard has become power-hungry, the state police are right there with them and the townspeople are going stir-crazy? Oh, and not to mention one of my deputies is critically injured and there's an escaped killer on the loose?"

Theo winced. "Sorry. Is there anything I can do to help?"

"Not with that. Unless you can wave a magic wand and make this damn virus disappear. It seems to be multiplying rapidly."

Theo's heart stopped. When he'd talked to Gemma

the day before, he was so worried about Amelia that he hadn't asked her anything about the virus. "How bad is it? Is it getting worse?"

"Yeah." His brother sounded grim. "More and more people are getting sick. Everyone else—those who don't have the virus—are being asked to stay home and wait out their symptoms." He took a deep breath. "Even so, the clinic's isolation area is bursting at the seams. The CDC has brought in temporary trailers to house more patients. They've also got some for the doctors and nurses to use, as many are working twelve-or-more-hour shifts all week trying to care for all the sick people."

"What about deaths? How many more people have died?"

"Last I heard it was close to a dozen."

Stunned, Theo wasn't sure how to respond.

"And then there's those idiots who decided the quarantine doesn't apply to them." The frustration and anger in Flint's voice came loud and clear over the phone. "Some of them are even our relatives. Couple of them got liquored up and decided to try to run the barricade. Damn fools almost got shot."

Theo cursed. "As if you don't have enough to worry about."

"Right." Flint went quiet. When he spoke again, he sounded worried. "It's going to happen again. Sooner or later someone's going to get hurt. Or killed."

"You really think they'll try again?"

"Maybe not them, but someone. You know how we Wyomingites are. They were even shouting the state motto, Equal Rights. Never mind that symbolizes the political status women have always enjoyed in our state."

"Was beer involved?" Theo asked, already knowing the answer.

"Isn't it always?"

"How's Mike? Is he still at the clinic?"

"Yeah. The good news is, they upgraded his status from serious to stable. Bittard stabbed him quite a few times."

"Any sign of him?" Theo asked.

"Not yet. I've been too busy to get together a search party. That's partly why I called you."

"Just say the word and I'll get it put together." Theo didn't tell his brother how badly he needed a distraction.

"Okay. Can you come by my office this afternoon?"

"Definitely," Theo agreed. "I was just about to leave."

"I can't meet for about an hour."

"No problem." Theo figured he'd stop by the café for lunch to kill time. "I've got a few other things to take care of."

After a pause, Flint asked how Theo was doing. "You sound a little weird."

Theo shrugged, then realized his brother couldn't see him over the phone. "Not bad. Considering. It was pretty damn scary when Amelia got sick."

"Are you getting used to being a daddy?"

If anyone else had asked that question, Theo might have come back with a flippant remark. But Flint shared the same past. More than anyone else, he knew Theo had no fatherly example to emulate.

"Little by little. Ellie's helping me learn," he allowed.

"Ah, Ellie." Something in Flint's tone…

Theo frowned. "What do you mean by that?"

"Just that you and she seem…close."

Familiar with his brother's teasing, Theo laughed, though he felt himself grow a little hot under the collar.

"She's really pretty," Flint continued. "Not your usual type, but I'd say an improvement."

"She's sweet, kind and a hard worker," Theo allowed. "But you know I don't mix business with pleasure." He winced, aware of the blatant lie. "She's my nanny and until the accident, she worked as the ranch cook, not my girlfriend."

Flint snorted. "Since when have details like that ever stopped you?"

"I don't know what you mean," Theo lied again. "But seriously, I can't afford to mess this up. If I didn't have her to take care of Amelia…" He shuddered. "I wouldn't survive."

Flint laughed. "Yeah, smart move, Hot Shot. Keeping your pants on. I have to say, I'm proud of you."

"Don't be." Unable to keep the glum note out of his voice, Theo continued, "Because I didn't."

"You slept with her?" Flint sounded shocked.

"We didn't do much sleeping." Though that was Theo's standard reply, this time it came out sounding flat.

"You don't sound overjoyed."

Theo sighed. "I have a feeling, no matter what I do from this point, she's going to get hurt. You know how women have a way of getting upset when you don't give them everything they want. I'm a one-night kind of guy. And she's—"

"White picket fence and minivan," Flint finished, making Theo laugh.

"Not really, though I bet she might want that someday. She talks a lot about traveling." Deciding it was time to change the subject, Theo asked about Molly's ex-fiancé. "Any luck locating him?"

"Nope. My only consolation is I know he hasn't left town. He stopped by the body shop to pick up his last paycheck on Friday afternoon. After the quarantine went into effect."

"He still picked up his paycheck after cleaning Molly out?"

"Yep." Flint's tone told what he thought about that. "I can't wait to get my hands on him."

Someone spoke in the background.

"I've got to go," Flint said. "See you in about an hour, give or take."

Theo agreed and ended the call. He grabbed his Stetson and put it on. Jingling his keys, he headed out.

He nearly made it to the front door, but Ellie's voice stopped him. "Are you going into town?"

Slowly, he turned. Despite steeling himself, his heart skipped a beat at her blue-eyed prettiness. "Yep. Why? Do you need more formula and diapers?"

Her slow smile didn't entirely hide the hurt in her expression. "Amelia really runs through them. I'm afraid I'm going to have to ask you to pick up a double batch."

"What about more infant Tylenol?" He flashed an impersonal smile when what he really wanted to do was kiss her goodbye.

"Oh, good idea. And I need one more thing, if you don't mind."

The slightest hesitation in her voice made him tense. He waited, wondering if she meant to ask to go with him.

"Would you mind picking up a few Halloween decorations?"

This stunned him. "What for?"

"It's my favorite holiday. I usually decorate. As a matter of fact, I have a list of supplies and I can get them, if you want to watch Ellie. Either way, we're running low on a few things."

He actually wished she could come with him. Of course, there was no way he wanted Amelia anywhere near town. Plus, he had the meeting with Flint, and a search to organize.

"I'll have one of my hands do the shopping for you, okay? I've got to meet up with Flint and won't have time."

Face expressionless, she nodded. Amelia fussed, and she turned her attention to the baby. "So far, she seems okay. No sign of fever or anything else."

"That's a relief," he said, and meant it. "Gemma said she'd try to come by and check her out, but she sounded so exhausted, I told her not to. I promised we'd call her if anything changed."

She nodded and turned away. But not before he caught himself longing to kiss the hurt from her bright blue eyes.

Theo took the opportunity to escape, feeling gutless, which unsettled him. He was many things, but a coward wasn't one of them. He stopped back by the barn, tagging one of the younger hands who'd just finished sweeping out the tack room and asking him to head up to the house, get the list and handle the shopping. Already disappointed at not being able to help round up cattle, the boy brightened at having an actual task.

Once that was handled, Theo got in his pickup and headed to town.

Chapter 14

The young ranch hand who showed up a few minutes later seemed nervous. Ellie smiled to put him at ease and handed him her list. She'd crossed off the Halloween decorations, as she didn't want to make anyone else try to decide what to buy. That was half the fun, after all.

She had a feeling this year Halloween wouldn't be the same.

Molly called, full of the news that her ex-fiancé had been spotted in town. Flint had two men searching for him right at this moment. "I might just maybe get my heirloom ring back," she said. "Plus, I really want to make him face me and explain why he did what he did."

"That might be interesting." Ellie could imagine what a fireball Molly would be, demanding to know why Jimmy had broken her heart.

"What about you and Theo?"

Ellie swallowed. "What about us?"

"Ellie! Did you try the negligee?"

Closing her eyes for a moment, Ellie debated whether or not to lie. What she and Theo had shared was private, but on the other hand, he'd been acting so strange since then, she'd like a second opinion.

"Yes," she finally allowed, wincing as Molly squealed.

"Then I can assume it accomplished the intended purpose?"

"It did."

Silence. Then Molly ventured, "You don't seem too happy about it. What's wrong?"

"We made love and it was…wonderful. I really think we had a connection." Ellie sighed. "But since then, Theo's been even more remote. It's like it never happened."

"You need to talk to him."

"I will," Ellie promised. "I don't know, maybe I'm afraid he'll think I'm making a mountain out of a molehill. I mean, isn't Theo the love-'em-and-leave-'em type?"

"Oh, Ellie." Molly sighed. "You knew that going in. I thought you just wanted to have a little fun."

"I was, I am…" Miserable with the lie, Ellie sighed. "I don't know. I'm a little confused right now. Anyway, enough about me. What's new with you?"

"Well, Flint has people looking for Jimmy and the pawnshop has been put on notice in case my ring shows up."

"That's good." Relieved, Ellie sighed. "Flint's not so bad, actually."

"No. I guess I was being silly. But I confess, I wanted to hug him when he told me what he wanted to do to Jimmy once he catches him. Of course, since Flint's the sheriff, he can't. But still."

"I hope he finds him soon."

"Me too. But since everyone in town is on the lookout for him, he can't spend much of my money. So there's that." Molly sounded upbeat. "And he must still have the ring. No doubt he's hanging on to it until he can get out of town and pawn it in Cheyenne or somewhere."

"I wonder if he'll try to sneak out of town."

"I wish he would. The way they're patrolling the borders would mean he'd get caught much more quickly. So far, every single person who's tried to leave has been caught."

"Seriously?" Impressed and appalled, both at the same time, Ellie shuddered. "I don't hear any of that stuff since we're so isolated out here at the ranch. What else is going on in town?"

Molly told her the townspeople had decided to cancel Halloween, because of the virus, which made Ellie wince.

"That makes me sad. It's my favorite holiday."

"Really?" Molly sounded surprised. "Even more than Christmas or Thanksgiving?"

"Yep. I've always loved Halloween. When I was younger, it had started as rebellion, since my parents disallowed Halloween, claiming it was a holiday for devil worshippers."

Molly gasped. "That's intense."

Used to this reaction, Ellie shrugged, even though Molly couldn't see her. "They're super religious. Right now they're missionaries in Africa."

"Oh. That makes more sense." Again Molly gave a light trill of laughter. "So that's why you love it so much? Rebellion?"

Ellie laughed. "Not anymore. As I grew older, I came to honestly love the decorations and the costumes, and the mystical aspects of All Hallows' Eve. I really like the artwork from Dia de Muertos, the Mexican Day of the Dead."

"Wow," Molly said. "I just like giving out candy."

"Oh, me too. Or at least, I used to."

"What about costumes?" Molly asked. "Since you love Halloween so much, I bet you have some amazing ones."

"Not really." Ellie had only dressed up once herself. As a bride. She smiled at the thought, remembering how excited she'd been when the family she was staying with had taken her trick-or-treating.

And how furious her parents had been when they learned of the event later. She'd been told she was never to wear a Halloween costume again. And she hadn't.

She told none of this to Molly. It was old news, history, and she refused to let it be part of her new life.

"Even though I don't dress up," Ellie said, "I still enjoy the holiday. Not that I think we'd get many trick-or-treaters out here at the ranch—we're a bit too isolated for that."

"You should try wearing a costume. I mean, another time when Halloween isn't canceled. The bar normally has a great costume party, and it's a lot of fun. They aren't having it this year."

"I'd like that," Ellie said softly. "Though I'd have to buy something to wear. Maybe another time."

"You could borrow one of mine." Enthusiasm made Molly pitch her voice higher. "I have a ton. Heck, I'm pretty sure even Theo has dressed up once or twice."

"What, as a cowboy?" Ellie couldn't resist, laughing along with Molly.

"No," Molly squealed. "Something else. But I can't remember what."

"I'm so glad you called," Ellie said, once they'd finished laughing. "I needed a bit of a distraction, even if you did give me bad news. I was really looking forward to Halloween."

"You can come to my place," Molly offered. "If they

hadn't canceled everything, I'd normally get tons of little rug rats here. Even without it, you and I can celebrate. It'd do you good to get off the ranch."

"I might take you up on that." The idea brought Ellie's excitement back. "I'll have to check with Theo, since I'd want to bring Amelia."

"Did you get her a costume?"

Ellie grinned. "Yes. I ordered her an adorable infant princess outfit. Originally, I planned to let her wear it on an excursion into town for the big night. Which now, since they've canceled it, won't happen."

"Well, just let me know," Molly said. "And I'll keep you informed if Flint's men have any luck finding Jimmy and my ring."

Ellie noticed she made no mention of her missing inheritance. "I will," she said, hanging up.

The rest of the afternoon, without food prep and cooking to keep her busy, moved slowly. Thoughts of Theo filled her mind constantly. They seemed to have reached a new point in their relationship—she thought. Though from the way he acted, in his thoughts nothing had changed.

In fact, she'd had enough of this evasive stuff. When he got home, she planned to confront him. Even though she knew he probably had a lot on his mind with all the goings-on in Dead River, it appeared they were going to be together awhile longer, and she had a right to know where they stood. Actually, she needed to know.

Molly's news about Halloween had felt like the last straw. While she could understand the reasons for canceling the holiday, she'd been looking forward to it for months.

Trick-or-treating might be gone, but nevertheless she

felt determined to celebrate one of her favorite holidays, no matter what. Even if she had to go buy her own bag of candy and eat it all herself.

After he passed through the barricade on the way into town, Theo couldn't believe his eyes. Dead River looked deserted, like a ghost town. Occasionally, as he drove slowly down Main Street, he'd see someone leaving a store and hustling to their car, but by and large the sidewalks were empty.

Even the few people he saw looked different. They were alone, for starters. Single individuals only, not even a few couples or groups of three. And their movements appeared afraid, almost furtive. They moved about quickly, hunched into themselves, clearly in town only out of necessity.

This was such a stark contrast to the other evening, he couldn't help wondering what new calamity had befallen the town.

He pulled into the diner parking lot, relieved to see quite a few cars. People had to eat, at least. Once he stepped inside it was like changing the channel on the television—leaving the surreal gray-scape of an old *Twilight Zone* episode for a modern, color show.

The diner appeared at least two-thirds full, not bad for a weekday afternoon, even under normal circumstances. He sat in his regular spot, a small booth by the kitchen door, which was empty as usual. Others might avoid sitting here, but Theo loved having a view of the hustle and bustle of the kitchen.

Wilma hurried over. As one of the long-term employees, she got to choose her section, and she always worked this area. Theo liked her too, as she was briskly efficient and friendly, without overdoing it.

"Hey, Hot Shot," she greeted him, having long ago picked up on his childhood nickname. "Are you having the usual?"

Theo cocked his head, pretending to have to consider. "Sure," he finally said, grinning. "Why would I mess with a good thing?"

She grinned back and set down his iced tea. "I already put the order in the minute I saw you walk through the door."

Another reason why he loved her. She knew him so well he imagined she might faint if he ever ordered something beside his bacon burger and fries. Of course, why would he?

"How's business?" he asked.

"Better than it is at a lot of other places." She gestured around the room. "The past couple of days, people have been acting like the virus is floating everywhere, waiting to grab them if they left their house." She sighed. "I imagine they must be getting tired of that. It's been slow. Today's the first day we had a decent-sized lunch crowd. I guess it'll be back to normal tomorrow."

He nodded and took a drink of his tea. "So, what's new? I mean we've been under the quarantine and dealt with the virus for a while now. Why is everyone acting so weird?"

Wilma leaned in closer. "Between that and Hank Bittard having escaped, plus Jimmy Johnson robbing sweet Molly blind, I think people are on edge. More than once, I've heard someone comment that if the virus doesn't get them, Hank will."

Theo found himself feeling sorry for his brother. He

could only imagine what kind of hell Flint's life must be, with the citizens of Dead River on the edge of panic.

Wilma headed off with a wink to help another table. While Theo waited, he took the opportunity to observe the other customers. As far as he could tell, everyone seemed relatively normal. A bit subdued, maybe. And perhaps there were more diners eating alone instead of with friends or family.

A few minutes later Wilma returned with Theo's burger, setting it in front of him with an admonishment to eat up. Since he was hungry, he gladly complied.

After lunch, Theo drove to the sheriff's department. The parking lot there also seemed unusually empty. He guessed people were taking their concerns to the state police or the National Guard. As he parked, he couldn't help wondering if Flint felt relief or frustration about that.

After Kendra buzzed him back, Theo crossed the nearly deserted squad room to Flint's office. Talking on the phone, Flint gestured toward a chair. A few second later, he finished his call.

"Thanks for coming in," he said, exhaustion plain in his face. "I've just about had it up to here with the military. They keep using the phrase *martial law.*"

Shocked, Theo stared. "Did I miss someone declaring a state of emergency?"

"No. You didn't. And they won't. At least not out loud, in public. Not with our citizens verging on panic. But with the National Guard shooting people when they try to escape, and their continued refusal to listen to reason, I think maybe someone somewhere has done so internally."

"What are you going to do?"

Flint spread his hands. "There's nothing we can do. They've got us under a rock and a barrel, to say the least.

So I'm just trying to focus on the things I *can* control. Like recapturing Hank Bittard. And locating Jimmy Johnson, and Ellie's stalker."

"I understand." Though Theo really didn't. But that was another reason he was glad he wasn't sheriff. If he couldn't be a rodeo star, he guessed a cattle rancher or a horse breeder wasn't such a bad thing to be.

The revelation stunned him. All along he'd considered his breeding program a second choice. Now, it sounded pretty damn appealing, actually.

"Theo, are you listening to me?" Flint demanded.

Blinking, Theo gave his brother a sheepish grin. "Sorry. What were you saying?"

"I was asking you if you'd mind lending me a few of your ranch hands—plus yourself—to head up a search for Bittard."

"I'd rather look for Jimmy," Theo said grimly. "But since a killer is more dangerous than a thief, I don't mind at all. When do you have in mind?"

Flint shrugged. "As soon as possible. I know your guys are bringing the cattle down from the higher pastures and I don't want to mess with that."

"I'll check with Slim George about the schedule and let you know."

"Thanks."

"I drove downtown," Theo began, not at all sure he should mention anything. "The place seemed pretty deserted."

"I know. With all the declarations and bulletins, the CDC has everyone pretty scared." Dragging a hand through his close-cropped hair, Flint shrugged. "I can't say I blame them. They've even canceled Halloween, for

Pete's sake, including the annual Dead River Bar party. They're believing all the B.S. the CDC is putting out."

"How do you know it's not true?"

Flint's mouth twisted in a mocking smile. "That's the thing. I don't. But the way they're acting, they apparently believe everyone in Dead River is pretty much doomed."

"I refuse to believe that," Theo said. "We're not. Especially if Dr. Rand or one of the others can find a cure."

"True."

Since there wasn't much else to say, Theo got to his feet. "Is Gemma all right?" he asked.

"I suppose so. I'm sure we would have heard from her if she wasn't. All I know is every time I talk to her, she sounds dog-tired. I know they've brought in RVs for the clinic staff to sleep in. They've got people working around the clock there. Not just ours, but the CDC people too."

On the drive home, Theo reflected how life could turn on a dime. When he'd gotten hurt trying to ride that crazy bronco, he had no idea in the instant before he hit the sawdust that his life as he knew it was over.

Nor had he realized when Mimi Rand showed up on his doorstep with a baby how his world would spin another 360.

And then Ellie. He'd felt that tug of attraction the day he hired her, but he hadn't known how much she would impact his life.

All this time, he should have been counting his blessings. Now he just needed to figure out where he wanted to go from here.

The quarantine could be lifted any day now. With Ellie's stalker still at large, he knew she'd leave town first chance she got if she thought she was protecting Amelia.

He didn't want her to go. Not just because he needed a nanny and a cook, but because he needed her. The time they'd spent side-by-side in the kitchen and caring for Amelia had made him realize what a relationship could be like. What building a life together could look like.

Though he needed to find out if Ellie felt the same.

And neither the damned stalker nor the virus had better not rob him of that chance.

Ellie heard Theo's truck returning. When the house was quiet, the sound of tires on gravel was unmistakable.

She brought Amelia into the den and perched on the sofa. Theo's hand had brought her the necessary supplies over an hour ago.

"Did you get everything you needed?" Theo asked as he strode into the room.

Ellie took in his cowboy hat and boots, unable to keep from admiring the way his Wranglers fit his tight butt. For a second, she lost track of what he'd asked her.

"Oh yes. The diapers and formula and other stuff."

"Right. And the Halloween decorations."

She smiled to hide her disappointment. "No decorations. I crossed them off the list. I didn't want to put that poor kid through the chore of trying to choose."

Regarding her with a quizzical look, he finally nodded. "So now you're not going to decorate at all?"

"No. I talked to Molly about Halloween," she said, keeping her voice bright. "Like I said, it's one of my favorite holidays."

After a moment, he nodded. "I guess you heard they've canceled it in town."

"Yes. I'm still going to dress Amelia up."

"You are?" At her nod, he cocked his head. "Let me

guess. You've got your own costume planned. Something elaborate and showy."

"No." She frowned. "I never dress up."

"Never?" His narrow-eyed gaze told her he wasn't sure she meant it. "Molly always does. There's usually a big party at the bar, and from what I hear, Molly has had a fancier costume each year."

This made her smile. "I can imagine," she said.

"Then why don't you? I think you'd actually enjoy it."

Why didn't she? So she'd had one bad experience as a kid. Maybe it was time to let go of the past and make one more change. "You know, I believe you're right. I would." She shrugged. "But since Halloween is canceled, it's a moot point now."

"I guess you're right." Oddly enough, she could have sworn he looked disappointed. "But you should still dress Amelia up. I don't think we should let that stupid virus ruin her very first Halloween."

"I agree. I'm going to let her wear her costume. Molly invited me over to her house, so I thought I'd bring Amelia with me, if it's okay with you. Even though there won't be any trick-or-treaters, I think it'd still be fun."

He gave her an odd look. "But this is Amelia's first Halloween. I'd kind of like to spend it with her. And you know—" he gave her a sheepish sort of smile "—take pictures, all that."

Stunned, she simply stared at him, her chest tight.

"You can go to Molly's if you want," he continued. "But leave Amelia here with me." He flashed a crooked smile. "You can even dress her up in her costume before you go."

Suddenly, the thought of going to Molly's held zero

appeal. Not only was Theo learning to be a daddy, but he'd come to love his infant daughter. They'd make Halloween a family event, the one aspect of the holiday she'd never been able to recreate.

Longing stabbed her. Once again, she was on the outside looking in. Theo and Amelia were a family of two. Ellie was merely the nanny. And no amount of wishing or wanting would change that.

Still, she wanted to experience this, even if it was mostly pretense on her part. No matter how great the potential for hurt.

"Would it be all right if I stayed with you two?" she asked, her voice tentative. "I'd really like to be a part of Amelia's first Halloween, also."

Just as Theo was about to reply, a sharp knock sounded on the back door.

Before either of them could react, the door flew open. One of the ranch hands rushed in, clearly agitated.

"Theo, you need to get out here," he said. "We spotted a stranger over on the west pasture near the woods. The guys think he might be that escaped killer, Hank Bittard."

Instantly alert, Theo nodded. "Let me get my gun. Are any of them men armed?"

The other man nodded.

"Good. Give me a second. I've got to unlock my gun safe."

Ellie watched wide-eyed as Theo disappeared. A moment later, he returned, carrying a deadly-looking rifle.

As he headed for the door, Theo glanced at Ellie. "You stay here with Amelia. Set the alarm after I leave."

Ellie nodded, her heartbeat ragged. The intruder might

very well be this Hank Bittard person, who from all accounts was armed and dangerous.

But he could also be her stalker. She wasn't sure which one would be worse.

Following his man down the ravine where the stranger had been spotted, Theo held his rifle ready. He hoped he wouldn't have to use it, but better safe than sorry.

In the meantime, he called Flint's cell. As soon as his brother answered, Theo relayed the info.

"I'll be right there," Flint said. "Don't do anything foolish. This guy's a killer and has nothing to lose."

Theo agreed and ended the call, cursing the ache in his still-healing bones that made it difficult to keep up with his ranch hand. He took consolation in the knowledge that at least, if needed, he was a crack shot with a rifle.

Once they reached the edge of the woods, they met up with three of Theo's other men, all armed.

"He went in there," one said, pointing toward the old hiking trail that led to one of Theo's summer pastures.

"Good. We'll split up," Theo decided. "Two of you go that way, and we'll go the other."

As they murmured their assent and started moving away, he called after them, "Be careful. And don't get too trigger-happy, understand?"

Carefully and quietly, Theo and his guy searched. After thirty minutes or so, they met up with the other two.

"Nothing."

While they debated whether to search some more, Flint pulled up on the road beside the pasture. He had his lights flashing and left them on as he got out of the car. Climbing the fence, he strode over to them.

"Any luck?"

"Nope." Theo pointed toward the area they'd searched. "We split up and came up with nothing. I think if it's Bittard, he's probably trying to make a run for it through the trees. Eventually, he'd come out on one of the forestry roads. I'm guessing there's no way the National Guard can police every single mile."

"No, they can't." Flint looked grim. "But you've heard the helicopters and low-flying planes. They're doing regular flyovers using heat-seeking eyewear. If anyone tried to get out, it's likely they'll be caught. Just this week alone, they've stopped two groups—one of four teenagers and the other three hunting buddies."

Stunned, Theo exchanged glances with his men. "Why didn't we hear about any of this?"

Flint shrugged. "What's the point? The last thing I need to do is incite more panic. I think we should—" His belt radio crackled. Someone spoke, but the speaker kept cutting in and out and the rest of the words were so full of static they were unintelligible.

Cursing, Flint used his cell phone to call in. As he listened, his normally tanned skin turned ashen.

Ending the call, he turned to Theo. For the first time Theo could remember, he saw panic in his brother's eyes. "Theo, get in my truck. It'll be faster. We gotta go. Now."

Without hesitation, Theo headed for the truck, Flint right beside him. Once they both were inside, Flint started the engine and hit the gas. The truck fishtailed on the gravel road. Flint straightened it out, his expression grim.

"What's going on?" Theo asked.

Flint swallowed. "A 911 call came in from your house. It was Ellie. She didn't manage to talk, but she left her phone on speaker. It sounds like an intruder broke in and is holding her hostage."

Ellie had just finished changing Amelia when a peculiar shadow on the wall had her straightening. She turned to see the man in the hoodie standing in the doorway between her room and the hallway.

She froze, her heartbeat hammering in her throat.

"Afternoon, Ellie," he drawled, pulling down his hood so she could get a good look at his face. High balding forehead, narrow nose and thin lips. Doug Gasper.

"You," she gasped, moving to stand protectively between him and Amelia's crib. She'd left her phone on the changing table, and she pressed the call screen, hitting 911 and speaker quickly before turning back around.

Doug had worked with her at the bookstore. "You're my stalker? I don't understand. We were friends."

"Were we?" he asked, his tone mild as he peered down his nose at her. "Maybe that was the problem, right there, in a nutshell."

Bewildered, she eyed him. She had trouble believing he was dangerous. "Us being friends was a problem?" She crossed her arms. "Doug, we had dinner together at least once a week. I thought you were one of my best friends. You even comforted me when my stalker left roses or one of those poems."

He didn't reply, just continued to stare at her.

The implications of this struck her. She and Doug had talked for hours at each dinner. She'd denigrated her stalker with his creepy black roses and frightening and awful poetry. Doug had pretended sympathy, when in reality he must have been furious that she didn't appreciate his efforts.

A chill snaked up her spine. Clearly, she'd severely misjudged him.

"I still don't understand why," she finally said. "I thought you liked me. Why would you do all that stuff to me?"

"Liked you?" He moved closer. She realized to her shock that he had a gun in his hand. "You never did get it, did you, Ellie? *Like* never factored into it."

Swallowing, she was afraid to ask what he meant.

A tic moved in his cheek as he sidled around to stand beside her, his back against the changing table. "Ellie, you were mine from the first moment I saw you, but you didn't realize it. Or care."

"I always cared," she protested, praying he wouldn't notice her cell phone. "We were friends, Doug."

"I thought I could win you," he snarled. "But the first time I left you a poem, instead of appreciating it or wondering who your secret admirer might be, you said horrible things about it. About *me.*"

Ellie inhaled sharply, struggling not to recoil. She sensed that the slightest wrong move would set him off. Whatever happened, she knew she must keep him away from the crib. And oddly enough, now that she had Amelia to protect, she was no longer worried about what he might do to her.

The baby, however, was another story.

"You're wrong," she said. "I remember that first poem. I can recite it from memory." She ought to. After all, she must have studied the damn thing hundreds of times trying to decipher its meaning.

He narrowed his brown eyes. "I don't believe you."

Keeping her tone measured and level, she began. "The darkness comes when I look in your eyes. No longer blue, but the inky color of the deepest corner of hell. You are mine and I find myself longing to bathe in your eternal fire, damned forever." She swallowed. "Come on, Doug. I don't think you can honestly tell me that anyone wouldn't find that terrifying."

His frown made a deep line appear between his bushy eyebrows. "It's romantic," he declared. "I can't help it if you don't appreciate a good literary work."

Wisely, she refrained from commenting.

"You never appreciated any of my efforts," he continued, his gaze burning. "The black roses were an ironic portrayal of the commercialization of red roses to symbolize love. I thought you'd get that, but instead you acted as if you found them creepy."

Trying to formulate a reply, Ellie jumped as the back door flew open and footsteps pounded down the hall toward them.

Moving swiftly, Doug grabbed her, holding her around the neck in front of him, his pistol pressed against her temple. She began to perspire, praying he didn't have an itchy trigger finger.

Chapter 15

Theo and Flint rushed into the room, stopping short as they took in the scene. Shocked, Ellie noted that both men had weapons drawn.

"Get Amelia out of here," Theo ordered. Flint glanced at him, and then hurried to do exactly that.

"No," Doug said, the single word stopping Flint in his tracks. "The baby stays."

"Why?" Ellie pleaded. "She's not mine. She has nothing to do with you and me. Let her go."

He pressed the muzzle harder into her temple, making her gasp with pain. "I might need her for a bargaining tool."

"Bargaining for what?" Flint asked, his voice deceptively calm. "What do you want?"

"My woman, for starters." He squeezed the arm he had around Ellie's neck, choking her. She began to struggle as her air supply was cut off, seeing stars.

"Let her breathe," Theo shouted. Though at first glance he appeared composed, Ellie could see the desperate fury in his eyes.

For some reason this reassured her. Doug wasn't going to get away with this. Theo wouldn't let him.

"Doug?" she rasped, her throat slightly raw. "If you

really want my undying love, you've got to be more romantic than this. What kind of story would this be to tell our children?"

Doug froze. She prayed he'd buy the complete and utter nonsense she'd just sprouted. It depended on how deep his delusions were.

"You're wrong," he finally said, sounding furious. "I might just kill you, and your baby, before I shoot myself. That way we'll be together forever."

A chill spread through her, turning her blood to ice. Doug sounded crazy enough to do exactly what he said.

"Now, hold on," Flint said, his tone reasonable and reassuring. "None of us want it to come to that. What would be the point?"

"You know nothing," Doug argued. Facing Flint, he slightly loosened his grip on her neck. Heart pounding, Ellie figured it'd be now or never.

She twisted her head back into his face, ducking and ramming her elbow up at the same time, knocking his pistol arm away from her head and using that momentum to jab again, this time her elbow into his stomach. Out of reflex, he fired. The shot went wild.

Theo jumped him, wrestling him to the floor, holding him down while Flint cuffed him. Doug continued to spew curses and nonsense about destiny and true love. Shaking his head, Flint led him out of the room.

Ellie's legs gave out and she crumpled, suddenly unable to stop shaking. Crouching beside her, Theo scooped her up, holding her close and murmuring soothing words.

"Amelia?" she managed to ask. "Is Amelia okay?"

"She slept through it all." His husky voice reverberated against her ear. "And believe it or not, she's still asleep."

Ellie nodded, shaking violently. She closed her eyes and let herself sag against him as she pushed back panic. She couldn't allow herself to think of how close she'd come to dying. Worse, how close Amelia had come to being hurt. She knew that would come later, no doubt tonight when she was alone in her bed trying to sleep.

At least Amelia and Theo were safe. That was the most important thing. And then it hit her. She couldn't imagine a life without the two of them, her makeshift family. Somehow she'd allowed a tiny baby and her cowboy father to worm their way into her heart. Which meant she had set herself up for a world of hurt.

To her consternation, her eyes filled with tears, which overflowed and began running down her cheeks. She turned her face into Theo, crying in earnest, her entire body shaking with the force of her sobs.

"It's over now," he said, smoothing his hand down her hair and massaging her shoulder. "Flint's taking him to the station and booking him. That crackpot won't bother you again."

And then she realized she no longer had a stalker.

"It's finally over," she managed, hardly able to believe it all, still floored with the realization of how much Theo and Amelia meant to her. Even though she was now free, she knew she wasn't. "He almost killed me."

"I wouldn't have let him," Theo said, his voice fierce. She remembered the feel of the cold metal against her temple and knew he wouldn't have been able to do anything.

No doubt he knew this too, which was why he continued to hold her.

She wiped her eyes, sniffling and wishing she had

a box of tissue. Pushing against Theo, she struggled to stand, unable to keep from checking on Amelia once more.

The baby still slept peacefully, oblivious of the craziness that had just occurred around her. Thankful, she clutched the edge of the crib, wondering why her legs felt hollow.

Theo came up behind her, his hand gentle on her shoulder. "Are you all right?"

Refusing to look at him since she knew if she did, she'd start crying again, she shrugged. "I don't know," she answered honestly, hating the quaver in her voice.

"Come in the kitchen and let me get you a glass of wine."

"As tempting as that sounds, I don't want to leave Amelia." Glancing at her hands, she realized she clutched the edge of the crib so hard her knuckles were white.

When he didn't reply, she raised her head to see him gazing down at his daughter, naked tenderness softening his rugged features.

Longing stabbed her, mixed all up with joy and relief and an odd sense of finality. "I'd like to rest," she said, again avoiding meeting his eyes. "Sometimes I nap when she does. I really need to lie down."

"Okay." Was that regret coloring his voice? "I'll be around if you need to talk, all right?"

Answering with a quick nod, she turned away and crossed to her bed, where she methodically began folding down the blanket, and then the sheet, using the busywork to keep her occupied until she heard the sound of the door closing behind him.

Then she crawled into her bed, buried her face in her pillow and allowed herself to weep.

"Ellie." As if he knew, somehow Theo was beside her, gathering her close, kissing the tears from her cheeks. Holding her tight, as if he never meant to let her go.

She kissed him back, mindless in her desperation, needing to feel alive. To feel real, to let her body speak for her heart. She clawed at his shirt, wanting nothing but skin between them.

Somehow they divested themselves of their clothing. Theo seemed to share her need, instinctively understanding that this was not a time to go slowly.

They met halfway, body to body. Not sure how, she ended up on top, mindless with desire. She rode him hard, letting herself go wild with her head back, a primal sound of need and wanting escaping her throat. She gave herself over to him, to his body and to his life.

When she reached the peak, she let herself go, hurtling toward fulfillment with a cry and a shudder. Theo wasn't far behind.

Holding each other close, they fell asleep in each other's arms.

Amelia's hungry cry woke Ellie a few hours later. She sat up and blinked for a moment at Theo, sound asleep in her bed. She slid from under his muscular arm and hurried to get to the baby before her crying escalated.

Feeling pleasantly sore, Ellie carried Amelia into the kitchen and began to prepare her formula. Outside, she saw dusk had fallen. Which meant she and Theo had missed the evening meal.

But inside the refrigerator, Mrs. Jay had made two

plates, covered in cellophane. Ellie smiled, silently thanking her.

After Amelia had finished her bottle, Ellie burped her. Then she went to wake Theo so they could eat. Grinning wickedly, Theo trailed his gaze over her, as hot as any caress. Wearing only his boxers, he followed her into the kitchen. He ate fast, though Ellie picked at her food. She couldn't concentrate, not with him sitting across from her practically naked.

The instant they'd finished, Theo stood and came over and kissed her. "I'll be waiting in your bed," he murmured, his voice husky with desire. "For you."

Her entire body blushing, Ellie nodded. She carried Amelia back to her room and changed her, feeling incredibly self-conscious with Theo's half-lidded gaze on her. She put the already sleepy baby in her crib, then turned to face him, already unbelievably aroused, dizzy with need.

"Come here, you," he said, holding out his arms.

So she did.

Wonder of wonders, Amelia slept through the night for the first time that evening. Sunlight had already begun to stream through the window when she made her first, gurgling baby sounds.

Ellie glanced at Theo, who still slept with one arm holding her close to him. Again she managed to wiggle out from under him without waking him, and changed Amelia before carrying her into the kitchen for her morning bottle.

A quick glance at the calendar, and she smiled. Halloween. Even though Dead River had canceled the holiday, she still got that expectant feeling she always had on holidays or her birthday. As if something wonderful would happen that day. Even though Dead River would not be celebrating, Ellie and Amelia and Theo would.

She thought it might be the best Halloween ever.

Theo kept his eyes closed when Ellie got up to tend to Amelia. This, he realized. This was how he wanted to start every morning from now on. With his arms around Ellie.

He'd spent way too much time bemoaning everything he had lost. The rodeo was out, his career, his life, vanished in the buck of a crazy bronco. Suddenly, he realized he could have a new life.

Ellie's words came back to him. *"For a man who has so much, you act like you have nothing. You're alive, you have family who loves you, a productive and profitable ranch and a beautiful baby girl. What more do you want?"*

Her, he realized. He wanted her. Ellie, to promise to stay with him and love him for the rest of her life.

She had no idea how he felt. He certainly had never told her, and he couldn't help but wonder how she'd react once he did. He knew she wanted to travel. What he didn't know was if she'd consider traveling with him rather than alone, at least once the quarantine was lifted.

No risk, no gain. That had always been his motto, part of what had made him so successful in pro rodeo.

Humming, he got up and headed for the shower. After he emerged, energized and clean, his cell phone rang.

Flint. "I need to officially take your and Ellie's statements. Can you come down and give them? You can even wear a costume if you want. Hell, it might brighten things up. It's Halloween, even if all festivities have been canceled."

"Halloween?" Ellie's favorite holiday. And just like that, he knew what he had to do.

He thought for a moment. "What's all this about a costume? You know I don't have any. I never dress up."

"I know. But I have, once or twice in the past. If I wasn't sheriff, I'd damn sure be wearing one of them."

Theo hesitated, and then decided what the hell? "I might want to borrow one. Would that be okay?"

"Sure." Flint sounded a bit mystified, but he didn't press for specifics. "So you'll pick it up when you bring Ellie in to give me your statements?"

"About that…I probably could come in, but I don't think we both can. I don't want to risk Amelia getting sick, especially after last time. And Ellie's too fragile right now to leave alone."

"Can't say I blame you." Flint sighed. "But what about the costume?"

"I'll send one of the hands over to get it." He decided not to mention to his brother that he had a bit of special shopping of his own to do. He knew Flint would tease him mercilessly if he did.

"Fine," Flint said. "I guess I can just take your statement over the phone. And when Ellie feels up to it, just have her call me. How about that?"

"Works for me," Theo replied. "But you were here. You know everything that happened."

"I do. But I still need you to go over the event in your own words."

Barely resisting the urge to roll his eyes, Theo did. After he'd finished, he headed into the kitchen to find

Ellie. He planned to watch Amelia so Ellie could shower. Then once she'd done that, he'd have her call Flint. He figured he'd wait until dinner to tell her he was planning something special for their first Halloween together.

In between, he needed to call Molly and send the same hand he'd be sending to Flint's to run by her house.

Ellie's cheeks reddened as he walked into the kitchen. "Good morning," she said, sounding shy.

He grinned, unable to keep himself from planting a kiss right on her still-swollen-from-last-night lips.

"Mornin' darlin'," he drawled. "How about I keep an eye on Amelia, so you can have a shower?"

Swallowing, she nodded. "That would be nice."

He thought she'd bolt or rush out of the room, but instead she reached up and cupped his face with her hands. "Thank you," she whispered, brushing her mouth over his, sending a jolt of desire straight to his groin. Then, looking pretty darn pleased with herself, she strolled away, hips swaying.

Theo grinned, watching her go. He waited until he heard the sound of the shower before he picked up the phone.

Molly sounded surprised and pleased when he heard his request. "I don't know if she'll go for it," she said. "But I really do think it would be great if she did. I'll help you in any way I can."

When he told her what costume he wanted for Ellie, she laughed. "That's perfect. I'll have it ready for you. When are you going to get it?"

"I'm going to send someone now," he said. "Since tonight is the night, I want to surprise her."

"Sounds good," she said. Relieved that she didn't ask

any more questions, he headed out to the barn to get all of the details taken care of. After that, Theo went down to the kitchen to see what kind of meal Mrs. Jay, his temporary cook who might be about to become permanent, planned to make for the evening meal.

"A nice pot roast," she said, smiling. "With new potatoes and carrots. Will that be all right with you?"

He nodded. "And biscuits?"

"Of course."

"What about dessert? Since it's Halloween, would you mind making some sort of special, themed dessert?"

Her smile widened. "Of course not. I know just the thing. My boys used to love Halloween when they were younger."

"Thank you," he said, turning to go. "Then I'll leave you to it."

"We're having chicken sandwiches for lunch," she called after him.

With a wave as his answer he left, his mood buoyant. If everything worked out as planned, Mrs. Jay would be offered a permanent job before she left for the day.

Theo skipped lunch, afraid he'd slip up and do something to make Ellie wonder what he had planned. More than anything, he wanted to surprise her so he could witness her joy firsthand.

If things went the way he hoped, Amelia's first Halloween would be the first of many holidays he and Ellie shared.

Claiming he needed to stop by the feed store, he drove to town and stopped at the lone jewelry store, Dead River Diamonds. The proprietor, Mr. Mauricio, squinted in surprise when Theo walked in.

"I've already told your brother I'd let him know if anyone tried to sell me your family heirloom ring," he said.

"That's not why I'm here," Theo said, walking to a case and peering down. Suddenly intimidated by all the dazzling choices, he looked at Mr. Mauricio for help. "I need to buy an engagement ring of my own," he said, glad the store was empty. "For a very special lady."

The older man's face lit up. "Why didn't you say so? What cut in the diamond?"

"Bear with me, I've never done this before." He watched while the jeweler brought out a tray of sparking rings and pointed to a square-cut diamond, surrounded by a complete circle of smaller diamonds. "I like that one."

"Good choice." Mr. Mauricio named a price and then followed up by stating he could offer an installment plan if Theo liked.

Smiling, Theo declined and wrote the man a check for the full amount.

"You can bring it back to be sized, at no charge." He handed Theo the ring in a black velvet box. "I sure hope your lady likes it."

Thanking him, Theo tucked the box in his jeans pocket and left. After he left the jewelry store, he stopped by the drugstore and bought decorations. Not scary spiders and skeletons, but streamers and lights and everything he could think of to make the living room magical.

Back home, he felt like a kid on Christmas morning as he tried to keep busy while unobtrusively watching the clock. He took the decorations to Mrs. Jay and asked her if she'd put them up when Ellie was out of the room. Giving him the smile of a conspirator, she agreed.

The ranch hand he'd sent to pick up the costumes arrived and handed them over, both in plastic dry cleaning bags. Theo hurried to get them to his room before Ellie saw.

Finally, it was time for the evening meal. Since they always ate pretty early, he knew the hands would be gone before dark.

"This is delicious, Mrs. Jay," Ellie said, smiling. She practically glowed with happiness tonight, despite the town's cancelation of Halloween and despite nixing her plans with Molly to stay home with Theo and Ellie.

Watching her while trying not to stare, he also thought she looked radiantly beautiful. Her pretty blue eyes shined with excitement.

Theo barely tasted his meal, though he was hungry since he'd skipped lunch. He managed to clean his plate, aware that tonight just might be the biggest night of his life.

"I can't wait to see Amelia in her costume," Ellie said, glancing over at the bassinette where the baby dozed. "I'm planning on taking some pictures and posting them on Facebook."

"I didn't know you were on there," he said, surprised.

"I wasn't." Her smile dazzled him. "But now that I no longer have to worry about a stalker, I've reactivated my account."

"I'll have to send you a friend request."

She stared, clearly astonished herself. "You have a Facebook account?"

He laughed. "Yes. It used to be for promoting my rodeo career. I used to have a virtual assistant to handle all my online activities. Of course, once I had the accident and lost my career, I had to let her go."

She nodded, watching him closely. "I'm sorry."

"Don't be." And he meant it. For the first time, he felt no despair when talking about his former rodeo days or his accident. "That's all in the past," he said. "I'm concentrating on looking forward, to the future."

"Me too." She lifted her chin. "Of course, that won't even be possible until they lift the quarantine."

Just like that, his confidence deflated. He knew he didn't know what she wanted out of life, other than she'd said she'd always wanted to travel to Australia. Would he be wasting his time asking her to spend the rest of her life with him?

No matter. He had to know. Theo had learned early on that the bigger the risk, the better the reward. Ellie had become his everything, and no way in hell was he going to let a bit of uncharacteristic self-doubt prevent him from going after what he wanted.

Mrs. Jay announced the time had come for their special dessert. As was customary, she served the ranch hands first. Guffaws and hoots greeted whatever she gave them. Amid teasing and laughter, the men got busy eating.

A moment later, Theo saw what all the commotion had been about. Mrs. Jay had made cupcakes, decorated to look like spiders.

When Ellie saw this, she clapped her hands with happiness. "Perfect," she said, jumping up and planting a quick kiss on the older woman's cheek. "Thank you so much. I love Halloween, and you've just helped make it even more special."

Theo watched in amazement as the normally confident cook blushed. "You're welcome, dear."

He choked down his cupcake, making the appropriate complimentary comments.

The men got up to leave, grumbling about how the annual Halloween party at the bar had been canceled. They were planning to have a poker game instead.

"You in, boss?" one of them asked Theo.

"Not this time," he answered. "It's my baby girl's first Halloween and I want to spend it with her."

The man smiled his approval, put his hat back on his head and left.

Ellie offered to help Mrs. Jay with the dishes. The older woman declined, shooing Ellie along. "You go celebrate with Amelia and Theo," she said. "Once I finish cleaning up, I'm taking myself home. I'm sure going to miss all the kids coming around for candy."

"Maybe they'll let them do it another day," Ellie said. "Once they find a cure for the virus."

"Maybe so." Mrs. Jay turned back to the dishes.

Ellie crossed to the bassinette and picked up Amelia. "I'm going to go get her cleaned up and changed and then put her in her costume." Her excited smile told him how much this meant to her.

He followed her down the hallway, stopping her with a touch on her arm when she got to her room. "Just a minute," he said. "I've got something I want you to put on once you're finished."

Though she gave him a quizzical look, she nodded.

Hurrying into his room, he opened his closet door and removed the elaborate and gaudy princess costume Molly had provided. It came complete with a sparkling crown and jewelry. Since Ellie and Molly were about the same size, he felt confident it would fit.

"Here you go." He handed her the plastic-wrapped gown. "Courtesy of Molly."

"A costume?" Her eyes sparkled with delight, though she appeared confused. "What for?"

"I thought we'd all three dress up tonight," he said, his heart thumping loud in his chest. "I really want this to be special for Amelia—and you."

Though she nodded and ducked her head, he could tell she was pleased. What woman—especially one who loved Halloween—wouldn't want to wear such a beautiful dress? Even if they weren't going to a party, she could pretend for a few hours.

Once she'd closed her door, he hurried to his room to don his own costume. He was going to be prince to her princess, and when he got down on one knee to offer her the ring, he wanted it to be the most magical moment of her life.

And hopefully of his.

Dressed, he checked himself out in the mirror. Surprised that he didn't feel even the slightest bit foolish, he didn't think he looked half-bad.

Satisfied, he turned to go check out the living room and see if Mrs. Jay needed any help.

"I'm nearly finished," she chirped when she saw him, and then her eyes went round. "You look stunning."

He grinned and thanked her, looking at the streamers and balloons and tiny orange lights. "This is perfect. You did a great job."

"That's good." She ducked her head, clearly pleased. "Especially, since I've never decorated inside for Halloween before."

She finished up and took herself off for home, still smiling, almost as if she knew what he intended.

A few minutes later, Ellie emerged. Theo heard the sound of her door opening and tensed. Telling himself to relax, he faced the hallway, eager to see her reaction when she saw what he had done.

But when she turned the corner, he found himself transfixed instead.

"Wow!" Ellie as a princess gliding into the room, transfixing him with her beauty. "This place looks amazing."

Speechless, he nodded, though he only could look at her. The deep purple velvet of the dress highlighted the perfection of her porcelain skin, which glowed with heightened color. Her soft brown hair hung in long, seductive swirls over her shoulders.

He lowered his gaze to her creamy throat begging for kisses above the low-cut bodice of the gown. She was exquisitely feminine. Slender, willowy, yet somehow dainty.

His.

Finding himself at a loss for words, he struggled to figure out the right thing to say.

At his silence, her lashes swept down over her cheeks. "What do you think?" she asked shyly.

Then, as he opened his mouth to respond, she held up Amelia, wearing an infant version of the princess gown, only in a cheerful, bright pink.

"Isn't she lovely?" Ellie said, smiling with joy. "I even bought this little flower headband to go on her sweet, bald head."

Enchanted, he crossed the room and took little Amelia from her. "She's beautiful," he said. "Just like you."

Though she blushed at his words, she didn't look away. "You're a prince," she said, her blue eyes sparkling.

"I am."

"I would have thought you'd go as a cowboy," she said. "But then I guess it wouldn't really be a costume, since you're a cowboy every day."

Normally, he would tease her. But the black velvet box inside his pocket made him tongue-tied. Panicking slightly, he realized he should have rehearsed this, maybe even practiced. A man only got one chance to propose, and he damn sure had better get it right.

Not yet, though. He planned to wait until the moment was right. First, he wanted to give her the special Halloween night she'd wanted.

"We never have trick-or-treaters out here at the ranch," he said. "And since Dead River canceled their festivities, including the annual party at the bar, I thought maybe you and I could have our own Halloween party."

She gave him a tentative smile. "Okay."

"You know, I have to tell you again how gorgeous you look. If the costume party at the bar hadn't been canceled and we'd gone, you would have had men fighting to dance with you."

Her delighted laugh lightened some of the tightness in his chest. "What about you?" she asked, her smile turning teasing. "You make a mighty handsome prince yourself."

Unable to resist, he placed Amelia in her bassinette and gave her the pacifier. Then he held out his hand. "May I have this dance?"

Her eyes widened. "But there's no music."

He lowered his voice. "We can make our own."

Shaking her head, nevertheless she slipped her fingers

into his. He pulled her close, one hand on her waist, and twirled her around the floor.

Laughter floated up from her throat as she spun, her skirt flaring out. He caught her and brought her back, realizing the moment could never be more perfect than it was at this very instant.

"I need to ask you something," he asked, his voice thick and unsteady.

Smiling up at him, she tilted her head. "If it's about my dancing, then no. I never did learn how to slow-dance properly."

Enchanted again, he nearly staggered at the intense flare of his emotions. "Not about your dancing," he managed. Letting go of her hand, he dropped to one knee.

Ellie stared at him, her hand creeping up to her throat, her lovely eyes huge in her pale face. "Theo…"

If he'd thought about it too much, he knew in this moment he might fumble taking the ring box from his pocket. But as certainty filled him, his hands were steady and sure.

He opened the black velvet box, letting her see the ring he'd chosen. "You've made me realize what kind of future I can have with you by my side. I'm tired of living in the past, especially since everything I want and need is right here, with you and Amelia. I'd be honored, Ellie Parker, if you'd agree to become this rancher's wife."

When she didn't immediately respond, he knew something had to be bothering her. Because deep in his heart he had to believe that Ellie loved him almost as much as he loved her.

"What is it?" he asked. "Is it because you wanted to go to Australia? We can do that for our honeymoon. I still have lots of money socked away from my prize-winning rodeo days. So if you're still wanting to travel Down Under—or anyplace else—we can take vacations there together."

"You know, I think I'd like that." Her sweet smile appeared a bit mischievous, though her eyes had grown wet with unshed tears. "Though I mainly wanted to get away because of my stalker. Now that he's out of the picture, I'm pretty darn happy right where I am."

Despite her words, she still looked troubled. "But Theo, I have to ask you something. I saw a notebook you had, and it looked like you were planning on trying to go back to the rodeo. Is that the case?"

Puzzled, he shook his head. "I can't go back, even if I wanted to. I'm not sure what you saw…" And then he realized what it had to have been. "I plan to start a breeding program to supply rodeo broncos. With my knowledge of rodeo and of ranching, I'm pretty confident I'll be a success. At least, once this quarantine is lifted, that is."

Her dazzling smile made him catch his breath. "That's absolutely wonderful," she said. "And you're completely right—I believe you will be very successful."

"Thanks." Eyeing her, he cleared his throat. "About my proposal?"

"Ah yes." Her smile broke into a watery grin. "About that. I'm thinking there's something you haven't yet said. I don't know if you're wanting to marry me just because of Amelia, or if you really want me for yourself."

She was right. Amused and chastened, he nodded. "You're correct. So here's the truth. I love you more than words can say, Ellie. I love you more than you could ever love a broken-down cowboy like me."

"Don't say that!" She dropped down beside him, cupping his face gently with her hands and caressing his mouth with hers. "I adore everything about you, Theo Colton. And yes, I'd love to be your wife."

Elation sang through his veins and he kissed her back. Then he broke away, slipping the ring on her finger. They both admired it for a moment and then, arms wrapped around each other, he reclaimed her lips.

The doctors might not have figured out the cure to the virus, and the future of Dead River might be uncertain. But this, his love for her would always be steady and sure.

"We're a family now, Ellie," he promised her, against her lips. "Together, we'll make it through all this craziness. You, me and our daughter."

She gave him a watery smile. "I believe we will." And then her expression turned mischievous. "You know what? Theo, what do you say we get married wearing these costumes?"

He gazed back, his heart full of amused wonder. "You know, I think that might be perfect. Once this virus gets cured, we'll have a costumed wedding, in honor of your favorite holiday."

Half laughing, half crying, she wrapped her arms around him again and buried her face against his throat.

"I want to spend the rest of my life showing you how much I love you."

Ducking her head, the rosy color in her cheeks told him his words had pleased her. "Me too," she replied. "That is, I want to do the same with you."

He couldn't help it, he laughed and pulled her close. "You're something else, Ellie."

"So are you, Theo Colton." She kissed him again, without hesitation, and full of love. "So are you."

Smoothing his hand down the silky length of her hair, he marveled at how quickly his life had changed for the better. "One year ago, I thought I'd lost everything. And now I've been given a second chance. My life is richer than I ever could have imagined."

"Mine too." She raised her head, a seductive softness in her baby blue eyes. "And I can think of a great way to celebrate."

Before he could ask, she kissed him once more and proceeded to show him exactly what she meant.

* * * * *

THE COLTONS: RETURN TO WYOMING
Don't miss a single story!

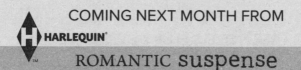
#1823 HER COLTON LAWMAN
The Coltons: Return to Wyoming
by Carla Cassidy

With his town under quarantine and an escaped killer on the loose, Sheriff Flint Colton must protect the one woman who can testify against the murderer. But getting close to Nina could just prove his undoing.

#1824 HIGH-STAKES BACHELOR
The Prescott Bachelors
by Cindy Dees

When stuntwoman Ana lands her first big role, she finds herself the target of an increasingly violent stalker. The movie's star, Jackson, insists she stay with him for her safety. Can she risk both her career and her heart?

#1825 TEXAS STAKEOUT
by Virna DePaul

An undercover stakeout becomes a mission to protect for U.S. marshal Dylan when the fugitive's widowed sister is targeted. Will he do his job and win the woman he's come to think of as his own?

#1826 DESIGNATED TARGET
To Protect and Serve
by Karen Anders

After rescuing the genius Dr. Skylar Baang, NCIS agent Fitzgerald must protect the beautiful scientist from betrayal by her own government—without falling too hard for her himself!

REQUEST YOUR FREE BOOKS!
2 FREE NOVELS PLUS 2 FREE GIFTS!

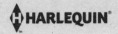

HARLEQUIN

ROMANTIC suspense

Sparked by danger, fueled by passion

YES! Please send me 2 FREE Harlequin® Romantic Suspense novels and my 2 FREE gifts (gifts are worth about $10). After receiving them, if I don't wish to receive any more books, I can return the shipping statement marked "cancel." If I don't cancel, I will receive 4 brand-new novels every month and be billed just $4.74 per book in the U.S. or $5.24 per book in Canada. That's a savings of at least 14% off the cover price! It's quite a bargain! Shipping and handling is just 50¢ per book in the U.S. and 75¢ per book in Canada.* I understand that accepting the 2 free books and gifts places me under no obligation to buy anything. I can always return a shipment and cancel at any time. Even if I never buy another book, the two free books and gifts are mine to keep forever.

240/340 HDN F45N

Name	(PLEASE PRINT)	
Address		Apt. #
City	State/Prov.	Zip/Postal Code

Signature (if under 18, a parent or guardian must sign)

Mail to the **Harlequin® Reader Service**:
IN U.S.A.: P.O. Box 1867, Buffalo, NY 14240-1867
IN CANADA: P.O. Box 609, Fort Erie, Ontario L2A 5X3

Want to try two free books from another line?
Call 1-800-873-8635 or visit www.ReaderService.com.

* Terms and prices subject to change without notice. Prices do not include applicable taxes. Sales tax applicable in N.Y. Canadian residents will be charged applicable taxes. Offer not valid in Quebec. This offer is limited to one order per household. Not valid for current subscribers to Harlequin Romantic Suspense books. All orders subject to credit approval. Credit or debit balances in a customer's account(s) may be offset by any other outstanding balance owed by or to the customer. Please allow 4 to 6 weeks for delivery. Offer available while quantities last.

Your Privacy—The Harlequin® Reader Service is committed to protecting your privacy. Our Privacy Policy is available online at www.ReaderService.com or upon request from the Harlequin Reader Service.

We make a portion of our mailing list available to reputable third parties that offer products we believe may interest you. If you prefer that we not exchange your name with third parties, or if you wish to clarify or modify your communication preferences, please visit us at www.ReaderService.com/consumerschoice or write to us at Harlequin Reader Service Preference Service, P.O. Box 9062, Buffalo, NY 14269. Include your complete name and address.

HRS13R

Pink panties.

Hot pink panties.

Flint closed the door to his master bedroom and began to
change out of his uniform.

He'd gone into the store on high alert, hovering near
Nina and watching to make sure that nobody else got close
to her.

What he hadn't realized was that shopping with a woman
could be such an intimate experience. He'd been fine as
she'd grabbed several T-shirts and sweatshirts, some jogging
pants and a nightshirt.

His close presence next to her felt a little more intrusive as
she shopped for toiletries. Peach-scented shampoo joined a
bottle of peach and vanilla scented body cream. It was then
that things began to get a little wonky in his head.

He imagined her slathering that lotion up and down her

shapely legs and rubbing it over her slender shoulders. He imagined the two of them showering together, the scent of peaches filling the steamy air as he washed the length of her glorious hair and then stroked a sponge all over her body.

He'd finally managed to snap himself back into professional mode when she'd headed to the intimates section. He was okay when she grabbed a white bra and threw it into the shopping basket. He even remained calm and cool when the bra was followed by a package of underpants.

It was when she tossed that single pair of hot pink panties in the cart that his head once again went a little wonky. Pink panties and peach lotion, those things had been all he'd been able to think about.

He sat on the edge of his bed to get every inappropriate vision and thought he'd had of Nina over the past couple of hours out of his head.

She was the witness to a vicious crime and a victim of arson. She was here to be in his protective custody, not to be an object of his sexual fantasies. Speaking of protective custody, he pulled himself off the bed, grabbed his gun and went in search of his houseguest.

Don't miss
HER COLTON LAWMAN
by *New York Times* bestselling author
Carla Cassidy, coming November 2014 from
HARLEQUIN®
ROMANTIC suspense

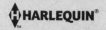

HARLEQUIN®

ROMANTIC suspense

Heart-racing romance, high-stakes suspense!

TEXAS STAKEOUT
by *New York Times* bestselling author
Virna DePaul

A killer in waiting. A brother in hiding.
Could they be the same person?

Dylan Rooney is out of his element. A U.S. marshal and
city-wrangler at heart, he must adopt a new cover—and a
new client—in the heart of Texas. The assignment: protect
Rachel Kincaid...a widow with a young son who realizes her
struggles are just beginning when her ranch hand is killed.
Posing as the new ranch hand, Dylan quickly learns that
catching a killer may not be so simple—especially when
Rachel's fugitive brother is the prime suspect. And the
woman he's vowed to protect is the same woman he's
falling in love with.

Available **NOVEMBER 2014**
Wherever books and ebooks are sold.

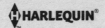

ROMANTIC suspense

Heart-racing romance, high-stakes suspense!

HIGH-STAKES BACHELOR
by Cindy Dees

More than hearts are at stake for a legendary Hollywood family in Cindy Dees' brand new miniseries, The Prescott Bachelors!

Wannabe stuntwoman Ana Izzolo can't believe she lands a starring role in actor-producer Jackson Prescott's new film. A plain-Jane nobody and a megastar? Their on-screen chemistry is electric, burning up the celluloid...but offscreen, Ana is stalked by danger.

Like a true Hollywood hero, Jackson whisks her to his oceanfront mansion, practicing love scenes while keeping her safe. But when their real-life relationship starts mirroring the movie's leading couple, the confirmed bachelor fears he may fall for the doe-eyed ingenue. If the stalker doesn't get her first....

Available **NOVEMBER 2014**

Wherever books and ebooks are sold

www.Harlequin.com

HRS78947

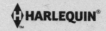

ROMANTIC suspense

Heart-racing romance, high-stakes suspense!

DESIGNATED TARGET
by **Karen Anders**

***A NCIS agent must protect a brainy scientist
who criminals are after—for her mind.***

NCIS special agent Vincent Fitzgerald's mission: to find
missing naval scientist Dr. Skylar Baang. The brilliant
American-Filipino beauty has been kidnapped for her brain
and research on top secret projects. But even as Vin rescues
her from a dangerous group, he knows they'll be back.

A long-ago promise has kept Skylar committed to her
work—love is a distraction she's never allowed herself. Now
in the protective custody of a complicated NCIS agent who
surprises her at every turn, Skylar wants to stop thinking and
start *feeling*. But as the thugs come after her, she'll need
everything she is—and smart, sexy Vin—to stay alive.

Available **NOVEMBER 2014**
Wherever books and ebooks are sold.

HRS78961